SIXKILLER, U.S. MARSHAL:
DEAD MAN WALKING

Look for these exciting Western series from bestselling authors
WILLIAM W. JOHNSTONE
and **J. A. JOHNSTONE**

The Mountain Man

Preacher: The First Mountain Man

Luke Jensen, Bounty Hunter

Those Jensen Boys!

The Jensen Brand

Matt Jensen

MacCallister

The Red Ryan Westerns

Perley Gates

Have Brides, Will Travel

The Hank Fallon Westerns

Will Tanner, Deputy U.S. Marshal

Shotgun Johnny

The Chuckwagon Trail

The Jackals

The Slash and Pecos Westerns

The Texas Moonshiners

AVAILABLE FROM PINNACLE BOOKS

SIXKILLER, U.S. MARSHAL: DEAD MAN WALKING

William W. Johnstone

and J. A. Johnstone

PINNACLE BOOKS
Kensington Publishing Corp.
www.kensingtonbooks.com

PINNACLE BOOKS are published by

Kensington Publishing Corp.
119 West 40th Street
New York, NY 10018

PUBLISHER'S NOTE
Following the death of William W. Johnstone, the Johnstone family is working with a carefully selected writer to organize and complete Mr. Johnstone's outlines and many unfinished manuscripts to create additional novels in all of his series like The Last Gunfighter, Mountain Man, and Eagles, among others. This novel was inspired by Mr. Johnstone's superb storytelling.

ISBN-13: 978-0-7860-4320-0
ISBN-10: 0-7860-4320-2

First printing: November 2013

10 9 8 7 6 5 4 3 2

Printed in the United States of America

Electronic edition:

ISBN-13: 978-0-7860-3129-0 (e-book)
ISBN-10: 0-7860-3129-8 (e-book)

Chapter One

A bullet smacked into the doorjamb about six inches from the crown of John Henry Sixkiller's pearl gray hat and sprayed wood splinters against it.

John Henry crouched and his Colt came up in his hand. He triggered two swift shots at the spot where flame had bloomed in the night like a crimson flower.

Then he threw himself out of the trading post doorway, hit the ground on his left shoulder, and rolled behind the long watering trough beside the hitch rail.

You asked for this, John Henry, he reminded himself as he came to a stop belly down. *You're the one who painted a big, fat target on yourself.*

He didn't have the patience to spend a week or more ferreting Valentine Starbird out of these rugged hills in eastern Indian Territory, though. It was easier and quicker to swagger around and boast about how he was a deputy United States marshal, by God, sent here by Judge Isaac Parker, the notorious Hanging Judge his own self, to bring in the infamous outlaw Starbird, dead or alive. Starbird was a prideful man, and John Henry figured such bragging would bring the fugitive to him, since Starbird would want to prove him wrong.

Evidently the plan had worked, John Henry thought as more bullets thudded into the thick boards of the trough.

Unfortunately, he hadn't planned on Starbird bringing help with him, and that seemed to be the case. At least two more guns opened up on him from the woods that came up almost right to the trading post's front door.

One of the extra men was off to the side, too, and had an angle on him. A slug plowed into the ground not far from John Henry's head and showered his face with dirt and grit. This wasn't working out at all.

At that moment a rifle started cracking nearby, but these shots weren't directed at John Henry. He twisted his head around and saw Doris Rainbow in the log building's doorway. The Winchester in her hands spat fire as she cranked off several rounds as fast as she could work the weapon's lever.

Over in the trees, somebody screamed, and the gun that had been homing in on John Henry abruptly fell silent.

"Clovis! Clovis, are you shot?"

John Henry recognized that voice. It belonged to Valentine Starbird, who was wanted on numerous counts of murder, robbery, and whiskey smuggling. He was a plague on the

Indian Territory and ran with several men who were almost as bad, including one Clovis Miller.

Nobody answered Starbird. After a moment he yelled, "You bitch! You killed Clovis!"

Doris had ducked back inside the building, John Henry saw when he glanced in her direction. That was good. He appreciated what she had done to help him, but he didn't want her to get killed or even hurt on his account.

Her involvement meant there was no question about what had to happen now. Her father owned this trading post, and if Starbird got away, he would come back here sometime in the future and take his revenge on Doris. John Henry couldn't allow that.

While lying there he had thumbed fresh rounds into his Colt until the chamber was full. He surged up now and dashed for the trees, triggering the revolver as fast as he could. His bullets slashed through the branches and made Starbird and whoever was with him duck for cover. John Henry left his feet in a dive that carried him into the thick shadows under the trees.

Now he and his enemies were on equal footing. He wasn't silhouetted in a doorway or pinned down behind a water trough anymore.

He reloaded again, then stood absolutely still and listened. Hearing wasn't the only sense he used. He drew in deep breaths as well, searching for the scents of whiskey, tobacco, and unwashed human flesh.

He was about to try tracking by smell, just like a droopy-faced old bloodhound, he thought as a faint smile touched his lips in the darkness.

It didn't come to that point, however, because one of the outlaws got careless as his nerves stretched out taut. The man moved, causing a crackling in the brush about ten feet from John Henry. As soundless as a ghost, John Henry glided toward the sound.

When he judged that he was close enough to his quarry, he let his foot press down a little harder on a twig underneath it. The twig snapped, which in the tense silence sounded almost as loud as a shot.

The man he was stalking jerked around and gasped, "Val?"

"Nope," John Henry said. He reached out with his left hand and grabbed a shirtfront. The gun in his right hand slashed down and crashed against the face of the other man. Swiftly, John Henry hit him again, knocking him out cold.

That left Starbird.

John Henry eased the unconscious man to the ground and hooted like an owl. It was a common signal among outlaws.

"Keller?"

Starbird's voice was a harsh whisper as he called softly to the man John Henry had just knocked out.

John Henry remained silent now.

Starbird's nerves couldn't take it, either. He yelled, "Keller, hit the dirt!" and opened fire, shooting blindly through the trees. Shots roared and flames spurted from the muzzle of Starbird's gun, tearing orange holes in the shadows.

John Henry had already dropped to one knee. He steadied his gun and fired twice, aiming carefully at the muzzle flashes. Starbird cried out, and a second later John Henry heard the heavy thud as the outlaw's body hit the ground.

Of course, Starbird could be shamming, John Henry thought, trying to trick him and draw him into the open. So he shifted position quickly, just in case Starbird tried to draw a bead on his muzzle flashes, and waited.

He heard a ragged, bubbling, whistling sound and realized after a few seconds that it was Starbird breathing. The outlaw was shot through the lungs and drowning in his own blood. Starbird began to thrash around.

It was an ugly way to die. But John Henry knew that Valentine Starbird had gunned down at least four men in cold blood, had raped two women and cut their throats, and committed Lord knew what other heinous crimes. So John Henry figured he wasn't going to lose one second of sleep over the suffering Starbird was going through now.

A few more rasping, strangling breaths and it was over. No tricks now. John Henry heard the death rattle in Starbird's throat as life departed.

He moved back over to the man he had knocked out, grasped his collar, and hauled Keller into the clearing between the woods and the trading post.

"Billy Rainbow!" he called. "Fetch a lantern."

Moments later the chunky, middle-aged owner of the trading post appeared, carrying a lantern. With a worried look on his face, he brought it out to John Henry.

"Are they all dead?" Billy asked.

"Starbird is." John Henry looked down at the man at his feet, who had a big bloody gash on his forehead and a broken nose from being pistol-whipped. "Looks like this one will live to hang in Fort Smith."

"I recognize him," Billy said. "That's Tupelo Keller. He held up the Tahlequah stage, stole a sawmill payroll, and killed the driver about a month ago."

"I remember. Well, he'll swing for it. Fetch some rope and tie him up while he's still out cold."

Billy nodded, handed the lantern to John Henry, and hurried back into the trading post, stepping past his daughter, who stood in the doorway watching.

Doris Rainbow was eighteen years old, with long, raven hair and expressive dark eyes. She was beautiful enough to take a man's breath away, and she had been in love with John Henry Sixkiller since she was twelve, when he'd been a dashing Cherokee Lighthorseman.

John Henry knew the way she felt about him. It was impossible not to. Any man with a lick of sense would have married Doris and given her half a dozen babies and spent the rest of his life fat and happy, he thought.

But nobody had ever accused him of having a lick of sense, which might explain why he had spent several years working as a deputy U.S. marshal for Judge Parker, putting his life in danger time and time again for damned little pay. Doris deserved better than that.

She started toward him, but he waved her back to the relative safety of the building.

"We don't know for sure that Clovis Miller is dead," he told her.

"He better be," she said. "I think I ventilated him good."

"Sounded like it, but I want to be sure."

With his Colt held ready in his right hand, he lifted the lantern in his left and advanced toward the trees where Miller had been taking those potshots at him a few minutes earlier. If he heard the slightest sound from in there, he planned to empty the revolver at it.

He had penetrated about ten feet into the trees when the lantern light revealed a man's bloody shape sprawled on the ground. Clovis Miller had fallen on his side and died pawing at his midsection where a bullet had ripped it open, trying to push his guts back into the hole.

John Henry remembered what Miller had done to a ten-year-old girl the year before. As far as he was concerned, the outlaw had died too quick and easy, just like Valentine Starbird.

He pouched the iron, took hold of Miller's left ankle, and dragged the body out into the open. Doris looked at the corpse and turned away in revulsion.

"I did that?" she said quietly.

"If you hadn't, he probably would have killed me in another minute or two," John Henry told her. "Don't worry about this one, Doris. You did the right thing . . . even though you never should have risked your life and gotten mixed up in this ruckus to start with. It was my fight."

"You just said that I saved your life."

"More than likely you did."

She sent a speculative glance his way and said, "Then I reckon you owe me something."

John Henry didn't like the turn this conversation was taking. Billy had finished tying Tupelo Keller's hands and feet, so John Henry said, "I'll need to borrow your wagon to take these men into Tahlequah with me, Billy. I'll fetch Keller on to Fort Smith, but Starbird and Miller will need planting right away."

Billy grunted and said, "Sure, but I'd be obliged if you'd wash the blood out of it when you're done. Just leave it at Harriman's Livery and I'll ride into town on my old mule in a day or two and pick it up."

"I'll sure see that it's taken care of," John Henry promised.

"And next time you set a trap for animals like these, I'd appreciate it if you didn't use my place to do it."

"My word on it. But this was really just the luck of the draw. They happened to catch up to me here."

Billy shook his head and said, "I can't imagine what it's like havin' people wantin' to kill you all the time. I swear, John Henry, you must feel like a dead man walkin'."

John Henry clucked his tongue, nodded sagely, and said, "It does get a mite wearisome."

Chapter Two

John Henry laid over at the trading post that night, and he was glad that Doris didn't try to sneak into the room where he was sleeping.

If she had, he would have been forced to either give in to temptation—which would leave him feeling guilty and Doris expecting him to marry her—or else send her packing in no uncertain terms, which would insult her and hurt her feelings. He didn't care for either of those options, so he was grateful he hadn't been forced to choose.

He was up early the next morning, before Doris was awake, and by first light was rolling toward Tahlequah in the borrowed wagon, with the corpses of Valentine Starbird and Clovis Miller laid out in the back.

Tupelo Keller was in the back of the wagon, too, riding stretched out with his wrists and ankles tied securely. John Henry had passed another rope around Keller's neck and tied it to a ring bolt set into the wagon bed.

Keller bitched and moaned the whole way. He complained about his broken nose and about the headache he had from being clouted with John Henry's gun. He bellyached about having to ride with a couple of dead men jostling him.

"This just ain't a proper way to treat a prisoner," Keller insisted.

"If you're going to complain no matter what I do, I might as well shove you off the back of the wagon and let you drag in the road for a while," John Henry pointed out. "Anyway, you should be grateful that I just cold-cocked you instead of blowing a hole in you. This ride would be a lot more quiet and peaceful if I had."

"You better take me to a sawbones when we get to town," Keller demanded. "This busted nose of mine is makin' it hard to breathe and it ain't never gonna heal right if a doctor don't set it pretty soon."

John Henry flicked the reins against the backs of the four mules hitched to the wagon. His saddle horse, a big, powerful gray named Iron Heart, was tied to the back of the vehicle.

"I don't believe you're thinking this through, Tupelo," John Henry said. "In a couple of weeks your looks aren't going to matter that much. By then you'll have paid a visit to the gallows in Fort Smith and left a mite abruptly."

"You like tormentin' me this way, don't you, Marshal?"

"To tell you the truth, I don't mind it all that much. How many innocent men is it that you've killed? And in case you didn't notice, those two hombres you were running with were just about the lowest trash you could find anywhere. You had to expect to come to a bad end when you threw in with the likes of Valentine Starbird and Clovis Miller."

"It still ain't proper to gloat over a man because he's gonna hang," Keller said sullenly.

John Henry nodded solemnly and said, "You're probably right about that. I won't say anything more about it. Maybe I'll just sing a little, instead."

He launched into an old Cherokee song. It wasn't long before Keller was cussing about that, too.

By the time the wagon reached Tahlequah, the capital of the Cherokee Nation, the prisoner had given up and gone to sleep, snoring raucously through his broken nose. John Henry had worked out of this pleasant little town when he was a member of the Cherokee Lighthorse, the tribal police force, and also when he was the Nation's chief sheriff.

He had given up those jobs to concentrate on being a deputy United States marshal, but he still had many friends here among the members of the Cherokee government, including Lighthorse Captain Charley LeFlores.

John Henry brought the wagon to a stop in front of Lighthorse headquarters, and while he was tying up the team he told a boy who was loitering on the porch to go inside and let Captain LeFlores know he was here.

When LeFlores stepped out onto the porch he craned his neck to look into the back of the wagon and said, "Are those dead men I see in there, John Henry?"

"Two of 'em are. The other one's still alive, unless corpses have taken to snoring."

"Just two out of three." LeFlores clucked his tongue and shook his head. "You're slipping. Must be slowing down a mite in your old age." He took another look. "Good Lord. Is that Valentine Starbird?"

"Yep. And Clovis Miller."

"Well, there's good riddance doubled. I heard you were hellin' around, making a lot of noise about bringing Starbird in. That was just bait, wasn't it?"

John Henry shrugged.

"Where'd you catch up to them?" LeFlores asked.

"Actually, they tried to bushwhack me up at Billy Rainbow's trading post. That's his wagon I borrowed."

LeFlores nodded and said, "Thought I recognized it. Rainbow's, eh?" He sighed wistfully. "Doris is still just as pretty as ever, I suppose?"

"Yes, and she's still young enough to be your daughter, too."

"When you get to be my age, it's perfectly acceptable to appreciate feminine beauty." The captain grimaced. "Truth be told, appreciating it is about all I can do these days—"

John Henry held up a hand to stop him and said, "You'll see to it that Starbird and Miller get planted, won't you?"

LeFlores slipped his hands into the back

pockets of his trousers and rocked forward and back on the balls of his feet.

"That depends. Will my office be reimbursed for any expenses incurred in the burial of said felons?"

"I'll make a note to tell Judge Parker about it."

"Well, then, I reckon we can take care of it."

"The jasper making all that racket with his busted snout is Tupelo Keller, by the way. I guess I'll have to rent a wagon to take him on over to Fort Smith, since Billy said to leave his wagon here in town at Harriman's."

"No, that won't do," LeFlores said.

John Henry frowned in surprise.

"Why not? I can charge the wagon rental to my expenses."

"You can't take the time to make a leisurely drive by wagon to Fort Smith," LeFlores explained. "I got a telegram from Judge Parker yesterday. It said that if I was to see you, I should tell you to get back to Fort Smith posthaste. I reckon that means you should rattle your hocks."

"You know good and well that's what it means," John Henry said. "You're an educated man, Charley."

"I'm smart enough to know that when the Hangin' Judge says to hurry, a fella better not waste any time. If I was you, I'd climb on that big gray horse of yours and head for Arkansas as soon as I picked up a few supplies for the trip."

John Henry jerked a thumb at the wagon bed and asked, "What about Keller?"

"I'll keep him locked up here until Judge

Parker can send somebody else after him. That sound all right to you?"

"Sure, I guess so. It's a generous gesture on your part, Charley."

"Here in the Territory we like to stay on good terms with the federal government, and that definitely includes federal district court judges."

"I'll tell Parker you passed along his message," John Henry promised.

"Anything else I can do to assist you, Marshal?"

"No . . . unless you can tell me why the judge is in such an all-fired hurry to see me."

"I don't have a clue," LeFlores said, "but given your history, I'd say there's a good chance he's eager to send you somewhere and have you shoot somebody."

Chapter Three

As usual, Iron Heart was eager to stretch his legs and run, especially after spending all morning plodding along behind a wagon. Every now and then during the trip from Billy Rainbow's trading post, Iron Heart had blown air loudly through his nose in what John Henry suspected was the equine equivalent of irritated muttering.

John Henry had fifty miles to cover between Tahlequah and Fort Smith, though, so he held Iron Heart in slightly to keep the gray from getting too worn out. There was no telling where Judge Parker was going to be sending him or when he'd have to leave. He might need his faithful trail partner almost right away.

He had started from Tahlequah too late in the day to finish the journey by nightfall, so he spent the night in a tiny hamlet that didn't amount to much more than a wide place in the road. There was no hotel, only a general store, a blacksmith shop, and a livery stable, but the owner of the stable was agreeable to John Henry bunking in the hayloft.

"Just don't get spooked and shoot Chester," the liveryman warned.

"Who's Chester?" John Henry asked. "Is somebody else already sleeping up there?"

"Chester's my tomcat. Best ratter in this whole part of the country."

"Oh." John Henry nodded in understanding. "I'll be careful."

The storekeeper shared his supper, for a price. Most people in this area knew John Henry from his time as a Lighthorseman and chief sheriff and were happy to assist him, but these were hardheaded businessmen and their hospitality came with a price. John Henry didn't mind. The judge might grouse a little about his expenses, but they always got paid.

Judge Parker knew that John Henry got results and was worth it.

After supper, a cup of coffee, and a cigar shared with the storekeeper, John Henry went back to the stable and climbed to the hayloft, where he had put his bedroll earlier. He stretched out and dozed off quickly, as he usually did, falling into the sort of light but restful sleep that good lawmen learned how to achieve. A man who packed a badge had to be able to wake up quickly and fully alert . . . if he wanted to stay alive for very long, that is.

A rustle in the hay, a heavy thud, and a sharp squeal roused him from that sleep. He sat up quickly with his Colt in his hand. He didn't remember drawing it from the holster attached to the coiled shell belt beside his head, but there it was. He looked around but couldn't see much in the gloom that shrouded the loft.

Then he stiffened slightly as he saw two large, glowing green eyes watching him.

John Henry trained the revolver on the eyes. Using his left hand, he slid a match from his shirt pocket and snapped the lucifer to life with his thumbnail.

As the glare spread across the loft, it revealed the largest yellow tabby cat John Henry had ever seen. The cat must have weighed twenty-five pounds, and not much of it was fat, either. A scarred nose and ragged ears testified to the epic feline battles the animal had waged.

Right now its jaws were clamped around the lifeless, furry corpse of a large rat with a long, naked tail. When John Henry leaned forward slightly, the cat growled, as if daring him to try to take the carcass away from it. He would pay dearly if he tried it, the cat seemed to be saying.

"I reckon you must be Chester," John Henry said as he slid the Colt back into its holster. "Don't worry, I'm not going to try to take your rat away from you. I've got more sense than that."

Chester stood up, turned, and stalked off haughtily into the bales of hay, twitching his tail at John Henry like some sort of obscene gesture.

"I've heard old granny women warn folks about cats!" John Henry called after the creature. "They say you're all possessed by devils. Might be something to that."

The match had just about burned down to his fingertips. He blew it out and pinched it between his fingers to make sure not even the faintest ember remained. You had to be mighty careful with fire around hay.

Then he stretched out again and fell back into an uneasy sleep, a part of his brain remembering the stories he'd heard as a boy about how cats would crouch on your chest and steal your breath. He figured Chester was big enough to do it, too.

Nothing of the sort happened, of course, and John Henry didn't even see the cat the next morning when he got up, settled accounts with the liveryman, and set out for Fort Smith again.

He arrived there without incident by midday and rode straight to the big, square block of a redbrick building that served as the federal courthouse.

Some of his fellow deputy marshals were loitering at the bottom of the steps leading up to the main entrance. They greeted John Henry warmly for the most part, although a couple of the men were a little surly, probably because they felt like John Henry sometimes got preferential treatment from the judge.

"If you're here to see Parker, court's in session right now, John Henry," said Tim Weatherbee, one of the lawmen. "He ought to be taking the noon recess pretty soon, though."

J.P. Harlingen, another of the marshals, said, "I heard you went over into the Nations after Valentine Starbird, Sixkiller. Don't see any prisoners with you, though."

"That's because Starbird and Clovis Miller are in pine boxes in Tahlequah by now," John Henry said. He didn't particularly like Harlingen, and the feeling was mutual. "Tupelo Keller is locked up in Charley LeFlores's jail." He paused and smiled. "I expect the judge will send one of you boys to fetch him in. Maybe you, J.P."

Harlingen scowled and said, "Why didn't you just bring him yourself?"

"Because the judge wanted to see me in a hurry. I reckon he's got an important job for me."

With that, John Henry went up the stairs and into the courthouse.

A bailiff stood outside the door to Parker's courtroom, hands folded behind his back. He nodded to John Henry and said, "The judge has been expecting you, Marshal Sixkiller. He said if you came in, you should go around to his chambers, and he'll meet you there as soon as court's adjourned."

John Henry nodded his thanks, then went around a corner and through a door into a room dominated by a big desk. Shelves filled with law books and other leather-bound volumes lined the walls. John Henry had been there only a moment when another door opened and Judge Isaac C. Parker came into the room.

Parker was a dark-haired man who sported a neat goatee. He wasn't very big, but the black robe he wore made him an impressive figure. He nodded to John Henry and said, "I knew you'd arrived in Fort Smith and would be waiting here for me, Marshal."

John Henry didn't ask how Parker had known that he'd ridden into Fort Smith. The judge had ways of finding things out. He had sources of information scattered all over town, but sometimes his knowledge seemed almost supernatural to John Henry.

"Sit down," Parker went on, and started divesting himself of the judicial robe. "We don't have a lot of time," he continued as he hung the robe on a brass hook attached to the wall. "I have an important trial going on."

"Big case?"

Parker sighed and said, "No, petty and sordid, the way most crime is. But it's caught the public's attention, and not only that, some blasted newspaper reporter wrote a story the other day about how it's been more than a month since I sentenced anybody to hang. Some people seem to think I'm letting them down when there's a shortage of gallows fruit."

"Well, there'll be work for George Maledon pretty soon," John Henry said, referring to the hangman who carried out the sentences of death imposed by Judge Parker. "Tupelo Keller is locked up in Tahlequah. I left him there so I could get back here faster. Charley LeFlores told me you sent him a telegram saying you were in a hurry to see me."

"Keller, eh? What about Starbird? He's the leader of that wicked bunch."

"Not anymore. He and Clovis Miller are dead."

Parker grunted and then jerked his head in a curt nod.

"Good work, Marshal. Although some people in town probably would have preferred it if I could have hanged all three of them at the same time. Ah, well, dead's dead, I suppose, and justice was done, which in the end is all that matters." Parker shoved a stack of papers across the desk toward John Henry, who had settled down in a chair of brown morocco leather in front of the desk, where he always sat when he visited Parker's chambers. "Here's some reading for you to do on the train."

"Train?" John Henry repeated, wincing slightly. "You're sending me somewhere so far away I have to go on a train?"

"Well, you can't ride all the way to California on that big gray horse of yours, now can you?" Parker leaned his head to the side. "Although I suppose you could, of course. But you probably wouldn't get there in time to catch the scoundrel I'm sending you after."

Chapter Four

"California? That's really out of our bailiwick, isn't it?"

"A federal marshal has jurisdiction throughout the entire country."

"I know," John Henry said, "but it seems like somebody closer to California could handle this job, whatever it is. That fella who works out of the Denver office, maybe?"

Judge Parker shook his head.

"This case originated in our jurisdiction, or at least the first reports of it did, so that gives us first claim on dealing with it," he said.

"*Us* meaning *me*," John Henry said.

"Your job is to apprehend the criminals, mine is to preside over their trials," Parker replied rather stiffly. "At any rate, you can see from those documents that the suspicious bills were first spotted in Wichita, Kansas."

"Suspicious bills," John Henry repeated. "So we're talking about counterfeiting?"

"Indeed we are, and on a fairly large scale,

too. The distribution hasn't been confined to one town or even one state. As I mentioned, the phony bills first turned up in Wichita, but since then they've surfaced in Denver, Santa Fe, and Tucson as well. The most recent report of them is in Los Angeles."

"Somebody's making their way across the Southwest, passing the bills," John Henry said. "The same person, or maybe a gang that he's running?"

"One of those two options, certainly. It would strain the bounds of credibility to have that many different counterfeiters suddenly operating independently at the same time. All the details are in those documents, along with information about the man the Justice Department believes to be ultimately responsible, a fellow named Ignatius O'Reilly."

John Henry had to smile at that. He repeated, "Ignatius O'Reilly, eh?"

"Don't let the colorful name fool you," Parker warned. "O'Reilly has a reputation as a ruthless master criminal and expert forger and counterfeiter. From what I've read about the man, it's possible that there's no one better at engraving phony printing plates. Authorities in Washington have examined some of the spurious bills from various locations and are convinced that they're all O'Reilly's work, although they're not considered to be some of the best examples of his illegal art."

"Well, everybody has an off day now and then," John Henry said with a shrug. "So I'll be picking up this fella O'Reilly's trail in Los Angeles?"

"That's right. There's a good chance he'll have moved on by the time you get there, but it's still the best lead we have. The only lead we have, actually. There's a westbound train leaving later today, I believe."

John Henry sighed and nodded.

"I'll be on it," he said. "It won't take me long to get Iron Heart settled at the livery stable and pack a few things."

"Do you have any questions?"

John Henry thought about it, then said, "One thing strikes me as a little odd about this, Your Honor."

"What might that be?"

"Counterfeiting isn't a hanging crime. At least it wasn't the last time I checked."

"So why am I interested in it, is that what you mean?" Parker snapped.

"Like I said, it just seems a little strange. No offense meant by it," John Henry added hastily, although he could tell that Parker was indeed a little offended.

"My job is to enforce the laws of the United States," Parker said, sounding a little pompous. The judge could be a bit of a stuffed shirt every now and then, although John Henry had never held that against the man. "Counterfeiting is against the law, and it's a crime that officials in Washington take very seriously."

"Yes, sir, I imagine they would."

John Henry understood now. For all the power that Isaac Parker wielded as a federal district court judge, he had people he answered to as well, and he was no more immune than anybody else to the desire to please the folks he worked for.

"I'd be obliged if you'd forget that I brought up the subject," John Henry added.

Parker just said, "Hmmph," then went on, "There's one more thing. When you catch up to O'Reilly, try not to kill him. There are those who would like to question him."

"I'll do my best," John Henry said as he got to his feet, figuring that Parker was talking about officials in the Justice Department. "But when you come right down to it, Your Honor, that'll sort of be up to him."

Several years earlier, John Henry had helped the railroad extend a spur line from Kansas down through Indian Territory to Texas. He hadn't toted rails or swung a sledgehammer to drive spikes, but rather had done battle as a lawman with forces that wanted to stop the expansion for greedy reasons of their own.

That didn't mean he particularly *liked* railroad trains. As far as he was concerned, they were loud, smoky, smelly critters, and traveling on one wasn't even really all that comfortable unless you were rich enough to have your own private car or at least a Pullman compartment.

He couldn't afford anything like that on the money he made as a deputy U.S. marshal. Like everybody else who worked for wages, he rode sitting up on hard wooden bench seats.

But he recognized the advantages of having rail lines connecting as many places in the country as possible. If you needed to get from where you were to somewhere far off in a hurry, you couldn't beat a train.

He was going to miss Iron Heart, though, he thought as he swayed gently to the train's rocking motion. On other cases in the past when he'd had to travel by train, he had taken the big gray horse with him, shipping him in a stable car and unloading him when they reached their destination.

That wasn't really feasible this time since he had to go halfway across the country and didn't know where the trail would lead him after that. If he needed a saddle mount he would have to rent one and hope that he found a good, dependable animal.

With nothing else to fill up the long hours, he began reading the reports that Judge Parker had given him.

One was a lengthy description and history of Ignatius O'Reilly. As a young man, some thirty years earlier, O'Reilly had been a member of one of the Irish gangs in New York, and he had gained a reputation there as a vicious, ruthless criminal. That quality had allowed him to rise rapidly in the gang.

O'Reilly had graduated from breaking legs and cutting throats to planning some of the schemes carried out by the gang. He had set up an operation to sell black market beef, much of which was rotten or contaminated.

Some people had died from the bad meat, and even though law enforcement in the city was particularly feeble, the deaths drew too much attention to O'Reilly and he moved on to smuggling.

He ran prostitutes as a sideline and even after he had become one of the gang's bosses, he wasn't above bashing in a man's head and robbing him from time to time. Just to keep his hand in, was the way he put it.

Somewhere along the way, O'Reilly had made the acquaintance of a man named Alfred Dean, who owned a printing shop and had a sideline of his own. By day Dean printed flyers and broadsides, and by night he printed money.

By this time the Civil War was being fought, and Confederate agents came to New York and engaged Dean to print bogus Union currency in an attempt to undermine the Northern economy and perhaps give the South a slight advantage.

That hadn't worked out, but Dean had discovered that he had a talent for engraving the plates used to print bills, and after the war, when he became friends with O'Reilly, he passed that on to the other man.

O'Reilly was even more skilled at counterfeiting, something he might never have discovered on his own. He soon surpassed Dean and moved to take over the operation. Dean had protested . . . and he was never seen again, at least not whole and alive. Some body parts turned up that might have belonged to him, but without a head, who could say for sure?

With his mentor out of the picture, O'Reilly began to expand . . . and he finally pushed his luck too far. The law caught up to him and he had gone away to prison, sentenced to twenty-five years in a federal penitentiary.

He had been behind bars less than a year, though, when he escaped, and he hadn't been caught since. He had continued to carry out his counterfeiting activities, surfacing long enough to pass some of the bogus bills here and there, then disappearing again. His current operation, which found the fake money being spread out across the Southwest, was his largest one to date.

The report also included a physical description of O'Reilly. He was in his late forties, of medium height, stockily built, and had curly red hair with a considerable amount of gray in it. His nose had been broken on a couple of occasions and had healed a little crookedly. He had a scar over his left eye from a fight, and a longer, thinner scar on the right side of his jaw where someone had cut him with a knife.

Ignatius O'Reilly was a vicious, cunning individual who had to be considered armed and extremely dangerous, the report concluded. When John Henry caught up to O'Reilly—and he had no doubt that he would—he would have to be careful and not take any unnecessary chances.

He was mulling over everything he had just read when a woman's voice asked quietly, "Excuse me, sir, do you mind if I sit here?"

John Henry looked up from the papers in his hands to see lovely green eyes, a tumbled mass of auburn hair, and full red lips curved in a smile. The young woman who stood in the aisle next to the bench seat was intriguingly curved in a bottle-green traveling gown. A stylish hat of the same shade, adorned by a feather, perched on that stunning red hair.

John Henry was sitting next to the window so that he could get some fresh air, hopefully without too many cinders from the locomotive's diamond-shaped smokestack mixed in with it. He stood up, stuffed the papers back in his coat, and took off his hat. Smiling at the woman, he said, "Ma'am, any man would have to be a puredee fool to turn down such a request."

"I'm glad you feel that way. Now please move back a little," the woman said with a touch of impatience in her voice.

As John Henry did so, she squeezed past him so that she was next to the window. He thought maybe she needed the fresh air, so he didn't complain.

The fact that she had to press against him to reach that side of the bench didn't hurt anything, either.

"Sit down," she said, and as he sank onto the bench beside her, she slid her hip against his with surprising intimacy and rested her head on his shoulder.

"Here he comes," she whispered. "Please don't give me away."

Chapter Five

John Henry almost said, "Ah!" as understanding dawned on him, but he reined in the impulse. He heard heavy footsteps advancing up the aisle toward the front of the car, so he glanced over his shoulder to have a look at their source.

The man was tall and thick and looked a little like a slab of beef in a brown tweed suit. A dark brown bowler hat was crammed down on what appeared to be a bald head. Black mustaches curled above a wide mouth. The man's jaw reminded John Henry of boulders he had seen.

Small, angry, piggish eyes darted back and forth as the man studied all the passengers he passed. Clearly, he was looking for someone, and when he found them, his intentions weren't very friendly.

John Henry lifted his left arm and put it around the redheaded woman's shoulders, urging her even closer to him. His embrace caused her to jump a little at first, but then she seemed to realize what he was doing and why. She snuggled against his side in the circle of his arm.

He leaned his head toward hers and tipped it slightly to the side. That caused his hat to block the woman's face from the view of anyone in the aisle. Probably not much of her head was visible past the hat's broad brim.

"I hope you'll forgive me for being forward, ma'am," he said in a half whisper.

"I'm the one who should be asking forgiveness," she said softly. "Thank you."

As he heard the searching man's footsteps close behind his right shoulder, he said in a normal voice, "That's right, darling, we'll be in St. Louis before you know it. I'm sure you'll be glad to see your mother again."

He turned his head even more toward her as the man moved past the seat. With her face right in front of his like that, and only inches away, what he did next seemed like the most natural thing in the world.

He kissed her.

Not a lingering, passionate, scandalous kiss of the sort that not even married couples exchanged in public, but rather just a quick but sweet peck on the lips, a gesture of affection. It served to shield her even more from view, however, and the charade seemed believable enough, John Henry thought.

It appeared to work, because the big man stomped on past the seat. The vestibule at the front of the car was only about ten feet away, and in a matter of seconds he had disappeared into it, obviously intending to carry on his search in the next car.

The redhead leaned back against the circle of John Henry's arm and heaved a sigh of relief.

"I can't thank you enough, Mr. . . . ?"

"Sixkiller," he told her. "John Henry Sixkiller."

She didn't act like she recognized the name, and there was no reason she should unless she'd had some dealings with the Cherokee Lighthorse or Judge Parker's court. She didn't exactly look like a criminal, he told himself, but you couldn't always tell about such things. He had run up against female outlaws who were just as bad as, if not worse than, their male counterparts.

"I'm very glad to meet you, Mr. Sixkiller." She held out a gloved hand. "My name is Emmaline Dolan."

He didn't elaborate and tell her that he was a deputy United States marshal. As he took her hand he said, "The pleasure is mine, Miss Dolan. It is *Miss* Dolan, isn't it?"

"That's right."

"And the, ah, gentleman . . . ?"

"Was no gentleman," she said firmly. "That was Walter Golliher."

She said the name like he ought to be familiar with it, but he had to shake his head and lift his eyebrows quizzically.

"Walter Golliher, the prizefighter," she said.

"I'm afraid I don't follow the sport," John Henry told her. He had wrestled with his friends when he was a boy, and as a lawman he'd been in plenty of fistfights, but those ruckuses were serious business, often life-and-death, not some sort of competition or exhibition.

If he was going to get hit, he wanted it to be for a good reason, not so somebody could win a bet or get a thrill from the sight of two men pounding on each other.

"Walter is on his way from New Orleans to Kansas City to fight a bout with Otto Mueller," Emmaline Dolan said.

"Ah, the Prussian."

"I thought you said you don't follow prize-fighting," Emmaline said with a slight frown.

"I don't, but I know a Prussian name when I hear one."

"It's true, that's where Mueller's family is from, but he was born and raised in Chicago."

"For an attractive young woman, you seem to know a lot about this prizefighting business," John Henry commented.

"My father is Henry Dolan. He's been training and managing pugilists since before I was born. I grew up around a prize ring."

"Well, that makes sense, I suppose." John Henry paused. "Why were you hiding from Golliher?" A possibility occurred to him. "Is he your fiancé? I sort of make it a habit to not get involved in romantic disputes."

Especially when he was on his way to track down a notorious counterfeiter, he added silently.

Emmaline said, "Wait . . . you think Walter and I . . . you're asking if we're engaged?"

"It seemed like a reasonable enough question," John Henry said mildly.

Emmaline leaned back against the hard bench seat and laughed.

"I guess somebody might think so," she said, "but I promise you, Mr. Sixkiller, that's not the case. Walter would like that, but I have no interest in him other than the fact that my father is his trainer and manager."

"So this *is* a romantic dispute," John Henry said. "An unrequited one."

"No, I told you . . . well, I guess you could say . . ." Emmaline sighed. "All right, I suppose it is. Let's just say that I'm grateful to you for helping me just now. Walter was being particularly stubborn today. He wanted me to take a walk with him to the observation platform at the rear of our car. I know perfectly well what he intended to do. He meant to steal a kiss."

"Sort of like I did," John Henry reminded her.

Emmaline's face glowed warmly. She said, "That was very forward of you."

Despite what she said, she didn't sound like she disapproved.

"I suppose I get that way when strange ladies ask to sit with me on trains."

"But it was quite nice . . ." Emmaline sighed again. "Anyway, I told Walter to go ahead to the observation platform and that I would meet him back there—"

"And then you went the other way as fast as you could," John Henry guessed.

"I panicked a little. He's so persistent."

"You said that your father is his manager. Can't he put a stop to this?"

Emmaline rolled those beautiful green eyes.

"With this bout coming up against Otto Mueller, Father just wants Walter kept happy. I mean, he wouldn't allow anything improper to happen, of course, but he's not going to try to discourage Walter and get him upset, either."

"So what are you going to do?"

"We'll be in Kansas City tonight," Emmaline said. "We have family there, and I'm going to stay with my cousins while Father is training Walter for the fight. Walter won't be able to bother me there. I just have to dodge him for the rest of the trip, until we reach Kansas City."

"Then I have an idea," John Henry said. "Let's go back to the caboose. I'll explain the situation to the conductor and ask him if you can ride back there until the train gets to Kansas City."

Emmaline frowned again and asked, "Do you really think he'll do that?"

"I think I can talk him into it," John Henry said.

He didn't add that he could always pull out his deputy marshal's badge if the conductor needed a little extra persuading. If he had to, he would stretch the truth and claim that Emmaline was a witness he needed to protect. Judge Parker didn't like it when his deputies bent the law, especially when it wasn't in the cause of bringing in some outlaw who needed hanging, but John Henry didn't see any reason why the judge ever had to know about this.

"All right," Emmaline said. "That would be wonderful. Thank you, Mr. Sixkiller."

"Glad to be of help," he said. He stood up and politely extended a hand to Emmaline Dolan.

She smiled and took it and let him help her to her feet. They moved down the aisle toward the rear of the car, John Henry keeping one hand lightly on her arm to steady her against the rocking of the train as it clattered over the rails.

They went through the rear vestibule and had just stepped out onto the platform when John Henry heard a bellow like a wounded bull behind them. He looked around, and through the glass in the vestibule door, he saw Walter Golliher standing at the other end of the car. The prizefighter had spotted him and Emmaline.

Then, still reminding John Henry of an angry bull, Golliher lowered his bowler-hatted head and charged.

Chapter Six

Emmaline had heard Golliher's shout, too, and she gasped in horror as she looked back at him.

"Oh, no!" she cried. "He's found us!"

John Henry pushed her toward the door of the next car.

"Go on back to the caboose," he told her. "I'll try to slow him down."

"Please be careful, Mr. Sixkiller. Walter is violently jealous."

Before John Henry could ask her what she meant by that, Emmaline Dolan was gone, vanishing through the vestibule of the next car.

He turned back and braced himself to meet the prizefighter's rush. Maybe he could talk some sense into Golliher's head, he thought.

To give himself some room, John Henry backed up onto the front platform of the next car. If he'd had time, he would have taken out the leather folder that contained his badge and bona fides and had them ready to display to

Golliher. The sight of a federal lawman's badge usually made people slow down and think twice about what they were doing.

John Henry didn't have a chance to do that. Golliher slowed down just enough to jerk the door open and then started to build up steam again as he rushed out onto the platform.

"Hold it!" John Henry ordered. "Mr. Golliher, don't—"

The prizefighter ignored the firm command and lunged across both platforms at John Henry. Instead of throwing a punch, as John Henry expected him to, Golliher reached for him with open hands, as if he intended to grab him and tear him limb from limb.

John Henry tried to twist out of the way, but one of Golliher's hamlike hands snagged his coat and used it to slam him against the front wall of the railroad car. The impact was enough to knock the breath from John Henry's lungs and leave him momentarily stunned. Golliher's other hand caught him by the throat.

That wasn't good. Long, thick fingers like sausages closed around John Henry's windpipe. He was already gasping for air from being rammed against the wall, and now he couldn't get any breath into his lungs. The world seemed to spin crazily around him, and it took on a reddish tint around the edges that told him he was about to pass out.

He could have drawn his Colt and shot Golliher, of course, and it would be justified as self-defense. At this moment, it certainly appeared that Golliher intended to choke him to death.

John Henry didn't think somebody ought to die just because of a jealous rage, however, so he cast around desperately for some nonlethal means of breaking Golliher's grip. He tried a tactic he had used before, cupping both hands and slamming them against Golliher's ears.

That made Golliher roar in pain, but his grip on John Henry's throat didn't loosen. He had the lawman pinned against the wall and leaned in closer to him.

That brought him close enough for John Henry to raise a knee up sharply into his groin. It was a dirty move, of course, but this was no time for worrying about the niceties. It was a matter of survival.

The blow landed solidly and would have devastated most men. Walter Golliher just groaned, his face darkened even more with rage, and he squeezed harder on John Henry's neck.

Shooting the big ox was starting to sound more appealing, John Henry thought wildly.

But when he drew his gun he didn't pull the trigger. Instead he reversed the weapon and slammed the butt against Golliher's head. Clearly, the prizefighter had a thick skull and was used to getting hit, but even so, his eyes went a little glassy.

John Henry didn't want to do any permanent damage to the man, but he couldn't worry about that too much. If he passed out, there was no telling what Golliher might do. So John Henry hit him again.

That made Golliher stagger back a step. His hand slipped from his opponent's neck. John

Henry gasped and gratefully dragged a deep draft of air into his lungs.

Golliher was quick to shake off the effects of being pistol-whipped. He lunged forward again and threw his arms around John Henry in a bear hug. Still light-headed and breathing heavily, John Henry wasn't able to avoid the tackle.

His hat flew off and his feet came off the platform as Golliher swung him around. Golliher rammed him into the iron railing around the platform. John Henry yelled in pain as the top bar of the railing dug into the small of his back. Golliher began bending him backward over it. John Henry's spine creaked in protest.

When he turned his head he could see the gravel of the roadbed rushing past below him. If Golliher kept pushing, John Henry was liable to flip up and over the rail. With the train racing along at close to sixty miles per hour, if he fell onto that gravel it would probably prove fatal. At the very least, the tumble would bust the hell out of him and maybe break most of the bones in his body.

Of course, considering the tremendous pressure that Golliher was putting on his ribs with that bear hug, they might snap before the prizefighter even had a chance to throw him off the train . . .

Since he couldn't get his arms free to throw a punch, John Henry drew his head back and butted Golliher in the face. Blood spurted from the man's nose as he howled in pain. John Henry butted him again. Golliher let go of him and reared back. Crimson flooded down over Golliher's mouth and chin.

That didn't stop him from attacking yet again. He barreled toward John Henry.

This time John Henry was able to get out of the way. Golliher's momentum carried him past John Henry and into the railing. A startled bleat of fear came from the big man as his weight tipped him over it.

Golliher clawed at the railing in an attempt to catch himself. His hands closed around it, but he couldn't stop himself from tumbling off the train. That desperate grip was all that kept him from falling to the roadbed or even under the deadly wheels.

John Henry took only a split second to react. He leaped forward, leaned over the rail, and grabbed hold of Golliher's coat.

"Hang on!" he shouted. "I'll pull you up!"

The problem was that Walter Golliher outweighed him by at least fifty pounds, and lifting that much dangling weight was going to be almost impossible. Golliher's legs were kicking and flailing only inches above the speeding ground, and that didn't make things any easier. If Golliher lost his grip on the railing, John Henry would have to let go of him or be dragged over, too.

He grunted and strained as he worked to haul Golliher to safety. His pulse pounded in his head and his lips pulled back from his teeth in a grimace of effort.

It was no good. He wasn't going to be able to

make it, and he could tell that Golliher's hold was weakening . . .

Suddenly, someone appeared beside him. John Henry glanced over and saw the conductor's blue uniform and black cap. The conductor leaned over the rail, reached down, and got hold of Golliher's coat, too.

Another man crowded onto the platform and came up to the railing on John Henry's other side. With all three of them hanging on to Golliher, the prizefighter was able to start lifting himself. The three men hauled harder. Golliher got a foot onto the platform through a gap between the iron posts. He pushed up with that leg and took more of his weight on it.

He came up and over the rail and sprawled forward onto the platform as the three men who had saved his life fell backward. All of them lay there panting with effort, a huddled heap of exhausted humanity.

"Walter!"

That was Emmaline Dolan's voice. She rushed onto the platform and dropped to her knees beside Golliher, obviously not worried about getting her dress dirty on the grimy boards. She pulled his bloody head into her lap.

"Oh, Walter, are you all right, darling?"

With his chest still heaving, John Henry raised his head and looked at the way Emmaline was carrying on over Golliher. She leaned down, kissed his forehead, patted his bloody cheeks.

"Walter, please be all right!"

John Henry's head fell back. He began to laugh. Everything was clear now. Emmaline wasn't nearly as averse to Golliher's affections as she had claimed to be, but she didn't want the big prizefighter to take her for granted, either. She'd wanted to arouse his jealousy by fleeing and making him look for her.

John Henry had been her unwitting pawn. Only he had done his job of being chivalrous almost too well. He had nearly gotten first himself and then Golliher killed.

The conductor pushed himself up on an elbow and asked, "What . . . what's going on here, mister? That young lady came rushing back to the caboose and said there was a fight."

"It's a long story," John Henry said. "You'll have to get her to tell it to you."

He rolled onto his side and pushed himself to his feet. Once he was there he helped the conductor and the other man, who was a brakeman, to stand up as well. He spotted his hat lying upside down on the platform where it had fallen when Golliher grabbed him. Surprised but grateful that it hadn't blown away, he picked it up, brushed it off, and put it on.

Then he went back into the car where he'd been sitting before he'd gotten mixed up in this little farce.

It was still a long way to Los Angeles, and he had reports to study.

Chapter Seven

John Henry saw Emmaline Dolan and Walter Golliher one more time, when the train stopped at a town up the line and he had to switch to a different one heading west. Some of the passengers going on to Kansas City got out to stretch their legs on the depot platform, and Emmaline and Golliher were among them.

Walking arm in arm along the platform, they stopped short at the sight of John Henry coming toward them carrying his war bag.

The simplest thing would have been for him to turn around and go the other way, but that smacked too much of running away from trouble. John Henry wasn't about to do that. He continued toward them without breaking stride.

Golliher had cleaned himself up and changed out of his bloodstained clothes, but his nose was red and swollen and a scowl darkened his face. Emmaline just looked uncomfortable and embarrassed.

As well she should have been, thought John Henry. Her little game could have cost him and Golliher their lives. They could have both fallen off the train while they were fighting.

As he passed the couple, John Henry touched a finger to the brim of his hat and said coldly, "Ma'am." He moved on by without slowing down.

"Sixkiller."

Walter Golliher's voice was flat and hard. Obviously, Emmaline had told him John Henry's name.

John Henry stopped and turned to face them. He was in no mood for any more trouble. If Golliher wanted another fight, John Henry was going to put a stop to it before it got started by revealing that he was a deputy United States marshal on official business. He figured Golliher would back off rather than risk being arrested.

Without saying anything, John Henry gave Golliher a cool, level stare and waited. The prizefighter surprised him by extending a big, knobby-knuckled paw, not in a threatening gesture but rather for a handshake.

"I just wanted to say thank you," Golliher went on. The words seemed to pain him, but he forced them out anyway. "I reckon you saved my life, and after what I did, you sure didn't have any reason to."

John Henry clasped Golliher's hand. The big man's grip was powerful but not bone crushing.

"I never wanted any trouble with you, Golliher," John Henry said.

"I know that . . . now." Golliher glanced over at Emmaline, who looked even more embarrassed, if that was possible. "Things shouldn't have gone like they did, but I reckon they could have turned out worse."

"I suppose so."

John Henry let go of Golliher's hand, nodded to the man, and started to turn away.

Emmaline said, "I'm sorry. I . . . I can't let you go without saying that."

John Henry smiled thinly.

"Reckon you had what you thought was a good reason for what you did, Miss Dolan," he said. "I hold no grudges over that or anything else."

"Then you're a very good man, Mr. Sixkiller."

"Marshal," John Henry said.

"I beg your pardon?"

"It's Marshal Sixkiller."

Golliher said, "You're a lawman?"

"Deputy U.S. marshal out of Fort Smith."

"You mean . . ." Golliher swallowed. "You mean you work for Judge Parker?"

"That's right."

John Henry's smile was more genuine now. Maybe it was a little petty of him, but he enjoyed the surprised expressions on their faces. They looked a little worried, too, and he didn't mind that, either.

He added to Golliher, "Good luck on your bout," and this time when he turned to walk away, they didn't stop him. He chuckled, then put the whole incident out of his mind.

He had work to do, after all.

* * *

The rest of the reports the judge had given him made for pretty dry reading. They told about how counterfeit ten- and twenty-dollar bills had been found first in Wichita and then in other cities across the Southwest. Judge Parker had mentioned a few of those cities, but there were a number of others involved as well.

As John Henry read, a small frown formed on his face. He thought about the places where the bogus bills had been found and realized that they were all located along the railroad. Some of them were on the Atchison, Topeka and Santa Fe line, the one he was riding now. Others were stops on the Southern Pacific, with which the AT&SF merged in El Paso. The Southern Pacific then ran on west to Los Angeles.

It seemed highly likely to John Henry that whoever was passing the counterfeit money had ridden the train. Knowing that might come in handy. The Southern Pacific ran on up the California coast from Los Angeles to San Francisco and then on into Oregon. It didn't take any great stretch of the imagination to figure that O'Reilly would probably continue riding the train when he left southern California.

The railroad car he was in now wasn't any more comfortable than the one he'd been in earlier. As night fell, weariness gripped him, and that, coupled with the gentle motion of the train, lulled him to sleep. The slumber wasn't very restful, but it was better than nothing. He dozed through the night as the train rolled on toward Los Angeles.

The next morning he had breakfast in the train's dining car, then paused on one of the platforms between cars to gaze out at what seemed like mile after endless mile of orange groves. He'd heard that a lot of tropical fruit grew here in California because of its climate, but now he was seeing it with his own eyes. This was the first time he'd been this far west. He was grateful now that Judge Parker had assigned him to this case.

He wondered if he would have a chance to see the ocean while he was here. Having grown up in Indian Territory and spent most of his life there and in Arkansas and Kansas, he had never laid eyes on the ocean, and he wouldn't want to miss the opportunity. Although his job came first, of course.

The train pulled into the station at Los Angeles at midmorning. The town, which had been a sleepy little farming community only a few years earlier, was now a bustling, booming city. John Henry had read about how people from all over the country were moving out here, drawn by the good weather.

He couldn't fault the climate, that was for sure. It was sunny and warm, but there was a nice breeze off the ocean a few miles away. Puffy white clouds hung in the blue sky over the mountains north of the city. The air was clear as a bell.

John Henry had no desire to uproot himself and move halfway across the country . . . but if he did, this wouldn't be a bad place to go, he thought.

As he was crossing the depot's cavernous lobby, he was surprised to hear his name called. He stopped and turned around and was surprised again to see a uniformed law officer hurrying after him.

The man was young, with an earnest, open face and a shock of sandy hair under his black-billed cap. He came up to John Henry and said, "Excuse me, sir, but are you Marshal Sixkiller?"

"That's right, son," John Henry said. "How did you recognize me? We've never met before, have we?"

"No, sir. I was given your description and told that you should be on the train that just came in. I've been watching all the passengers get off. The chief of police received a telegram from Judge Isaac Parker in Fort Smith, Arkansas, and requested that someone meet you and pass it along to you."

"From Judge Parker, eh? You've got that wire with you?"

"Yes, sir." The young officer started to reach inside his blue coat but then paused. "I suppose the proper thing to do would be to see some identification." He seemed uneasy about saying that. "So if you wouldn't mind . . ."

"Sure," John Henry replied with a smile.

He took out the leather wallet with his badge and identification papers, opened it, and handed it to the officer, who took it with some obvious trepidation, looked at the bona fides, and handed it back quickly.

"Satisfied?" John Henry asked.

"Yes, sir. I just wouldn't have wanted to hand over that telegram to the wrong person." The young officer let out an awkward chuckle. "I mean, Judge Parker, he's the one they call the Hanging Judge, right? The one I've read about in *Harper's Weekly*?"

"He's the one," John Henry agreed.

"Is it true? About the gallows, I mean? You can hang a dozen men at once?"

"Oh, that's just some wild yarn," John Henry said with a dismissive wave of his hand. "A dozen executions at once? Shoot, we can only hang 'em six at a time. We have to run 'em through in shifts."

The young man's eyes widened.

"What's your name, son?" John Henry went on.

"My name? It's, uh, Wendell. Wendell McCormick."

John Henry held out his hand and said, "Well, Wendell, I believe you have something for me."

"I do? I mean, oh, yes, sir, Marshal Sixkiller, I do!"

Wendell reached in his pocket and brought out a folded telegraph flimsy. He handed it to John Henry, who unfolded it and scanned the words printed on it in pencil.

TO SIXKILLER STOP ADDITIONAL
INFORMATION RE O'REILLY STOP

REPORTED TO HAVE OPIUM HABIT
STOP SUGGEST CHECK WITH
SUPPLIERS IN LA STOP PARKER

John Henry folded the telegram again and slipped it in his own pocket.

"I'm obliged to you, Wendell," he said.

"Yes, sir, my pleasure. Is there anything else I can do for you?"

"Well . . ." John Henry thought about it, then drawled, "I reckon you could tell me how to find the nearest opium den."

Chapter Eight

Wendell McCormick had no idea how to answer that, so he did the next best thing. He took John Henry back to police headquarters with him and introduced him to Captain Ed Sawyer.

Sawyer was a stocky, blunt-faced man with graying dark hair. He had an unlit cigar clamped between his teeth and didn't remove it when he shook hands with John Henry and waved him into a chair in front of a paper-littered desk.

"So you're a deputy U.S. marshal," Sawyer said as he leaned back in his own chair and laced his fingers together over his ample stomach. "You look more like a cowboy."

"I've done a little cowboying," John Henry admitted. "Most of my adult life I've been a lawman, though."

"Sixkiller's an Indian name, ain't it?"

"I'm half Cherokee."

Sawyer grunted.

"Don't really look it," he said.

John Henry shrugged.

"I am what I am," he said. To change the subject, he went on, "Officer McCormick seemed to think you could tell me something about the opium trade in this city."

"Why's Uncle Sam interested in opium? If the government's gonna try to shut down the fellas bringing the stuff into the country, that's gonna be a mighty big job. There are China clippers full of it landing at isolated coves up and down the coast every night."

"My job isn't to stop the Chinese from bringing in opium," John Henry said. "I'm looking for a man who has an opium habit. He was here in Los Angeles not long ago. Maybe he still is, or maybe he's moved on. I'm just trying to get on his trail."

He didn't give Sawyer any other details about the case. The local lawman didn't really need to know about the counterfeiting, at least not at this point.

Sawyer used his tongue to roll the unlit cigar from one side of his mouth to the other, then chewed on the stogie for a moment while he frowned in apparent thought.

Then he said, "We've got our own Chinatown here, of course. Reckon every city of any size along the coast does. Plenty of joss houses and opium dens. From time to time we'll raid one and close it down, but another one just pops up somewhere else by the next night. What you need to do is talk to Wing Ko."

"Who's that?"

"Some sort of Chinese muckety-muck. He runs things in that part of town."

"You mean the law doesn't run things?" John Henry asked mildly.

That put a scowl on Sawyer's beefy face, as John Henry had figured it would. Sawyer finally took the cigar from his mouth and set it on a tin ashtray as he leaned forward in his chair.

"Part of upholding the law is knowing what you've got to work with," he snapped. "Sometimes you can do more good in the long run by acknowledging that you can't solve every problem right away."

"That's fair enough," John Henry said.

"Wing Ko knows there are certain lines he can't cross," Sawyer went on. "But we don't waste his time and he doesn't waste ours. He'll give us a hand from time to time as long as it doesn't hurt any of his people."

"Sounds like a good arrangement. You think he'd know something about the man I'm after?"

"Wing Ko's got eyes and ears in just about every nook and cranny in Chinatown. At the very least he can tell you where to start looking."

"Why would he do that?" John Henry asked. "I'd be a stranger to him. Surely he wouldn't want to spill a lot of secrets to somebody he didn't know."

"I can't make any guarantees," Sawyer said, "but he'll be more likely to talk to you if I send one of my men along with a note from me asking him to help you."

"You'd do that?"

Sawyer shrugged.

"We like to stay on Uncle Sam's good side, at least as long as it doesn't hurt our own cause. I'll write the note, and Wendell can take you to see Wing Ko."

"Officer McCormick?"

Sawyer chuckled and said, "Yeah, I know, he looks like he just fell off a hay wagon, doesn't he? But he's smarter than he looks, and he's ambitious."

"I guess I'll have to take your word for it."

"Come back here this evening," Sawyer said. "Wendell will have the note and be ready to take you where you need to go."

"Any suggestions what I should do in the meantime?"

"Ever seen the ocean?" Sawyer asked.

John Henry got himself a hotel room so he'd have a place to leave his war bag, then rode a horse-drawn trolley out to the end of the line, where a short walk brought him to a beach. In front of him the Pacific stretched out to the horizon, and it was an awe-inspiring sight. John Henry wouldn't have imagined there was that much water in the world.

The thought of sailing out onto that ocean in a ship, sailing so far that nothing but water was visible everywhere you looked, made him vaguely nervous. Some men were destined to travel the seas, he supposed, but he wasn't one of them. He was a land animal at heart.

There was something tranquil about just standing there at the water's edge, though, and watching it roll onto the beach in endless, gentle blue waves. The peacefulness of it washed through him. For a time he could forget about all the violence and trouble that usually filled his life.

After half an hour of standing there, he shook himself free of the ocean's hypnotic hold and went back to swing up onto another trolley and ride back to his hotel. Maybe he would return someday when he didn't have a job to do, he told himself . . . if that day ever came.

After eating supper in the hotel dining room, he walked back to the police station and met Wendell McCormick in front of the building. The young officer was waiting for him.

Wendell was dressed in civilian clothes this evening, a gray tweed suit and a dark gray hat. He patted the breast pocket of his jacket and said, "I have that note for Wing Ko from Captain Sawyer."

"You carrying a gun, Wendell?" John Henry asked.

Wendell moved his jacket back to reveal the checkered grips of a short-barreled revolver holstered on his left side in a cross-draw rig.

"We shouldn't run into any trouble tonight, but I figured it wouldn't hurt to be ready for some, anyway."

Sawyer had said that Wendell was pretty smart. The gun was evidence of that, John Henry thought.

"Lead on," he told the young man. "You're the one who knows where we're going."

They took a trolley to the edge of a district

where the streets seemed narrower and more twisting, whether they really were or not. Buildings were crammed in along those streets, and there were no sidewalks.

John Henry had seen a few Chinese people back in Indian Territory, but never this many in one place. They were like the ocean in that respect, something totally foreign to his experience. They clogged the streets and they all seemed to be in a hurry, although John Henry had no idea where they were going.

When he asked Wendell about that, the young man shook his head.

"I don't know. The Celestials are a very busy, industrious race. Except when they've been smoking opium. Then you never saw anybody move any slower."

John Henry saw a few white faces in Chinatown, but not many. Most of those he saw were furtive, telling him that the white men had come here in search of vice of some sort. If they had realized that he and Wendell were lawmen, they probably would have ducked their heads and hurried out of sight.

He supposed that he and Wendell looked like hombres in search of women or drugs or some other illicit thrill, too, because no one paid much attention to them.

Wendell seemed to know where he was going. John Henry was glad of that, because after the first few turns they made, he was lost. His frontiersman's instincts were next to useless in a place like this where buildings and people crowded in on him and the air was full of strange and somehow sinister smells and a man couldn't even see the stars when he looked up. Lines strung over the streets between the buildings were hung thickly with laundry.

Wendell opened the door into one of the buildings and told John Henry, "Wing Ko owns this restaurant and is usually here. If he's not, someone should be able to tell us where to find him."

"Do they know you here?" John Henry asked.

"Some of them do," Wendell answered somewhat cryptically. "Have you already eaten?"

"Yeah, at the hotel."

"Good. You might not want most of the things they serve here. The Chinese have, ah, different ideas about what constitutes delicacies than we do."

John Henry wasn't sure what Wendell meant by that, and he figured it would probably be smart not to ask.

The restaurant was crowded, as everywhere else in Chinatown seemed to be. Tables were small. Lanterns hung from the ceiling and cast a smoky glow over the room.

John Henry frowned as he saw that some of the diners had colorful birds with them in wicker cages that they could pick up and carry around. Some Chinese custom, he supposed, that he had never seen the like of before.

"Wing Ko's private room is back here," Wendell said, raising his voice slightly to be heard over the discordant strains of music that were coming from somewhere, although John Henry couldn't tell exactly where. The young man led him toward an arched doorway that was closed off by a curtain formed from close-packed strands of beads.

Wendell was just about to push through the curtain when a sudden commotion broke out in the room beyond. Men shouted angrily, and sounds of struggle could be heard. Wendell pushed his coat back with one hand so that he could reach his gun while his other arm swept the beads aside.

Both lawmen burst into the room. John Henry saw a big table with an inlaid marble top. Around it men were fighting, some with fists, others kicking at each other, others using knives or hatchets. On the other side of the table, atop a small dais, a man wearing a green and golden silk robe sat in an ornate chair, watching the battle with apparently only casual interest. John Henry realized that some of the men were trying to protect this man from being attacked.

Then one of the men involved in the ruckus burst through the defenders and leaped toward the man in the thronelike chair. He let out a strident shout and swung a hatchet high above his head, obviously intending to bring it down and cleave the skull of the man in the chair.

John Henry's instincts as a lawman took over. He wasn't going to stand there and watch cold-blooded murder being committed. He did the first thing that came naturally to his mind in a situation such as this.

He slapped leather.

Chapter Nine

The speed of his draw made the Colt seem to leap from its holster into his hand. He couldn't fire from the hip; the room was too crowded for that.

Instead he raised the revolver and took aim during the split second in which the hatchet man's hand paused at the top of its swing. The Colt blasted, and John Henry saw the hatchet fly from the man's fingers as the slug tore through the back of his hand and exploded out the palm. The would-be killer howled in pain as he stumbled and fell to his knees.

The seated man leaned forward then. His hand seemed to float out, not in any hurry at all, and lightly strike the wounded man's neck. The man collapsed, either dead or out cold.

The sound of the shot had made everybody else in the room freeze. John Henry heard a lot of clattering and the rush of feet behind him as the diners in the restaurant fled. Obviously none of them wanted to be caught here.

The tableau held for only a moment. Then the men who had been attacking turned to flee. John Henry and Wendell were blocking the door. John Henry knew he could cut down some more of them, but if those knives and hatchets started flying, he and Wendell wouldn't have much of a chance.

"Let them go."

The order came from the man on the thronelike chair, and to John Henry's surprise it was given in English. He nodded to Wendell, and both of them stepped aside to let the men rush out. The defenders left behind closed ranks around their leader on the dais.

"Wing Ko," Wendell said to the man. "You know me. Wendell McCormick. I work for Captain Sawyer."

The man on the chair nodded. He was middle-aged, clean-shaven, with sleek dark hair and a round, friendly face. To John Henry he looked like he ought to be running a laundry somewhere with a wife and a passel of kids, but he realized that wasn't fair, any more than it was fair when people thought his father's people, the Cherokee, were no different from the Sioux or the Comanche and ought to gallop around wearing war paint and feathered headdresses.

Wing Ko spoke in Chinese to his protectors. They cleared a path, and he beckoned to John Henry and Wendell.

"Please approach, my friends," he said. "The

troublemakers are gone. They will be dealt with in suitable fashion later."

Despite Wing Ko's pleasant expression and mild tone, John Henry thought that last statement sounded vaguely sinister. "Suitable fashion" could mean just about anything, very little of it good for the men toward whom it was directed.

John Henry saw the remnants of a meal scattered around the big, fancy table. He figured there had been some sort of negotiation taking place here . . . and it had gone badly.

That was really none of his business, though, legal or otherwise. He was just here to see if Wing Ko could tell him where to look for Ignatius O'Reilly.

As John Henry and Wendell stepped forward, some of the men around Wing Ko's chair tensed. They were all clad in white, pajama-like trousers and embroidered tunics of various colors, and their dark hair was twisted into short braids that hung down behind their necks. Several of them held hatchets.

"Holster your gun," Wendell whispered. "Wing Ko has given us leave to approach, but his guardians still don't like anybody coming near him holding a weapon."

John Henry grunted and pouched the iron. He said, "Makes sense, I reckon."

The guardians, as Wendell had called them, relaxed slightly but remained vigilant. John Henry and Wendell went around the table and stopped in front of Wing Ko's chair.

"Who is your friend, Wendell?" Wing Ko asked.

"This is Marshal Sixkiller," Wendell said. "He's a deputy U.S. marshal."

"A federal lawman, eh?" Wing Ko smiled and nodded to John Henry. "An honor to make your acquaintance, Marshal."

"The honor is mine, sir," John Henry said.

"You are an excellent shot." Wing Ko gestured dismissively at the unconscious man still lying on the floor practically at his feet, and went on, "This unworthy one would not have harmed me, but still it was exciting to see a demonstration of such skill with firearms. My people invented them, you know."

"Seems like I've heard that," John Henry said.

Wing Ko pointed at the unconscious man again and nodded, and a couple of his retainers dragged the man through a side door and out of the room. John Henry wondered if they were going to kill him, then decided that it wouldn't pay to speculate too much about that. He was in the middle of hostile territory right now, and the best thing he could do was concentrate on the job that had brought him here.

"I assume you're the reason for my young friend being here tonight, Marshal," Wing Ko continued. "Have you come to ask a boon of me?"

Wendell said, "Honorable sir, if I might . . . ?"

Wing Ko nodded. Wendell took the note from his pocket and handed it to him. Wing Ko unfolded it and glanced at it briefly.

"You will pass along my greetings to your

esteemed captain Sawyer and tell him that I was honored to offer my assistance to his guest?"

"Of course," Wendell said.

John Henry felt himself getting a little impatient. There had been enough of this oblique, overly formal give-and-take. He was a straightforward sort of hombre and wanted to get down to business.

Thankfully, the next thing Wing Ko said was, "What can I do for you, Marshal?"

"I'm looking for a man who might have been in Los Angeles as recently as a week or so ago," John Henry said. "His name is Ignatius O'Reilly."

Wing Ko smiled again and said, "Not a common name, I am sure. Also, not one that I have ever heard before. Why do you think I would know this man, Marshal?"

"He's reported to have a fondness for opium."

"Ah." Wing Ko nodded. "And Captain Sawyer told you that I was the one to ask about such things."

John Henry inclined his head in acknowledgment of that point.

"I do not deny that many of my countrymen have a fondness for the smoke of the lotus, and I am, above all else, a businessman. As such, when there is a demand I seek to supply it. But I know nothing of this man O'Reilly." Wing Ko spread his hands. "So in the face of this ignorance, what can I do to assist you?"

Wendell said, "Captain Sawyer thought you might put out the word to your places. You've got eyes and ears all over, Wing Ko. Someone might have seen or heard of the man the marshal is after."

"This is true," Wing Ko admitted. "You have told me his name, Marshal. Can you tell me what he looks like?"

John Henry repeated the description of O'Reilly he had been given. Wing Ko listened attentively, nodding now and then. When John Henry was finished, he turned to his men and spoke in rapid Chinese. A couple of them hurried from the room.

"I have instructed that O'Reilly's name and description be spread throughout Chinatown," Wing Ko said. "If he is within these environs, we will know soon. In the meantime, you and my young friend may wait here, Marshal. I have other business to attend to."

"Thank you," John Henry said.

"Yes, thank you, Wing Ko," Wendell added.

Striding serenely, Wing Ko left the room through the side door, followed by all of his guardians except for two men who stayed there, obviously to keep an eye on John Henry and Wendell. From the side of his mouth, John Henry asked the young officer, "Now what do we do?"

Before Wendell could answer, the curtain of beads rattled behind them, and a woman's voice said, "Now you sit down, enjoy a drink, and wait for the search my father put in motion to bear fruit."

John Henry turned. The young woman who had spoken stood there with the slim hands she had used to part the beads still raised. She was tall, elegantly slender in a dark blue silk gown, and had long, straight hair the color of midnight. She was also exceedingly beautiful when she smiled.

"I am Wing Sun," she said, "also called by some . . . the Black Lotus."

Chapter Ten

John Henry heard Wendell swallow hard. Evidently the young police officer was just as impressed by the woman's beauty as he was.

Wing Sun came into the room, her movements full of sensuous grace as she walked. A man carrying a tray with a bottle and glasses followed her. He set it down on the marble-topped table and backed off.

There were three glasses. Wing Sun poured what looked like wine from the bottle into each of them, then handed a glass to John Henry and another to Wendell, taking one for herself.

Up close she was even more lovely. Her eyes were so dark that they appeared to be almost as black as her hair, and her skin was flawless.

"To the success of your mission, gentlemen," Wing Sun said as she lifted her glass.

John Henry drank. The wine was potent. He wasn't a big drinker, so he hoped Wing Sun wouldn't be offended that he took only a sip and then set the glass back on the table.

"I didn't know Wing Ko had a daughter, ma'am," Wendell said.

"I have only recently arrived from China," she murmured.

John Henry told her, "You speak English very well for a newcomer."

"A missionary to our land, a man who was a doctor as well as a minister, taught me. I knew that someday I would follow my father here, and that when I did, I would need to know the language."

"You speak it very well," Wendell said.

Wing Sun smiled indulgently at him.

"Your friend just said that," she pointed out.

"Oh. Yes, of course. I'm sorry."

"No need to apologize," she told him with a shake of her head. She turned back to John Henry and went on, "I was told that you saved my father's life from one of the treacherous assassins sent by Ling Yuan."

"Well . . . your father claimed he would have stopped the fella himself."

"Perhaps he would have. Perhaps not. We will never know, will we? The important thing is that Wing Ko lives."

"Who's this fella Ling Yuan you mentioned?" John Henry asked.

Wing Sun's face hardened into a mask. A lovely mask, to be sure.

"Ling Yuan is a dog who believes that he should run things here in Chinatown instead of my father. He sent emissaries here tonight, to discuss a truce, he said. And my father, in his boundless generosity of spirit, welcomed them, dined with them, only to discover that they were snakes. Assassins sent to kill him, even if they lost their own lives in the process."

"Bushwhackers, I'd call 'em," John Henry said.

A low, musical laugh came from Wing Sun's gracefully curved lips.

"Bushwhackers," she repeated. "An American word I have not heard before now. A harsh word, as well. It suits them. Yes, Ling Yuan's men were . . . what would you call them? . . . dirty bushwhackers."

John Henry chuckled.

"If you stay here, I reckon you'll pick up even more of the lingo," he told her.

"There is no doubt that I will stay. There is nothing for me back in China. My mother and all the rest of our family are dead, killed by a warlord who is my family's ancestral enemy."

"I'm sorry," John Henry said.

"Our land is a violent one at times. But the same is true here. As long as people want more than they have, there will be struggles."

"That's true. But if people didn't want more than they have, there never would be any progress, would there?"

"In China, at least, we are more patient. We are an old, old people. We think in terms of centuries, not years."

John Henry was enjoying this conversation, but again he could feel impatience brewing inside him. If he found out for sure that O'Reilly had been in Los Angeles at the same time as the counterfeit money was being distributed, it would confirm what the Justice Department officials in Washington believed about him being behind this fresh batch of bogus bills.

"How long do you think it'll take for your father to find out if the man I'm looking for has been around here?" he asked.

"Not long. Runners have gone out to every joss house and opium den in the neighborhood. You should know what you seek within the hour."

"That would be good. I appreciate the help."

"One thing you should remember," Wing Sun said. "Favors come with a price. Someday my father . . . or I . . . may ask something of you."

"If it's legal and within my power, I'd be glad to do it."

"We shall see," the Black Lotus said with a smile.

True to her prediction, in less than an hour Wing Ko reappeared, coming into the private room trailed by some of his men. His hands were hidden in the voluminous sleeves of his robe as he gave a slight bow to John Henry and Wendell, a bow that the two men instinctively returned.

"I regret to tell you, Marshal Sixkiller, that I have found no trace of the man you seek," Wing Ko said. "No man using the name Ignatius O'Reilly, or matching the description you gave me, has been seen in Chinatown in recent weeks."

"You're sure?" John Henry asked as disappointment filled him. O'Reilly's opium habit was really the only lead he had to the man.

"If he had been here, my men would have discovered that fact," Wing Ko replied without hesitation. "I am sorry I could be of no help."

John Henry sighed and nodded. He said, "Well, at least we got to meet your charming daughter."

Wing Ko looked over at Wing Sun and smiled.

"Someday when I am gone, as my only child she will carry on my legacy," he said.

So he was grooming her to take over as the boss of all the crime in Chinatown, John Henry thought. That had to be sort of unusual for the Chinese, putting a woman in a position of such power, but like Wing Ko had said, she was his only child.

Wing Ko went on, "Daughter, be so kind as to escort these gentlemen out."

"Of course, Father."

She led John Henry and Wendell through the restaurant, which was crowded again. The customers had filtered back in once the fight between Wing Ko's guardians and the assassins sent by Ling Yuan was over.

They paused on the street outside the restaurant. John Henry touched a finger to the brim of his hat and said, "It was a pleasure to meet you, Wing Sun."

"Here," she said. "I have something for you."

She held out her hand, and in the light that came from inside the restaurant, John Henry was able to make out the object that lay on her palm.

It was a medallion of sorts, an oval of jade with a ring of gold around its outer edge. Painted on the jade was a black flower.

"A black lotus," John Henry said.

"If you ever have to come here again, show

this," she told him. "It will protect you and open many doors. And if you never return . . . keep it so that you will remember me, even though we met only briefly."

John Henry smiled and said, "I don't think I'm likely to forget you, Wing Sun, but I'll keep this with me from now on anyway."

He slipped the medallion into his pocket.

While they were talking, a wagon pulled by a pair of draft horses had been trundling its way along the narrow street toward them. A drooping canvas cover hung over the back of the wagon. John Henry had barely paid any attention to the vehicle. With such radiant loveliness as Wing Sun standing right in front of him, it was hard to look anywhere else.

That changed abruptly as Wendell let out a startled exclamation. John Henry swung around to see that the wagon had come to a stop, and the canvas cover over its bed was thrown back to reveal a handful of men and the ugly snout of a Gatling gun. Tongues of flame spurted from the gun's muzzle as it began its deadly chatter and sent a hail of bullets sweeping toward the front of the restaurant, and toward John Henry, Wendell, and Wing Sun.

Chapter Eleven

John Henry's left arm shot out and shoved Wing Sun off her feet. She let out a startled cry that was all but drowned out by the deadly sputtering of the Gatling gun. Bullets slashed through the space where the beautiful young woman had been standing only an instant earlier and crashed into the restaurant, shattering the big windows and sending millions of shards of glass spraying into the air.

At the same time, John Henry dropped to one knee and drew his Colt with the same sort of blinding speed he had demonstrated earlier. The barrel tilted up as he fired, instinct guiding his aim so that the slug struck the gunner just under the nose and angled on up into his brain.

The man died without a sound, falling backward as he let go of the gun's firing handles. One of his companions sprang to take his place.

The Gatling gun wasn't the only danger. Several of the men pulled hatchets from under their loose coats and let fly with them. John Henry spotted one of the glittering blades spinning through the air toward him and dived out of the way just in time to keep the hatchet from splitting his head open.

He fired again as he hit the street, and one of the men in the wagon bed spun off his feet as the bullet ripped through him.

Wendell hadn't reacted quite as fast and wasn't so lucky. One of the hatchets had lodged in his left shoulder. Blood poured from the wound as Wendell lay on the cobblestone street, but the young officer wasn't out of the fight just yet. He had been able to draw his revolver before he was injured, and now he fired it toward the men in the wagon.

The Gatling gun had fallen silent only for a moment. As it started singing its lethal song again, John Henry grabbed Wing Sun and rolled toward the mouth of an alley, taking her with him. As they came to a stop, she cried, "Let me go!" and twisted out of his grip.

The dress she wore was slit up the sides, and her long, slim legs flashed in the dim light as she pulled the dress up even more and reached under it. Lying in the alley's mouth, she raised the small-caliber pistol she had taken from a hidden holster and opened fire on the wagon.

John Henry knelt beside her and triggered off several more shots as well. Under the barrage from the two of them, and also Wendell, the men on the wagon lost their nerve, even though they had far superior firepower with the Gatling.

They didn't have the deadly aim of John Henry Sixkiller, though, and the shots from

Wing Sun and Wendell McCormick were taking a toll as well.

The man on the seats whipped his team and shouted at them. The horses lunged forward. The would-be killer manning the Gatling gun squeezed off a final burst, then dived for the floor of the wagon bed as bullets whistled around his ears.

John Henry, Wendell, and Wing Sun didn't stop firing until the wagon careened around a corner with its canvas cover flapping and vanished into the night.

With the immediate threat over, John Henry turned to Wing Sun and asked, "Are you all right?"

"Yes," she said. "The dogs didn't hit me. But this dress will never be the same after rolling around in the street."

"Better that than catching a bullet," John Henry said as he automatically reloaded the Colt. When he was finished, he holstered the weapon and ran along the street toward the fallen police officer. "Wendell! How bad are you hurt?"

Wendell sat up and grimaced. The hatchet was still lodged in his shoulder.

"I'm afraid to pull it out," he said. "I think I'd lose too much blood if I did."

"Let's get you inside."

John Henry bent to get his arms around the wounded young man. As carefully as he could, he lifted Wendell to his feet. Wing Sun came up on Wendell's other side to help support him. Broken glass crunched under their feet as they walked toward the restaurant entrance.

Thousands of rounds had smashed into the front of the building, blowing out every window and gouging great chunks from the bricks. A great deal of frantic yelling and screaming came from inside. John Henry knew the bullets that had gone through the windows must have inflicted terrible damage on the people in the restaurant.

The carnage was even worse than he expected. The inside of the place looked like a war had been fought in it. Blood was everywhere, on the floor, the walls, the overturned and broken tables. Bodies chewed to pieces by flying lead littered the floor. The screaming and crying sounded like something you'd expect to hear in the bowels of hell, John Henry thought.

With several of his guardians surrounding him, Wing Ko rushed through the devastation. He stopped short at the sight of his daughter and cried, "Wing Sun!"

She went to him and embraced him.

"I am unharmed," she assured him, "thanks to Marshal Sixkiller."

"Marshal, you have my eternal gratitude," Wing Ko said fervently. Then he exclaimed, "Wendell! You are hurt!"

The pale-faced young officer nodded as he clutched at his shoulder with the hatchet embedded in it.

"I'm not the only one, though," he said. "You've got a lot of injured to take care of—"

The loss of blood caught up to him then. His eyes rolled up in their sockets, and his knees unhinged. John Henry still had hold of him, though, and kept him from falling.

Wing Ko gestured to his men, several of whom hurried forward to take Wendell from John Henry.

"He will receive the finest of care," Wing Ko told John Henry as the men carried Wendell out of the wrecked dining room. "Did you see who committed this . . . this atrocity?"

"I did, but I'm afraid I didn't get a good enough look at any of them to know for sure if it was the same bunch who left here earlier."

"They had to be Ling Yuan's men, Father," Wing Sun said. "Who else would have done such a thing?"

"Who else indeed? Ling Yuan shall pay dearly for this. Earlier tonight, I was merciful to his men." Wing Ko's face was as hard as stone now. "Never again. There will be no mercy, there will be no peace in Chinatown until this bloody savagery is avenged."

It sounded to John Henry like war had broken out tonight. He was glad that Captain Sawyer and the rest of the police force here in Los Angeles would have to deal with it, not him.

Wing Sun asked, "Where would Ling Yuan get a gun such as that one, that fires so much and so fast?"

"That was a Gatling gun," John Henry said. "The army has them, but they're supposed to be the only ones. So I reckon Ling Yuan stole it from an armory somewhere."

Now that he thought about it, the theft of a weapon belonging to the United States Army did sort of give him jurisdiction here. That was a federal matter.

But he already had a job to do, and while passing counterfeit bills didn't strike him as being nearly as important as mass murder, he couldn't go against his orders, no matter how much he might want to strike back at Ling Yuan.

A couple of police wagons arrived outside the restaurant, and uniformed officers led by Captain Sawyer swarmed inside. The captain's teeth clamped down harder on the usual unlit cigar in his mouth as he burst out, "Good Lord! This looks almost like Gettysburg!" He spotted John Henry and went on, "Are you all right, Marshal?"

"I'm fine," John Henry told him.

"If I had known all hell was going to break loose, I wouldn't have sent you down here tonight. Where's Wendell?"

Wing Ko said, "The young officer was injured in the attack, Captain. His wounds are being tended to. As soon as possible, you can take him to the hospital."

Sawyer nodded and said, "I'm obliged to you for that, Wing Ko. Do you know who's responsible for this?"

Wing Ko glanced at John Henry for a second, then told Sawyer, "I have no idea, Captain."

John Henry knew what Wing Ko was asking of him. He wanted to deal with Ling Yuan himself, in "suitable fashion." But in order to do that, John Henry had to keep quiet about what he knew.

Wing Sun was looking at him, too, obviously waiting to see what he would do. John Henry supposed it wouldn't hurt anything to bend the rules that far.

"How about you, Marshal?" Sawyer asked. "Did you see the men who did this?"

"Yeah, I did, but . . ." John Henry shrugged. "You know how it is."

"Yeah," Sawyer said disgustedly. "All these Chinamen look alike."

Chapter Twelve

John Henry stayed there at the restaurant to help out any way he could in the aftermath of the deadly attack. Eleven people were dead, another two dozen wounded. As he told Sawyer, he estimated that he, Wendell, and Wing Sun had killed or badly wounded five or six of the attackers during the gunfight in the street, but that was impossible to confirm because all of them had still been on the wagon when it careened away.

"It's not like we'd have been able to identify any of them anyway," Sawyer grumbled. "People down here are the most closemouthed bunch you've ever seen. They won't tell you a damned thing, even when you're just trying to help them."

"Sounds a lot like the hillbillies back where I'm from," John Henry commented. He smiled slightly. "And I can say that because I'm sorta one of them."

"Well, I expect that blood will be running in the streets for a while," Sawyer said with a sigh.

"Old Wing Ko won't let whoever did this get away with it. And no matter what he says, he knows who's responsible for it, don't think for a second that he doesn't. But what can the police do? Come along afterward, cart away the bodies, and mop up the blood, that's what we can do. And that's about all."

John Henry waited until they got word from the hospital that Wendell McCormick was in stable condition and was expected to recover, then he went back to his hotel, weary and frustrated because it seemed that O'Reilly's trail had petered out before he could even find it.

He had taken off his shirt to wash up but still wore his boots and trousers when a soft knock sounded on the door. He had already coiled his gun belt around the holstered Colt and placed them on a chair next to the bed. A quick step brought him to the bedside, where he reached down and slid the revolver from leather. With his thumb over the hammer as he held the gun ready, he moved to the door and called, "Who is it?"

"Wing Sun."

He was surprised to hear her voice. Relaxing slightly, he lowered the gun and reached for the doorknob. He remained vigilant as he opened the door, however, wary of some trick.

There was no trick. The beautiful young woman known as the Black Lotus was alone in the hotel corridor. She wore a different dress now, but it fit her as sleekly as the other one had. A jacket was draped around her shoulders. Her head was bare.

"I didn't expect to see you again tonight," John Henry said.

"Aren't you going to invite me in?" Wing Sun asked.

"It's not really proper. An unmarried young woman, in a hotel room with a strange man. A strange man with no shirt on, I might add."

She said coolly, "We just met this evening, Marshal, but if you believe that I worry a great deal about what is proper, then you really do not know me."

John Henry had to laugh at that. He stepped back to let her in and tucked the Colt into his waistband. He picked up his shirt from the end of the bed where he had tossed it and shrugged into it, but he left it unbuttoned.

"So, what does bring you here?" he asked.

Wing Sun eased the door closed behind her. She said, "If you believe I've come because of some immediate, irresistible romantic attraction I feel for you, Marshal, please do not flatter yourself."

"The thought never crossed my mind," John Henry lied. He was as human as the next man. Of course the thought had crossed his mind.

"My father feels a great debt of gratitude toward you. Not only did you save his life this night, but you saved the life of his only child as well. So even though he has much to occupy his mind right now, he made inquiries about this man you seek, Ignatius O'Reilly."

John Henry frowned a little and shook his head.

"Wing Ko already put out the word. There's been no sign of O'Reilly in Chinatown."

"No . . . but he was curious what your interest in the man is. He assumed it must be serious to put a federal lawman on O'Reilly's trail. Though in Chinatown my father's word is law with most, his contacts and influence extend far past the boundaries of one small neighborhood. He discovered that this man O'Reilly is known to be a criminal, a counterfeiter."

John Henry didn't see any harm in admitting that, so he shrugged and said, "That's true."

"Armed with that additional piece of information, he sent word to all parts of the city. Counterfeit bills have made their way to Chinatown, but from only one source: a gambler who indulges in our games of chance. A man named Quentin Ross."

John Henry felt his pulse speed up. He had thought the trail was at a dead end, but Wing Sun had just given him a potential new lead.

"What do you know about Ross?" he asked.

Wing Sun smiled.

"He is playing in a high-stakes poker game tonight at a roadhouse in the hills. Perhaps if you ask him, he will tell you where he got the false bills."

John Henry took the gun from his waistband, slid it back into the holster, and started buttoning his shirt. He had been tired, wanting only to clean up a little and get some sleep, but that weariness had vanished when his manhunter's instincts were aroused.

"I hope you can tell me where to find this roadhouse," he said.

"I can do better than that. I can show you." Wing Sun reached into the bag she carried and brought out a small stack of bills tied together with string. "And I can give you the money you need to buy into the game with Ross, courtesy of Wing Ko . . . and the Black Lotus."

No amount of argument could persuade Wing Sun it wasn't a good idea for her to come with him, or for Wing Ko to finance his entry into the game. Wing Ko could easily afford it, she insisted. She knew where the roadhouse was, and it was the sort of place where he was more likely to be accepted as a high-rolling gambler if he had a beautiful woman on his arm.

"I have never been bothered with a sense of false modesty," she told him. "I know I'm beautiful."

"You won't get any argument from me about that," John Henry muttered. He had finished getting dressed again. "All right, let's go."

A carriage hitched to a pair of fine black horses was waiting outside the hotel. Two of Wing Ko's men were on the high seat, one handling the reins, the other holding a shotgun. Both men wore brocaded jackets and round black caps.

"When I told my father I wished to come and help you with your mission, he would not allow it unless I brought two of his men to protect me," Wing Sun explained. "With a war with Ling Yuan looming, he did not want to risk my safety. I insisted that we owe you a debt, however, and that I should help pay it in any way that I can."

"And you didn't want to pass up a chance for a little adventure at the same time," John Henry guessed.

Wing Sun smiled as she held out her hand so he could help her into the carriage.

"I am but a submissive Chinese girl," she murmured.

John Henry thought about the way she had pulled that gun from a holster hidden under her dress, probably strapped to her thigh, and blazed away at Ling Yuan's men. *Submissive* wasn't exactly the word he would use to describe her.

He didn't see any point in mentioning that, however, so he handed her up into the carriage and then followed her in. The driver got the team moving.

He must have known already where he was going, because Wing Sun didn't give him any instructions. The carriage rolled through the streets of Los Angeles and then started up into the hills overlooking the city on a broad, well-packed trail. At times the route was pretty steep, but the driver guided the horses with an expert hand.

John Henry was sitting on the front seat, facing backward. The carriage had lamps burning at the corners of its roof, but they didn't cast much light inside, so he couldn't see Wing Sun very well. He said, "What do you know about this man Ross?"

"Not a great deal," she replied. "His family owns a ranch and is respected, but he is regarded as a wastrel. A black sheep, I believe you Americans call it. He is fond of liquor, gambling, young girls. Too fond of those things. But he has plenty of money, so he has always been able to skirt around trouble that might otherwise have claimed him."

"Your father found out all this in a matter of an hour or so?"

Wing Sun laughed and said, "My father has tentacles like the octopus. They spread everywhere. They give him his power . . . and that power is what men such as Ling Yuan seek to wrest from him by any means necessary."

"I wish him luck," John Henry said sincerely, although a part of him knew that he shouldn't be sympathizing with a crime lord. Wing Ko had all but admitted that he was responsible for the opium that was brought in from China up and down the coast.

But as Captain Sawyer had said, sometimes a lawman had to work with what was available to him. Tonight, the best way John Henry could proceed with the job that had brought him here was to accept help from a criminal . . . and that criminal's beautiful daughter.

The carriage turned off the trail and followed a path that wound through some trees. It emerged onto a shoulder of ground that jutted out from a hillside. Dotted across the valley below were the lights of Los Angeles, scattered at this time of night since most people had already turned in.

The large house built in Spanish style that sat on the promontory, though, was lit up brightly. Carriages, buggies, and buckboards were parked at the end of a flagstone path leading to the house. A number of saddle horses were tied to several hitching posts.

"When you called it a roadhouse, this isn't exactly what I figured you meant," John Henry said to Wing Sun. "Back where I come from, most roadhouses are just run-down taverns."

"This is the old Campos estate," Wing Sun said. "A proud old Californio family fallen on hard times, according to my father. Once they owned much of these hills and a large portion of the valley as a land grant from the King of Spain. But everything is gone now except the old villa. Matteo Campos provides games of chance, food and drink, and women for those who seek a discreet venue for their vices."

"Men like Quentin Ross."

"Especially men like Quentin Ross."

John Henry opened the door and stepped out. As he turned to take Wing Sun's hand and help her to the ground, he said, "We'll have to be careful in there."

"One must always be careful. Danger lurks in unexpected places."

"Chinese wisdom?"

"Common sense." Wing Sun linked her arm with his. "Come on. Let's find the man passing those counterfeit bills."

As they started up the flagstone path toward

the house, John Henry was struck by the thought that so far, this night sure wasn't turning out the way he had expected it to. He had found himself in the middle of a fight between Chinese hatchet men, nearly been mowed down by a Gatling gun, and now he was waltzing into a gambling den run by a dissolute Californio with the beautiful, dangerous daughter of a Chinese crime lord on his arm.

Yeah, he mused, this was a pretty far cry from Indian Territory.

Chapter Thirteen

A swarthy man in tight trousers, a short charro jacket, and white shirt met them at the double doors of the entrance. He had thick, graying dark hair and a drooping mustache, and he wore a long-barreled Remington revolver holstered on his hip. He rested a hand on the gun's walnut grips as he confronted John Henry and Wing Sun.

"You and the señorita have not been here before, señor," the man said. "I have an excellent memory for faces."

"Then you probably recognize the faces on these," John Henry said as he opened his coat enough for the man to see the sheaf of bills stuck in his shirt pocket.

"Of course, my old amigos," the man said without a trace of humor on his solemn, flinty face. "Come in, *por favor.* If I may ask . . . how did you become aware of our establishment?"

Wing Sun said, "Captain Phillip Armistead told us about it."

"Ah, *el capitán* Armistead. Very well." The door guardian waved them into a tiled foyer. "Enjoy your evening."

As they walked along a short hallway, following the sounds of laughter, talking, and the rapid clicking of a roulette wheel, John Henry asked quietly, "Who's Armistead?"

"A former military man who patronizes one of my father's establishments. He's some sort of politician now, I believe. He was eager to assist us in our quest for information."

Which probably meant that Wing Ko had blackmailed him into helping, John Henry mused. He wondered if Armistead was addicted to opium.

This job was leading him down murkier and murkier pathways, John Henry thought, and it made him uneasy. He had always been a pretty straightforward hombre, wise enough to be aware that not everything in the world was always black-and-white but knowing as well that it didn't pay to stray too far into the gray area between right and wrong.

They emerged into a large central courtyard open to the stars overhead. It was surrounded by a second-floor balcony bordered with wrought iron railings. Flowering vines grew on those railings. The water in a constantly running fountain in the center of the courtyard tinkled merrily.

It was an unusual location for a gambling setup, but that's what John Henry saw before him. Tables for poker and blackjack, faro layouts, the roulette wheel he had heard on their way in . . . along with a bar on each side of the courtyard and a number of tables where men and women sat drinking.

A man in a considerably fancier version of the outfit worn by the doorman came toward John Henry and Wing Sun. He was young, probably in his midtwenties, with a handsome, olive-skinned face and a stiff brush of dark hair. He smiled as he stopped in front of them and said, "I know you, señorita, or I should say that I know who you are, since we've not had the pleasure of meeting before now. You are the honorable Wing Ko's daughter."

"And you are Matteo Campos," Wing Sun said.

Campos inclined his head in acknowledgment of her statement.

"It is an honor to have you visit my humble home," he said. "If anyone had asked me, I would have said it was unlikely that you would grace us with your presence, considering the number of establishments belonging to your father where similar entertainment can be sought."

"Exactly," Wing Sun said. "Those places belong to my father. I seek something . . . different."

Campos's smile widened. He said, "Ah. I understand. In that case, allow me to welcome you and your friend . . . ?"

"Señor Sixkiller," Wing Sun said.

"John Henry Sixkiller," John Henry supplied. He extended a hand to Campos. Very few people in southern California knew that he was a deputy U.S. marshal, so he didn't see how it would do any harm to use his real name. Anyway,

Wing Sun had rendered that question moot by introducing him to Campos.

"The pleasure is mine," Campos said as he shook hands. "What can we interest you in this evening? Blackjack, roulette . . . ?"

"Actually, I was thinking more of poker," John Henry said. "The higher the stakes, the better."

"Ah. You prefer a game of skill, rather than chance."

John Henry nodded and said, "That's what I had in mind. It's got to have enough riding on it to make it truly interesting, though."

"Of course. Some of my customers see things the same way you do. If you and the señorita would like to come with me . . ."

He swept an elegantly manicured hand toward a broad staircase that led up to the balcony. They climbed the stairs and Campos led them along the balcony to an arched doorway where another armed guard stood. The man moved aside to let them into the room.

The chamber was luxuriously appointed with heavy sofas and chairs, thick rugs on the hardwood floor, a large fireplace on one side of the room. A crystal chandelier hung from an exposed ceiling beam above the baize-covered poker table in the center of the room.

Six men sat at the table, concentrating on the cards in their hands. Three women, all young and beautiful, lounged in armchairs arranged to the side, near the fireplace, and sipped from the drinks they held.

Wing Sun was lovelier than any of the three women, John Henry thought.

One of the men at the table had the look of a professional gambler. John Henry suspected that he worked for Campos. Three of the others appeared to be local businessmen out for some excitement. The fifth man looked like a Spanish grandee with his elegant suit and pointed goatee, and the sixth . . .

The sixth had to be Quentin Ross, John Henry thought. Young, handsome in a dissolute, going-to-seed manner, with tightly curled fair hair and a seemingly permanent arrogant sneer. As John Henry, Wing Sun, and Campos approached the table, the man John Henry had pegged as Ross folded, throwing in his cards with a curse.

"Your luck is bound to change, Mr. Ross," the professional gambler said, confirming John Henry's hunch.

"Yeah," one of the businessmen agreed with a grin. "It can't stay that bad all night . . . or can it?"

"Just finish the damn hand," Ross snapped, "so I can have another chance to get even with you pikers."

Since he was out of the game for the moment, Ross turned his attention elsewhere. John Henry saw the young man's eyes swing toward Wing Sun and light up with curiosity. More than curiosity . . .

Lust burned in those eyes, too.

Unaccountably, that made John Henry angry even though he knew there was nothing between him and Wing Sun other than mutual respect. He didn't like the way Ross was looking at her. Judging by the way she stiffened as she stood arm in arm with him, neither did she.

Ross scraped his chair back and stood up.

"Leaving the game?" the grandee asked him.

"Not hardly," Ross said. "I just want to make the acquaintance of this lovely lady. Introduce us, Matteo."

Campos said, "Allow me to present Señorita Wing Sun and Señor Sixkiller."

"Wing Sun," Ross repeated, ignoring John Henry. "Wait a minute, I know who you are. I've heard rumors about old Wing Ko having a daughter."

"That venerable one is my father," Wing Sun admitted.

"I never figured the old boy would have a gal who's so pretty. You must have gotten your looks from your mama. What are you doing outside of Chinatown?"

"She's with me," John Henry said, leaning forward slightly and speaking sharply enough that Ross had to acknowledge him.

"Well, then, you're a lucky son of a gun, aren't you?" Ross said with a sneer that made John Henry want to punch him in the face.

"That's what I'm here to find out. I'm here to play cards."

To emphasize his point, John Henry drew the stack of bills from his pocket.

At that point, the hand going on at the table ended, with the grandee taking the pot. Quentin Ross glanced back and forth, obviously torn between paying attention to Wing Sun and wanting to get back into the game.

John Henry wanted to get into the game himself, and one of the businessmen made that possible by heaving a sigh and saying, "That's enough for me, I'm afraid." He put his hands on the edge of the table and pushed himself to his feet. "I think I'd better go home while I still have a home to go to."

One of the other men at the table laughed. He was big, well dressed, with a rough-hewn face and a shock of dark hair. At first glance John Henry had taken him for a businessman, but on second look he wasn't so sure. The man's features had a certain cruel, piratical cast to them.

"That's what happens when you go swimming with sharks," he commented. "Why don't you join us, Mr. . . . Sixkiller, was it?"

"That's right." John Henry leaned over the table to shake hands with the man. "John Henry Sixkiller."

"Nick Prentice," the man introduced himself. He nodded toward the chair the businessman had just vacated.

John Henry looked around the table at the other men and said, "With your permission . . . ?"

The house gambler waved him into the empty chair, and the others nodded.

John Henry turned to Wing Sun and said, "Why don't you get yourself something to drink, honey, and bring me a drink, too?"

She smiled, but her eyes glittered and he could tell she was annoyed by the dismissive tone he had taken. It was all part of the act, though, and he figured she understood that.

"Of course, darling," she murmured.

John Henry sat down. These men didn't bother with chips. They just piled money in the center of the table. He threw in his own ante, and the grandee, who had won the previous hand, began to deal.

Wing Sun came back to the table a couple of minutes later as the men were studying the hands they'd been dealt. She placed a glass of champagne next to the stack of bills in front of John Henry and leaned over to nuzzle her lips against his ear.

"Good luck, darling," she said so the others could hear her, then breathed, "I'll get even with you for the way you spoke to me just now."

John Henry just smiled.

Somehow, he was looking forward to Wing Sun making good on that "threat."

Chapter Fourteen

The game was high stakes right from the start. John Henry knew he wasn't playing with his own money, but he resisted plunging too much anyway. As a result, he stayed mostly even for the first hour as he gauged the skills of the other players.

The house gambler, as house gamblers tend to be, was steady and unspectacular, winning more than he lost but seldom taking a big pot. The grandee was a little more daring, losing more hands but staying slightly ahead overall. A man who introduced himself as Harvey Court explained to John Henry that he owned a hardware store; he was cautious but not very good at the game, so he lost money, but slowly.

Nick Prentice was more daring than the grandee and lost considerably more than he won, but when he won it tended to be a big pot, so he was ahead of the game, too.

All that meant most of the losses had to come from one place, and so they did: Quentin Ross.

He bet wildly, recklessly, cackling with glee when luck favored him and he won, more often cursing bitterly when his bluffs failed or when he reached to fill a hand and missed out on the cards he needed. The pile of money in front of him dwindled steadily, and the smaller it got, the angrier Ross became.

After one particularly stinging loss in a hand that Prentice won, Ross blustered, "If I didn't know better, I'd say that somebody was—"

Prentice cut in, his voice icy as he told Ross, "You don't want to finish that sentence, my friend."

John Henry knew that Ross had been about to accuse Prentice of cheating. That likely would have been a mistake. Ross was fairly big and looked like he could handle himself in a fight, but John Henry figured Prentice could probably break the young wastrel in half.

That wouldn't do. John Henry needed information from Ross. He said, "Why don't we take a break, maybe step out on the balcony and smoke a cigar? What do you say, Ross?"

"I'm not leaving the game, damn it—"

The house man said, "I think a break is a good idea. You won't lose your seat, Quentin."

Ross took a deep breath, then jerked his head in a curt nod.

"All right. Fine. We'll take a break."

He shoved his chair back and stood up.

One of the young women sitting near the fireplace stood up and came over to Ross. She had a thick mane of curly blond hair and sported a tiny beauty mark near her mouth. She asked, "Would you like me to come with you, Quentin?"

"Go back and sit down, Penelope," Ross told her.

She didn't seem offended by his sharp tone. She went back to her chair like he had told her to.

John Henry stood up as well, leaving his glass of champagne on the table. He had taken only small sips from it all evening, making it look like he was drinking more than he really was. He wasn't going to take a chance on anything muddling his mind.

Except for one twenty-dollar bill that he surreptitiously slipped in his pocket, he left his winnings on the table, too, knowing that they would be safe. Matteo Campos couldn't afford to allow any thievery in his place, because of the damage that would do to its reputation.

John Henry and Ross stepped out onto the balcony. The fragrance of honeysuckle and flowering blossoms filled the night air, along with the sounds coming from the gambling layouts in the courtyard below. John Henry had a couple of cigars in his coat pocket. He took them out and offered one to Ross.

"Thanks," the man said, not sounding too sincere about it. John Henry struck a lucifer and lit both cheroots.

"Your name strikes me as familiar, Ross," John Henry said, making it sound like he was just making small talk. "Your family owns a big ranch, isn't that right?"

"Yeah."

"I reckon that explains how you can afford a high-stakes game like this one."

"I don't take any money from my family," Ross said, not bothering to conceal the irritation he felt. "I make my own way."

"Oh? What do you do?"

"That's my business."

"Sure," John Henry said easily. "Didn't mean to pry. I don't talk much about my business, either."

"It must be crooked, or else you wouldn't be thick as thieves with Wing Ko. He wouldn't allow you to squire his daughter around unless he trusted you."

"That's true," John Henry agreed. "Wing Ko's got some other things on his mind these days, though. Trouble with another fella, named Ling Yuan."

"Really?" For the first time, Ross sounded like he was actually interested in something John Henry had to say. "I hadn't heard about that."

"Yeah, there was some sort of trouble at Wing Ko's restaurant tonight. Twice, from what I understand."

John Henry didn't mention that he had been right in the middle of both of those incidents.

Ross puffed on his cigar and mused, "I enjoy going to Chinatown."

"And I'll bet the folks there are glad to see you. American bills spend just fine, don't they? Even some of the bogus ones."

Ross glanced over sharply at him.

"What are you talking about? What bogus bills?"

John Henry shrugged and said, "I don't know.

I just heard some rumors about counterfeit money showing up in Chinatown and other places around Los Angeles recently." He took the twenty from his pocket and held it up, rubbing the bill between his thumb and forefinger. "Like this one, maybe."

Among the thick stack of documents that Judge Parker had given him to read on the train had been one that explained how to spot the false bills produced by Ignatius O'Reilly. It wasn't easy. The paper was infinitesimally thinner, the ink lines broken almost invisibly here and there. If a person didn't know what to look for, it would be almost impossible to notice that the money was fake.

The printing was slightly off-register in this current batch, which had led the officials in Washington to conclude that O'Reilly was getting a little sloppy in his work. Even that flaw was difficult for a layman to detect.

During the poker game, John Henry had been making an unobtrusive study of the bills that came his way from Ross. Although he was far from an expert, he was convinced there was at least a good chance some of the bills were counterfeit, including the one he had brought out to the balcony.

As John Henry held that twenty up now, Ross said angrily, "What the hell are you talking about? What's your game, Sixkiller?"

"Poker," John Henry said. "I thought you knew."

Ross threw the cigar onto the balcony and crushed it out with his heel. He said, "That's not all you're up to, and you damned well know it. What's all this talk about counterfeit money?"

"I'm always on the lookout for . . . let's call it a good business opportunity. I can probably help you, Ross. I have contacts in several of the banks here in Los Angeles. Put me in touch with your supplier, and I can make both of us rich men."

A harsh laugh came from Ross.

"You're trying to butt in on things you don't know anything about. I've seen your type before. You waltz in and try to take over—"

"Quentin."

The soft voice belonged to a woman. John Henry looked over his shoulder and saw that the blonde called Penelope had come onto the balcony.

"What is it?" Ross asked impatiently.

"Señor Campos wants to see you."

"Can't it wait?"

"He said it was urgent."

"Oh, all right." Ross cast a withering look toward John Henry. "We're done out here, anyway."

He stalked back into the room where the private game had been going on. John Henry tried not to sigh in disappointment. He had tried the subtle approach, and it hadn't worked at all.

Now he would have to consider getting Ross somewhere alone, putting a gun to the man's head, and forcing him to reveal the source of the fake money he'd been passing. The simple ways were usually the best, and nothing convinced a man to talk faster than the feel of a gun muzzle digging into his ear.

John Henry was going to follow Ross back into the room, but Penelope slid over gracefully to intercept him. She stopped him with a hand on his arm.

"Mr. Sixkiller, isn't that right?" she said.

"That's right," he said as he tried to move around her. He didn't really have time right now to deal with Ross's mistress, whatever she wanted from him.

"That's a fascinating name," Penelope went on, gracefully moving to the side so that she was still in his way. "Are you an Indian? You don't look like an Indian."

"Half Cherokee. No offense, miss—"

"Smith," she supplied, even though he hadn't really asked. "Penelope Smith."

"No offense, Miss Smith, but—"

She threw back her head and screamed.

Chapter Fifteen

John Henry liked to think that he didn't surprise easily, but he was so taken aback by the blonde's sudden outburst that for a moment all he could do was stand there and stare at her.

Then she yelled, "Rape! Oh, my God, somebody stop him! Help me! Rape!"

She still had hold of John Henry's arm. She gave him a hard shove and staggered away from him as if he had been holding her and she had broken free. Reaching quickly to the neckline of her gown, she grasped it and ripped the fabric so that it hung down, revealing a considerable expanse of her creamy breasts.

"What the devil's wrong with you?" John Henry finally asked.

For a split second, she gave him a sly smile, then lunged to the balcony railing and hung over it, a position that revealed even more of her lush figure to the people in the courtyard who were looking up to see what all the commotion was about.

"Help me!" she cried again. "He's attacking me!"

John Henry had no idea what the motivation was for this farce, but he knew what the outcome was likely to be. Angry shouts rose from the men in the courtyard, and several figures ran onto the balcony from the private gaming room, led by Quentin Ross.

"Sixkiller!" Ross yelled. "Get away from her, you bastard!"

John Henry lifted his left hand toward Ross as the man closed in on him. He said, "Now, hold on just a min—"

Ross didn't let him finish. Instead he swung a punch at John Henry's head with all the power of his charge behind it.

John Henry twisted aside. Ross was fast, and even with John Henry's quick reaction, Ross's fist scraped along the side of his head and sent his hat flying off. John Henry grappled with the man, swung him around, and shoved him toward the balcony railing.

Ross caught himself and was ready to attack again, but this time John Henry had time to say, "Wait just a blasted minute! I didn't do anything. The girl's lying."

Penelope started to sob. Big tears ran down her smooth cheeks. She covered her face with her hands and wailed, "Don't listen to him, Quentin! He attacked me! He tried to rape me!"

Everybody in the place was watching the scene on the balcony now. They had forgotten about the games. The group from the poker room, including Matteo Campos and Nick Prentice, stood to one side. Wing Sun was just behind them, and John Henry felt her coolly speculative gaze on him. He could tell that she was wondering if there was any truth to Penelope's lurid accusations.

She should have known better, John Henry thought . . . but how could she be sure of anything where he was concerned? They had met only a few hours earlier and were practically strangers themselves.

Ross started to claw under his coat as he snarled, "I ought to kill you!"

John Henry knew the man was reaching for a gun. This was quickly going from bad to worse. He didn't want to be forced to kill Ross before he even learned anything. He couldn't just stand there and let Ross shoot him, though.

"Enough!"

The powerful, commanding voice belonged to Matteo Campos. He strode forward, putting himself between John Henry and Ross, who stopped trying to drag a pistol from a shoulder holster.

"This is my home, and you people are my guests," Campos went on. "I will not allow a gunfight in the house my great-grandfather built!"

"Sixkiller attacked me," Penelope insisted. "Somebody's got to do something about it!"

Ross said, "A man like you ought to know something about honor, Campos."

"Because of my Spanish heritage, you mean?" Campos looked back and forth between John Henry, Ross, and Penelope. Clearly he was torn about how to proceed. After a moment he said, "Señor Sixkiller, is there any truth to this?"

"Not a bit," John Henry answered without hesitation.

Penelope gasped and said, "Now he's calling me a liar!"

"I demand satisfaction for my fiancée's honor," Ross said.

John Henry hadn't realized the two of them were engaged to be married, not that that had any relevance to anything. Maybe the best thing to do was just back off, he told himself. He could confront Ross again later, somewhere else.

"Let me understand," Campos said to Ross. "You are challenging Señor Sixkiller to a duel?"

"That's exactly what I'm doing!" Ross declared.

John Henry bit back a groan. The complications were just piling up deeper and deeper. The evening had already been packed with violence, and he had no desire to finish it off with some stupid duel.

"Forget it," he snapped. "I didn't do anything wrong, and I'm not going to fight a duel."

"Traditionally, this is the way such things are settled," Campos said. He made a small gesture, and several of his armed guards moved closer. "Refusal to fight could be taken by some as an admission of guilt, Señor Sixkiller."

"Take it for anything you want," John Henry said. "Wing Sun and I are leaving."

Again he was surprised. Wing Sun said, "Don't be so sure about that, John Henry. I believe you, but I think there's only one way for you to prove you're telling the truth. Honor demands it."

Somehow the whole world had gone loco when he wasn't looking, John Henry thought.

Ross sneered and said, "I'm gonna take great pleasure in shooting you, Sixkiller."

"No shooting!" Campos said. "There is a better way. The traditional way of my people. The test of the lash! Duel by bullwhip!"

Everyone in the courtyard heard him. A cheer went up. To the gamblers who had come here to the old villa, such a duel would be something new and exciting to bet on.

Campos snapped his fingers at one of his men, who turned and hurried away.

"Jorge will bring the whips," Campos said. "You will fight in the back, near the stables."

John Henry said, "I haven't agreed to fight anybody."

Campos inclined his head and said, "In that case I would have no choice but to allow Señor Ross to shoot you. Honor must be satisfied."

And as the owner of the place, Campos would probably insist on taking a cut from all the bets placed on the outcome of such a battle, John Henry thought cynically.

"Fine," he heard himself saying. "If that's what it's going to take to settle this madness."

More cheers came from the people in the courtyard. Campos smiled and gestured for John Henry and Ross to precede him down the stairs.

John Henry glanced again at Wing Sun but couldn't read her expression. Her face was a smooth mask.

He picked up his hat and started down the stairs.

Excited babble rose around John Henry and Ross as they descended to the courtyard. Men called bets back and forth. A lot of money would change hands tonight, and Matteo Campos probably would find his fingers clutching a significant chunk of it, John Henry thought.

Campos came down the stairs behind them and then took the lead, heading out the rear of the villa with the large crowd trailing him. The man he had sent after the bullwhips hurried after them and caught up, carrying a pair of the coiled, sinister-looking whips. He handed them to Campos.

They stopped at a large stretch of open ground next to the stables, which appeared to be empty in the light cast by torches carried by several of Campos's men. The vast hacienda had shrunk to just this villa, so there was no longer a need for a big remuda of horses.

"Have either of you ever used a bullwhip before?" Campos asked John Henry and Ross.

"I have," Ross answered immediately. "I used one on the ranch all the time."

"So have I," John Henry said, although in truth his experience with a whip was very limited. There was a good chance Ross was more skilled with the thing than he was.

But Ross had been drinking heavily all evening, so it was possible the liquor had slowed his reflexes considerably. John Henry would have to put his faith in his own speed and strength, which he already did every time he entered a fight.

"These whips are identical," Campos said, "so there's no point in letting either of you choose your weapon. However, tradition demands that practice in a duel, so as the challenged, Señor Sixkiller, you have the right to pick whichever one you want."

John Henry could see that the whips were the same. He reached out and took the one that was in Campos's right hand, since that was the one closest to him. Ross snatched the one from Campos's left hand.

"You will remove your guns," Campos continued.

John Henry didn't like that idea very much, but he didn't see any way to avoid it. He unbuckled his gunbelt and handed it over to one of Campos's men, who stepped forward to take it. Ross took off his coat and peeled out of the shoulder rig.

John Henry looked around and found Wing Sun in the crowd. He took off his hat and handed it to her.

"Hang on to that for me," he said. "If you don't mind."

"I don't," she said. She didn't look quite so expressionless now. In fact, he saw a few worried lines on her face. "Are you sure this is a good idea, John Henry?"

He wasn't sure of it at all, but events had snowballed beyond his control. He still had no idea why Penelope Smith had set him up this way, but she had and now he had to deal with it.

"I'll be all right," he told Wing Sun.

Behind him, a sharp crack brought admiring exclamations from the crowd. John Henry looked over his shoulder as Quentin Ross cracked the bullwhip again. A cocky grin spread across Ross's face. He was playing to the crowd.

"Anybody who bets on that redskin is a damned fool," he said.

John Henry ignored that. He knew Ross was just trying to get a rise out of him.

He walked into the center of the big ring formed by the crowd. Ross continued showing off, but John Henry took the time to study his whip, to get used to the feel of the leather-wrapped wooden handle, to gauge the weight and balance of the weapon. He let the long, braided strips of leather fall free. The slightest motion of the handle made them writhe sinuously like a serpent at his feet.

John Henry cracked the whip once, popping the weighted tip, then nodded to Campos, who strolled into the center of the impromptu ring and held up his hands for quiet.

"You will fight until one man can no longer continue, or until one of you begs for mercy. You may use your fists or your feet, but the whip is the only weapon which you are allowed."

"This isn't a fight to the death?" Ross asked.

Campos spread his hands and said, "I suppose that depends on how stubborn the two of you are. Now, are you both ready?"

"I'm ready," Ross said. "I'm ready to cut this bastard's hide off him in bloody strips."

"I'm ready," John Henry said simply.

"Very well," Campos said.

With his hands still raised, he backed off until he was out of reach of the whips. Then with a sudden motion he dropped his arms.

"Fight!"

Chapter Sixteen

Quentin Ross didn't waste any time. He lunged at John Henry when the command was barely out of Campos's mouth. The whip leaped toward John Henry's face like a striking snake.

John Henry knew the weighted tip could pop one of his eyes out if it landed right. He darted aside. Ross's whip cracked, but it was a few inches away from his left ear, rather than in his face. He swung his arm up and then forward, sending his whip at Ross.

The man was ready for John Henry's counter-strike. He leaned away from the whip and threw up his left arm. The whip coiled around Ross's forearm, but before John Henry could jerk it back and cut the shirt sleeve, along with the flesh underneath, Ross grabbed the plaited leather strip and hauled hard on it.

The move pulled John Henry forward a couple of steps and threw him off balance. He caught himself, but just as he did Ross's whip curled around his left calf. John Henry grunted in pain as Ross jerked it back. He immediately felt the warm trickle of blood down his leg where the lash had cut it.

Even though the wound hurt, John Henry could tell that it was superficial. He limped as he lunged to the side, but only slightly. Caught up in the heat of battle as he was, the injury didn't even slow him down.

Ross still had hold of John Henry's whip. John Henry circled rapidly, which meant Ross had to either let go or allow the whip to wrap around his body. He let go and slashed at John Henry again. The whip hit John Henry's shoulder but slid off, not hurting him.

John Henry pulled his whip back and snapped it forward again. The tip caught Ross on the meaty part of his right thigh. Ross yelled and grimaced. He staggered back a step. In the torchlight, John Henry saw the dark stain on Ross's trousers where blood welled from the wound.

This was ridiculous, John Henry thought. They could stand here slashing at each other all night, gradually cutting each other to ribbons. That would entertain the wildly shouting crowd, but it wouldn't do anything to help John Henry's mission. It would be better to end this as quickly as he could.

He pulled back his whip and got ready to strike again, but his movements were deliberately slow. Scowling furiously, Ross took the bait and tried to seize the advantage. He whirled the whip around his head once and then sent it speeding toward John Henry again.

John Henry lowered his head and charged.

He heard the lash whisper past his ear. It landed on his back and hurt, but he ignored the pain.

Ross stood there flat-footed, taken by surprise as John Henry crashed into him.

The two men went down hard, with John Henry landing on top. He rammed a knee into Ross's belly and used the whip handle as a club to batter his opponent.

Ross recovered quickly, though, and drove the handle of his whip into John Henry's belly. Gasping for breath, John Henry struck again, but Ross jerked his head aside so that the blow missed. Ross lifted a leg, hooked the calf in front of John Henry's throat, and levered the lawman off him. John Henry rolled across the dirt.

Still on the ground himself, Ross brought the whip up and slashed down with it. The leather strands landed on John Henry's back and cut through his coat and shirt, but they didn't draw blood. The stroke just hurt like blazes.

John Henry rolled onto his side and struck out with the whip. It was an awkward position, and he didn't really expect to do anything except distract Ross and maybe give himself a chance to get on his feet again.

But luck guided the blow, and the tip of John Henry's whip raked across Ross's cheek, opening up a bloody gash. Ross screamed and clapped a hand to the wound.

John Henry surged up and threw himself toward Ross in a diving tackle. He hammered the butt of the whip handle against Ross's jaw, then looped the whip itself around Ross's neck. While Ross was still stunned, he rolled the man onto his belly, planted a knee in the small of his back, and tightened the makeshift noose. Ross began to flail and writhe as the whip cut off his air, but he couldn't free himself.

John Henry's teeth clenched as he increased the pressure. He knew that if he wanted to, he could kill Ross. All he had to do was keep choking him with the whip.

Instead, he leaned over and brought his mouth close to Ross's ear. The crowd shouted, many of them in dismay because they had wagered on Ross, others crying out for John Henry to go ahead and kill him in as bloodthirsty a display as any staged in the gladiatorial arenas of ancient Rome.

"Throw your whip away," John Henry grated into Ross's ear. The spectators couldn't hear the words, but Ross could. "Throw it away or I'll kill you."

Ross stopped struggling. Feebly, he lifted his right arm and cast the bullwhip away from him. It didn't go very far, but it fell out of reach.

"Now," John Henry went on, "you're going to tell me where you got those counterfeit bills." Ross couldn't say anything with the whip coiled so tightly around his throat, so John Henry added, "Nod if you understand me."

A couple of heartbeats went by, then Ross jerked his head in a weak nod.

"I'm going to let off the pressure on the

whip," John Henry told him. "The first words I want to hear out of your mouth are the name of your source for the money."

He eased off on the whip. Ross's breath rasped in his throat as he desperately dragged air down his windpipe. John Henry kept the whip in place so he could tighten it again anytime he needed to.

"Tell me!" he prodded.

"P-Penelope!"

The name came out of Ross's mouth in a gasp. John Henry grimaced angrily and said, "Don't waste your breath calling for your lady friend, Ross. Tell me what I want to know, now!"

The air must have revitalized Ross. He reared up suddenly. The back of his head crashed into John Henry's jaw. Ross arched his back and bucked up from the ground. The crowd roared with excitement as John Henry was thrown to the side.

Ross scrambled to his knees as John Henry landed on the ground a few feet away. John Henry was on his back, still holding on to the whip, which had come loose from Ross's neck. In a darting move, Ross reached under his shirt, and when his hand emerged, it was clutching an over-and-under derringer. At this range even such a small gun could be deadly, and John Henry didn't figure he was good enough with the whip to knock the weapon out of Ross's hands.

Before Ross could fire, a shot blasted. Ross rocked backward as the bullet struck him in the chest. He caught himself and tried to raise the derringer again, but his strength failed him. The little gun slipped from his fingers and thudded to the ground, the sound clearly audible in the sudden shocked silence that gripped the crowd.

Ross pitched forward onto his face and didn't move again.

John Henry looked in the direction the shot had come from and saw Wing Sun standing there with his own Colt gripped in both of her hands. The holster and shell belt lay at her feet where she had dropped them when she drew the revolver. The people around her edged away, clearly nervous about what she might do next.

Several of Campos's men had drawn their guns and were covering Wing Sun. Campos barked an order at them in Spanish. With obvious reluctance, they pouched their irons.

"You can put the gun away, señorita," Campos told Wing Sun. "You fired in defense of Señor Sixkiller's life. Everyone here can bear witness to that, if need be." He glanced at Ross's body in disdain. "More important, Señor Ross broke the rules of the duel. Code duello demanded that he die for that. Had you not shot him down before he could fire, I would have."

Wing Sun lowered the Colt as John Henry climbed to his feet, leaving the whip on the ground. He stepped over to her and took the weapon from her hand.

"You saved my life earlier tonight," she said quietly. "I suppose that makes us even."

"I suppose so," John Henry agreed.

Even so, a part of him wished that Wing Sun hadn't shot Ross. Now he was dead, and he hadn't revealed his source for the counterfeit bills.

Or had he?

That thought burst in John Henry's brain with enough force to make his breath catch in his throat. When Ross had said, "Penelope," John Henry had assumed the man was calling for his fiancée, mistress, whatever she was.

But what if he had been answering the question John Henry had asked?

What if Penelope Smith was the one who had been supplying him with the bogus bills?

The possibility made John Henry turn quickly and look through the crowd, searching for the blonde. He didn't see her anywhere. Everyone else who had been involved in that private, high-stakes game was here, their faces revealed in the garish torchlight, but not Penelope.

"Where's the girl who was with Ross?" John Henry asked.

Campos frowned in confusion and said, "Why do you care about her? Did you really attack her, Señor Sixkiller?"

"Good Lord, no. She came out onto the balcony and told Ross that you were looking for him, then ripped her own dress and started caterwauling about how I'd attacked her."

"That bitch," Wing Sun said, tight-lipped.

Campos shook his head and said, "I did not send her to find Ross, señor. This is the first I've heard of it. She must have had her own reasons for that deception."

"Maybe it was just a distraction to get everyone outside," John Henry suggested. "And that left her . . ."

Campos's eyes widened with alarm.

"Come! We should get back in."

Everything looked fine in the courtyard, but as they started up the stairs toward the balcony, John Henry spotted a man lying sprawled on the floor near the landing. He and Campos rushed the rest of the way up with Wing Sun trailing closely behind them.

The man lying facedown was one of the guards. A large, bloody lump was visible on the back of his head where someone had hit him, probably with a gun or some other sort of blunt instrument. Campos rolled him over and found that he was still breathing.

John Henry stood in the doorway of the room where the high-stakes game had been held and said grimly, "Looks like she cleaned off the table. Chances are she stole a horse and is long gone by now."

Campos cursed in Spanish and paced back and forth, agitated and furious.

"So she was a thief," Wing Sun said.

"Maybe," John Henry said as the wheels of his brain turned over rapidly. "Maybe more than that."

He was thinking about Ross's admission that Penelope was supplying the counterfeit money. Maybe she had wanted to recover the fake bills and staged the distraction in order to do so. It was possible, too, that she had been trying to get John Henry killed because she'd figured out somehow that he was a lawman and might be on the trail of the counterfeit money.

The only way to get any real answers, he realized, was to find Penelope Smith.

While he was mulling over that, Wing Sun asked, "Are you going to turn me over to the law for shooting Ross, John Henry?"

"Like Señor Campos said, you shot Ross to save my life. That makes killing him justified as far as I'm concerned. I suppose there'll have to be a report, but saving the life of a deputy U.S. marshal ought to count for something."

Campos's eyes got wide with alarm again.

"A deputy marshal?" he echoed. "You are a lawman, Señor Sixkiller?"

"That's right. But don't worry, Campos, I don't care about this gambling operation you're running. My interest in Ross is part of something else entirely. If you want to help me out, though, you can tell me if he had a place here in town."

"He always stayed in a hotel," Campos said. "I had to send one of my men there once to pick up some money when Ross made good on a marker."

"When was this?"

"A couple of months ago," Campos replied with a shrug.

Before Ross was involved with the counterfeiting ring, thought John Henry. And he was convinced now that it *was* a ring. More than just

Ignatius O'Reilly were involved. O'Reilly had to have at least one confederate . . .

A beautiful blond-haired she-devil named Penelope.

And the next step was finding her.

Chapter Seventeen

Campos told John Henry how to find the hotel where Ross had been staying in Los Angeles, then said, "I'll send one of my men for the police, Marshal, and report Ross's death."

"Talk to Captain Sawyer," John Henry suggested, "and when you do, tell him that I'll check in with him later and explain the whole story to him."

"I may have to close down for a while until all this blows over," Campos said glumly. "But I suppose that would be better than going to jail."

"I'll put in as much of a good word for you as I can," John Henry promised.

"What about me?" Wing Sun asked. "I'm the one who shot him, after all."

"And I'll testify that you did it to keep Ross from shooting me. The word of a federal lawman ought to be enough. They shouldn't press any charges against you."

"I hope you're right. In the meantime, I'm coming with you to Ross's hotel, John Henry."

He frowned and said, "I don't know if that's a good idea."

Depending on how big the counterfeiting gang was, he might wind up involved in yet another shoot-out on this night when trouble seemed never-ending.

"I'm coming along anyway," Wing Sun insisted. "If you run into that blond woman, you might need help with the treacherous witch. After the way she tried to get you killed, I'd like to settle that score with her."

Obviously, Wing Sun was a good shot, John Henry thought. He had seen evidence of that twice already tonight. It might be handy to have her around.

On the other hand, she was a civilian, and he didn't want her to come to any harm. It would be on his conscience if she did. So he said, "You can come with me to the hotel, but you'll have to stay in the carriage."

"Fine," she said with a smile, and he warned himself that she might be agreeing just to placate him, with no intention of keeping her promise.

By now just about everyone who had been at the villa for a night of gambling and other assorted vices had scattered. A shooting tended to have that effect. Nobody wanted to be questioned by the authorities, especially when they'd been patronizing a place such as this.

John Henry said good night to Campos and helped Wing Sun into the carriage that had brought them there. Her driver slapped the reins against the backs of the team, and the vehicle rolled through the trees and back down the steep trails to the valley.

Twenty minutes later the driver brought the carriage to a stop in front of a hotel in downtown Los Angeles. It was a two-story adobe building, either one of the older structures in town or at least made to look like one. John Henry got out and told Wing Sun, “Wait here.”

“Of course,” she said.

Again, he wasn’t sure just how sincere she was, but he had to trust her for the moment.

He went into the quiet, well-appointed hotel lobby, which was empty at the moment, and approached the desk, limping a little from that cut on his calf the whip had inflicted. He knew the cuts on his clothes from the whip and the grime from rolling around on the ground made him look pretty disheveled, so he wasn’t surprised when the clerk gave him a frown of disapproval.

That frown turned into a worried look when John Henry took out the folder with his badge in it, slapped it down on the desk, and said, “Quentin Ross. Which room is his?”

“It . . . it’s Number 7, second floor front, Marshal,” the man said. “Mr. Ross isn’t in, though.”

“I know that,” John Henry said. “He won’t be coming back, either. What about Miss Penelope Smith? Has she been staying with Ross?”

Despite being worried, the clerk drew himself up slightly and said, “This isn’t that sort of establishment, Marshal. Miss Smith has her own accommodations.”

“Adjoining?” John Henry asked, cocking his head to the side.

"Well . . . yes. But there's nothing improper about that, I assure you."

"Uh-huh. She in Room Five or Nine?"

"Nine," the clerk said. As John Henry turned away from the desk to start toward the staircase, the man went on, "But she's not there now, either."

John Henry looked back over his shoulder at the clerk.

"You know that for a fact?"

"Yes, sir. I had a bellboy help her with her luggage. She left rather hurriedly, about half an hour ago."

John Henry bit back a curse and settled for a groan. He said, "You didn't find anything unusual about that?"

"Well . . . I just assumed that since Mr. Ross wasn't with her, that the two of them had had some sort of, well, falling-out. Such things happen, you know."

"Yeah. She took all her bags?"

"I assume so."

"Was anybody with her?"

The clerk shook his head and said, "I didn't see anyone. She had hired a buggy and driver. I saw the bellboy loading her bags into the back."

"You got any idea where she was going?"

"No, but Tom might."

"Tom?" John Henry said.

"The bellboy."

"Is *he* around?"

"Of course." The clerk hit a bell on the desk with his palm and called, "Tom!"

The summons made a middle-aged, balding

man with a close-cropped brown beard appear in a doorway at the side of the lobby. As usual in most hotels, the bellboy wasn't an actual boy. This one moved like his feet were stuck in molasses as he shuffled toward the desk.

"What . . . is . . . it . . . Mr. . . . Chambers?" he asked in the slowest drawl John Henry had ever heard.

"This man is a deputy U.S. marshal," the clerk said with a nod toward John Henry. "He has some questions about Miss Smith. You know, Mr. Ross's, ah, friend."

"Oh . . . her," Tom said. "Howdy . . . Marshal . . . What is it . . . you . . . want to know?"

With an effort, John Henry reined in the impatience he felt. Losing his temper with this old-timer would probably just delay things that much more. He said, "You loaded Miss Smith's things into that buggy. Did you hear her tell the driver where she was going?"

"Matter of fact . . . I did."

John Henry waited, and when Tom didn't go on, he asked, "What did she tell him?"

"Oh . . . you wanted to . . . know what she said. Lemme see now . . . what was it . . ."

John Henry clenched his teeth and resisted the impulse to grab the bellboy's shoulders and try to shake the words out faster.

"Oh, yeah . . . She told the fella . . . she told the fella to take her . . . to the train station."

"Thanks!" John Henry called over his shoulder as he broke into a run for the hotel's front door. Behind him, the clerk and the bellboy stared after him. The bellboy's head moved back and forth as if he were shaking it in amazement that anybody could move that fast.

"The train station!" John Henry told Wing Sun's driver as he swung up into the carriage.

When the man hesitated at taking John Henry's orders, Wing Sun leaned from one of the carriage's windows and spoke to him sharply in Chinese. The vehicle lurched into motion, throwing John Henry onto the rear seat where Wing Sun was. She surprised him by turning toward him, wrapping her arms around his neck, and pressing her mouth to his.

"What was that for?" John Henry asked when Wing Sun broke the kiss. "I thought we were already square when it comes to saving each other's lives."

"We are," she said. "But I've been wanting to kiss you, and the way this night has been going I didn't know if I'd get another chance."

She had a point there, and the whole thing had been pleasant enough that he thought it was worth doing again. Since it was going to take several minutes to reach the train station, he put his arms around her and urged her lips back toward his.

When the carriage rocked to a stop in front of the station, Wing Sun said a little breathlessly, "I'm coming with you this time. I know you're worried that this Smith woman has some sort of gang with her, but there's not going to be a gun battle in the middle of the train station."

John Henry didn't figure they could be sure of that, but he wasn't going to waste time arguing. He said, "Come on. Maybe you'd better bring those two hombres who work for your father, too."

With the driver and the guard following closely behind them, John Henry and Wing Sun trotted into the depot. There were quite a few people around, even at this late hour. John Henry's gaze darted around the big, cavernous lobby as he searched for Penelope Smith.

"I don't see her," Wing Sun said.

"Neither do I," John Henry said. He headed for the row of ticket windows.

Once again the sight of his badge brought immediate cooperation. Three ticket clerks were on duty at the moment. John Henry gathered all of them behind one of the windows and described Penelope to them.

"I'm pretty sure I sold a ticket to a woman who looked like that," one of the men said. "About twenty minutes ago, it was."

"Do you know where she is now?" John Henry asked.

"On her way to San Francisco, I suppose. She barely made the train."

John Henry drew in a deep breath and blew it out in an exasperated sigh. So close. So blasted close.

"She got on the train by herself, did she?"

"As far as I know, Marshal." The ticket clerk paused. "She wasn't the only one who cut it close, though. A fella came along and jumped on the train just as it was pulling out. He'll have to buy his ticket from the conductor, or get thrown off at the next stop."

Lawman's instinct made John Henry ask,

"What did he look like, the man who almost missed the train?"

"I didn't really get that good a look at him. He was big, though, and well dressed, I know that. Good-looking in a way, I guess, although I'm no judge of that. Oh, and he had dark hair, I'm pretty sure of that. Clean-shaven."

That description could fit dozens, if not hundreds of men in Los Angeles, John Henry thought.

But it also fit somebody he had seen earlier tonight at Matteo Campos's villa, and John Henry couldn't help but wonder if it was the same man.

He was thinking about Nick Prentice, who had sat in on that high-stakes game.

Maybe Prentice had been playing a game with even higher stakes.

"What are you going to do now?" Wing Sun asked.

"There's only one thing I can do," John Henry replied as he shook his head. "Reckon I'm going to need a ticket on the next train to San Francisco."

Chapter Eighteen

He could tell that Wing Sun wanted to come with him, but that just wasn't feasible, not with war looming in Los Angeles's Chinatown. She knew that, too.

"My father will need me by his side," she said while they waited at the train station for her carriage to return from John Henry's hotel. She had sent her father's men to the hotel to fetch John Henry's gear, what little of it there was. He was looking forward to putting on some clean clothes as soon as he got the chance.

"I know that," he told her. "The Black Lotus's place is here, after all. You came all the way from China to be with your father. You can't run out on him."

"If not for the trouble with Ling Yuan . . ."

"I know."

John Henry put his hand under her chin and tilted her head back slightly so he could meet the gaze of her dark, compelling eyes. He didn't have to look down much, since she was almost as tall as he was.

"I might be coming back this way, once this case is over. You can't ever tell."

"If fate smiles and you do come back, you know now where to find me. And the talisman I gave you will keep you safe no matter where you go in Chinatown."

"I'll remember that," John Henry promised.

The next northbound train left at four in the morning. After he said good-bye to Wing Sun, John Henry dozed on one of the benches in the station lobby and thought about everything that had happened.

The only thing he felt reasonably certain about was that Penelope Smith was part of the counterfeiting ring. She had to be working for Ignatius O'Reilly, distributing the phony bills to confederates such as Quentin Ross. John Henry didn't know how Ross had gotten involved, whether through sheer greed or if Penelope had seduced him into taking part in the operation.

That mystery would probably never be solved since Ross was dead, and it didn't really matter anyway. The important thing now was to catch up to Penelope, stop her before she could spread more of the bogus bills, and use her to lead him to the mastermind, O'Reilly.

John Henry's thoughts turned to Nick Prentice. His involvement was a lot more uncertain. The man who had caught the train for San Francisco at the last moment—in pursuit of Penelope?—might have been Prentice, or it might have been someone else entirely. He might not have any connection with the case at all.

But if it had been Prentice, was he really pursuing Penelope? Or was he her partner, who had been delayed for some reason and almost missed the train? John Henry had no way of knowing if either of those scenarios was true.

Again, the only way to know for sure was to catch up to Penelope and force her to talk.

The time passed slowly. John Henry had never been the sort of man to be content just sitting and waiting. He always wanted to be doing something.

At last a conductor in blue walked through the lobby and called out that the northbound was now boarding. The place was mostly empty at this early hour of the morning, but half a dozen people got up from the benches and moved toward the doors leading to the platform. John Henry studied them with narrowed eyes, trying to see if any of them might be connected to the case, but all the passengers looked completely innocuous.

He got onto the train, found an empty bench in one of the cars, and placed his war bag beside him as he sat down. He intended to stay awake and mull over the case some more, but after the train rolled out and the conductor came through the cars punching the passengers' tickets, weariness caught up to John Henry. It had been a long, long night, full of action and fury. He had been shot at, whipped, and pummeled. He had uncovered leads only to have them crash into dead ends. All that took a toll on a man.

He went to sleep and didn't wake up until the conductor came back through the car, bawling that they were arriving in San Francisco.

Hours had passed. The sun was up. It was a new day, and John Henry had slept through all the stops the train had made on its way up the coast.

He stood up and stretched. His muscles creaked and his bones popped like those of an old man. That was what sleeping on a train would do for you, he thought as he lifted his war bag to his shoulder and left the car.

Penelope Smith had bought a ticket for San Francisco. But once she was on the train, she could have bought another ticket from the conductor, one that would carry her past the so-called city by the bay. That would have been a good dodge on her part to throw off any possible pursuit.

On the other hand, she really could have been bound for San Francisco, and John Henry couldn't afford to assume that she hadn't stopped here. He got off the train, walked through the lobby, and found the stationmaster's office.

The man had a stove in the corner with a coffeepot sitting on it, and the smell of the strong black brew almost made John Henry groan from wanting a cup of it. He had business to tend to first, though.

The stationmaster was a burly, bald man in a brown tweed suit. He glanced up from his desk and asked, "What can I do for you, mister?"

"Marshal," John Henry corrected. "Deputy United States Marshal Sixkiller."

He took out his badge and identification papers and let the stationmaster take a good look at them.

The man seemed to be impressed but cautious. He asked, "What brings you to San Francisco, Marshal?"

"I'm looking for a woman who left Los Angeles on the midnight train."

"That train got in several hours ago, around dawn," the stationmaster said as he spread his hands. "I'm afraid the woman could be almost anywhere by now."

"I know that, but I'd like to question your porters. She had several bags and likely would have wanted help with them. Are the same men still on duty now who were working when that train came in?"

"That's right. Would you like me to call them in here one by one so you can talk to them?"

"That would be mighty helpful," John Henry said. "And there's one other thing . . . You reckon you could spare a cup of that coffee?"

That put a grin on the stationmaster's pleasantly ugly face. He waved a hand at the stove and said, "There are cups on that shelf there. Help yourself, Marshal. I warn you, though. I'm not known for the quality of my coffee."

"As long as it's got a bite to it, that's all I'm interested in right now," John Henry said. "I got a little sleep on the train, but other than that it was a mighty long night."

The stationmaster left the office. John Henry poured a cup of coffee and sipped it gratefully. The stuff was strong enough to get up and walk around on its own hind legs, as folks said back home, and it had an immediate bracing effect on him.

A few minutes later the stationmaster came back with an elderly black man, the first of the porters that John Henry would interview. The man was friendly and obviously eager to help. John Henry described Penelope Smith to him and said, "She would have come in very early in the morning on a train from Los Angeles, and I need to know where she went from here."

"I sure wish I could help you, Marshal," the porter said. "I don't recollect seein' any young lady who looked like that, though. The station ain't too busy at that hour, so I sees just about ever'body who comes an' goes."

John Henry had worried that that was the answer he would get. He nodded and thanked the man anyway, and the stationmaster told the porter, "Send the next fellow in."

Over the next few minutes, John Henry questioned four more porters, and they all told the same story. John Henry's frustration was growing as it began to appear that Penelope hadn't stopped in San Francisco after all. If she had continued on northward into Oregon, he might never find her. All he could do was head in that direction himself and check with all the local lawmen along the way to find out if any counterfeit money had been passed recently in their jurisdiction.

"There's only one more porter who was on duty when that train came in," the stationmaster said. "I'll get him, but it's not looking very good for you, Marshal."

"I know," John Henry replied with a sigh. "But I might as well talk to everybody."

The stationmaster called in the last porter, another elderly black man with white hair.

"This is Carl," he said to John Henry. "Carl, this is a U.S. marshal. He wants to ask you some questions."

"And I want to answer 'em," Carl said. "How do, Marshal."

"Carl," John Henry said. "Earlier this morning, did you happen to help a young blond woman with her bags? She might have been traveling alone, or she might have been with a dark-haired man a little taller and heavier than me."

"Sure, I seen her," Carl replied without hesitation. "And she was alone, all right, didn't have nobody with her. That's why I remember her, in fact. We don't see too many young ladies come through here travelin' by theirselves. Sure don't see many who are that pretty."

John Henry's pulse quickened at the old man's answer. For the first time, this was an indication that maybe he was still on the right trail after all. He said, "The woman I'm looking for has a beauty mark—"

"Right here," Carl broke in as he lifted a hand and touched his finger to a spot on his face near his mouth. "I recollect that, too."

That confirmed it. Penelope Smith had gotten off the train here in San Francisco.

Now it was a matter of trying to find out where she had gone next.

"Did she take a cab, hire a buggy, something like that?"

"I put her bags in a cab for her," Carl said. Without waiting for John Henry to ask, he went on, "She told the driver to take her to the ferry. She was goin' over to Oakland."

"Then that's where I'm going," John Henry said.

Chapter Nineteen

The cab ride to the ferry landing was . . . spectacular, that was the only word for it, John Henry decided. The hills covered with buildings, the water—bay on one side, endless ocean on the other—the towering clouds and the blue sky . . . There was nothing like this back in Indian Territory. Or Arkansas. Or Kansas or anywhere else he'd ever been.

Los Angeles had been interesting. San Francisco was beautiful.

He was just passing through, though, on the trail of an outlaw. When you got right down to it, that's all Penelope Smith was. Just another outlaw to chase down and bring to justice.

John Henry bought passage on the Oakland ferry, then had to wait for a while before one of the big boats returned to the San Francisco side of the bay. The vaguely uneasy feeling he'd had when he looked at the ocean in Los Angeles returned as he gazed out over the wide, dark blue expanse. He could see the hills rising on the other side of the bay, but between here and there was an awful lot of water.

He had to cross it in order to find Penelope. The trip would be fine, he told himself. Ferries crossed the bay dozens of times a day without incident.

The big, bargelike vessel had two levels, John Henry saw as he stood on the landing and watched it chug toward the shore. Wagons and other horse-drawn vehicles entered the lower level directly from the landing. Passengers who didn't have a horse or a wagon were supposed to climb a set of stairs to the upper deck. That was where he would ride, John Henry thought.

After the ferry docked, it was several minutes before everyone on it had gotten off and the passengers and vehicles from this side were allowed aboard. Carrying his war bag, John Henry went up the stairs and came out on a broad deck with the ferry's pilothouse set in the center of it. In a way, the ferry reminded him of riverboats he had seen on the Mississippi, although it completely lacked the grace and elegance of those paddle-wheel-driven vessels.

Not many people were headed for Oakland this morning. About a dozen passengers shared the upper deck with John Henry. As the ferry got under way, he stood at the railing with a cool wind blowing in his face and watched the seagulls soaring around the boat. He saw a couple of desolate-looking islands in the bay, one of them with some forbidding buildings on it. He didn't know what the place was, but it looked like a prison to him.

A man came up to the railing beside him. John Henry glanced over and gave the hombre a pleasant nod. The man wore a bowler hat and a gray tweed suit. He had sandy hair and a neatly trimmed mustache, and he reminded John Henry of a teller in a bank.

"Morning," the man said as he returned John Henry's nod. "Beautiful day, isn't it?"

"I reckon," John Henry replied. "I'm not too fond of boats."

The stranger chuckled.

"You get used to them, I suppose. I've ridden this ferry so many times I don't think anything about it anymore." He put out his hand. "I'm Clive Denton."

"John Henry Sixkiller," John Henry introduced himself. He left off the part about being a deputy U.S. marshal.

"Not from around here, eh?"

"Indian Territory."

"Out here on business, or is it a pleasure trip?"

John Henry didn't particularly want to make friendly conversation with Denton, but his natural politeness kept him from saying that. He said, "Business . . . but it'll be a pleasure if I get what I'm after."

That brought another laugh from Denton, who said, "Isn't that always the way? I hope it works out for you."

Clive Denton wandered off, and John Henry was glad to see him go. He would be even happier when the ferry reached the Oakland side of the bay and he could get dry, solid ground under his feet again.

The trip seemed to take longer than it really did, but finally the ferry docked and John Henry walked off as soon as the rope across the broad gangplank was unfastened. Several horse-drawn cabs were parked nearby, their drivers waiting for passengers from the ferry to hire them.

John Henry approached one of the men, a big fellow wearing a derby and sporting a rusty handlebar mustache. The man rumbled, "Need to go somewhere, mister?"

"That depends," John Henry said. "I'm looking for a woman."

The man's rough-hewn face immediately pinched into a scowl. He said, "I don't go in for that sort of thing. I'm a decent, God-fearin' gent with a wife and kiddies. Anyway, it ain't even noon yet! Can't you wait until nightfall like all the other degenerates?"

"You misunderstand me," John Henry said with a smile. "I'm looking for a particular woman who would have gotten off the ferry earlier this morning." He described Penelope Smith, making sure to mention the distinctive beauty mark.

"Why are you lookin' for her?" the man asked when John Henry was finished. Obviously, he was still a little suspicious.

John Henry heaved a sigh.

"She's my sister," he lied, taking a tack he thought might work with this fella. "She had an argument with our father—over a man that Pa and I both think can't be trusted—and left our home. I want to find her and bring her back before she does something that she'll regret for the rest of her life."

The cabman's wariness disappeared and was replaced by a look of concern. He said, "Dang it, that's a sad story. I wish I could help you, mister, but I just can't. I ain't picked up a passenger like that all day, and I been here since pretty early. Tell you what you do, though. Go talk to Simeon."

"Who's that?"

The cabman pointed with a thick, blunt finger. "He knows most everything that goes on around here. It's liable to cost you a little, but you can trust whatever he tells you."

John Henry looked where the cabman was pointing and saw a short, fat man holding a banjo. A hat sat on the ground at his feet, upside down. When people walked by, he began to pluck at the banjo strings and started singing. Most folks just passed on by without paying any attention to him, but a few of them paused long enough to listen to a little of the fast-paced, raucous song and then tossed a coin in the hat before they moved on.

"Thanks," John Henry told the cabman with a nod. He started toward the banjo player.

The man began playing even faster as John Henry approached. He wore a big grin on his moon-shaped face as he sang a slightly bawdy song about a girl named Sal. When the song came to an end, John Henry took a five-dollar gold piece from his pocket, started to toss it into the hat, then paused and held up the coin. The banjo player's eyes got bigger when he saw what it was.

"That was a good song," John Henry said, "but I'd like some information to go with it."

"Mister, for five dollars I'll tell you everything I know," Simeon said. "And some things that I don't."

"I don't want you making up anything just to get the money," John Henry said. "Just tell me what you saw with your own eyes. I'm looking for a pretty blonde with a beauty mark beside her mouth. She would have gotten off the ferry earlier this morning."

"Sure. Not long after dawn, it was. I'd just gotten here to catch the traffic from the early ferries."

"You're certain about that?" John Henry pressed.

"Absolutely. I make a habit of studying folks, mister. I can generally tell who's going to pitch something into the hat and who ain't. This young lady . . ." Simeon shrugged. "She went right on by. Looked like she had plenty on her mind."

"Where did she go?"

"Somebody met her. A fella in a buggy."

Nick Prentice? John Henry had to wonder about that. But Prentice would have had a hard time getting ahead of Penelope, since he had come north on the same train she had. Or at least somebody matching his description had.

John Henry was starting to think he wasn't cut out for this sort of detective work. Dealing with people shooting at him was a lot simpler, anyway.

"Did you see the hombre in the buggy?"

Simeon shook his head and said, "No, I didn't get a good look at him. It was early, so the weather was still pretty cold and damp. He had on an overcoat, and his hat was pulled down low. Wouldn't know him if I saw him again, if that's what you're getting at, Sheriff."

"I'm not a sheriff."

"Maybe not, but you're a lawman of some kind. Like I told you, I'm pretty good at figuring folks out."

John Henry let that go. He didn't see any point in explaining to Simeon who he really was.

"If you didn't see the man in the buggy, I'm betting you don't know where it was going, either."

Simeon shook his head and said, "I'm afraid not. I can tell you that it headed off toward town, but with the bay on the other side, where else could it go?"

Simeon was eyeing the coin John Henry still held. John Henry was convinced that the banjo player had told him the truth, so even though Simeon hadn't been all that helpful, he tossed the half eagle into the hat anyway. Simeon's eyes lit up.

"Lord bless you, sir," he said. "Good luck finding the young lady."

John Henry started to turn away, but he stopped when Simeon cleared his throat.

"One more thing, since you were so generous . . ."

"You were holding back to see whether I was really going to pay you," John Henry accused.

"You might not believe it, but there are some folks who seem to enjoy tormenting those who are more down on their luck."

Now that John Henry had gotten a closer look at Simeon, he saw the red nose, the veins in the face, the somewhat bleary eyes of a heavy drinker. Simeon might like to think that he was down on his luck, but John Henry had a hunch the man was right where he really wanted to be.

None of which mattered at the moment. Keeping any note of disapproval out of his voice, John Henry asked, "What else did you think of, Simeon?"

"That buggy didn't belong to the fella inside it. It was rented from Patrick Dunleavy's wagon yard. I see 'em all the time. Mr. Dunleavy ought to be able to tell you more about those folks."

John Henry reached for his pocket.

Simeon held up a hand to stop him and said, "You already paid. You don't have to throw in anything else."

"This is for the other information you're about to give me," John Henry said as he tossed a silver dollar into the hat. "Where do I find Dunleavy's place?"

Simeon told him. John Henry touched a finger to the brim on his hat and said, "You know, back in the hills where I come from, we have some pretty good banjo players, too."

With a big grin on his face, Simeon accepted that veiled challenge and said, "Can they do this?"

He started picking out a sprightly tune, his fingers flying so fast that it was hard for the eye to follow them. John Henry laughed, shook his head, and walked away, heading for the wagon yard where he hoped to find another lead on Penelope Smith's trail.

Chapter Twenty

Patrick Dunleavy's wagon yard appeared to be a thriving business. Dunleavy not only built wagons, he ran a livery stable as well and rented out horses, wagons, buggies, and carriages. John Henry talked to the man in the business's office, and this time he pulled out his marshal's badge to ensure Dunleavy's cooperation.

"You rented a buggy to a man earlier this morning," John Henry said. "I'd like to know who he was."

Dunleavy had a full head of brown hair and muttonchop whiskers that would have done a Union army officer proud during the Late Unpleasantness. He frowned and said, "I didn't rent a buggy to anybody this morning, Marshal."

"Somebody saw it and recognized it as coming from your place," John Henry said.

"I don't doubt it, but I didn't rent it to the man this morning. I rented it to him last night."

John Henry reined in the angry, impatient words that tried to well up in his throat at that pedantic response. He said, "Are you sure we're talking about the same buggy?"

"I'm positive. It's the only one I've rented in the past week. The man engaged it yesterday evening. He said that he had to meet someone at the ferry early this morning and wanted to be sure of having transportation."

John Henry had to think about that for a moment. Penelope had been at the Campos villa in the hills above Los Angeles the previous evening. But earlier, before she and Quentin Ross went up there, she could have sent a telegram to whoever had picked her up, letting him know to make the arrangements.

That would mean she had already planned to leave for San Francisco on that late train. John Henry had assumed she was fleeing from him, but that didn't necessarily have to be the case. She could have planned on leaving all along. If she was responsible for spreading the counterfeit money across the Southwest, as John Henry suspected, she had never stayed in any one place for too long.

That left Nick Prentice out. Penelope couldn't have wired him in Oakland when Prentice was still in Los Angeles. Of course, Prentice could still be part of the gang.

"Did the fella give you his name? The one who rented the buggy?"

"I believe so. Let me check my records." Dunleavy opened a ledger and flipped through the pages until he found the entry he wanted. Resting a fingertip on it, he said, "Alfred Hanson."

The name didn't mean anything to John Henry.

Anyway, there was a good chance it was every bit as fake as those ten- and twenty-dollar bills the gang had been passing out.

"He give you an address where he's staying?"

"The Golden State Hotel. But I don't think you'll find him there, Marshal."

"Why not?"

"I assume that he's checked out. He engaged the buggy for a period of two weeks. Paid quite a substantial fee to do so."

John Henry's eyes narrowed.

"This was last night, you said?"

"That's right."

"Have you deposited the money that Hanson paid you?"

"No, I haven't been to the bank yet." For the first time in this conversation, Dunleavy began to look less than absolutely sure of himself. "The money is still in my safe. Why do you ask, Marshal?"

"We might want to take a look at it," John Henry suggested.

Dunleavy came to his feet and said, "You don't think there's something wrong with it, do you?"

"Let's just have a look-see."

Dunleavy went to a squat, sturdy-looking safe in the corner of the office and bent to twirl the knob and work its combination. When he swung the door open, he reached inside and brought out a stack of bills tied together with twine.

"You understand, the money Hanson paid me is mixed in with the other bills we took in yesterday," he said.

"Yes, sir. I'll look at them one by one."

Hanson looked positively green now as he set the money on the desk and untied the string. John Henry picked up the stack and sorted out the tens and twenties. Then he began taking a closer look at each one of them, turning slightly toward the window so the light would be better.

Now that he knew what he was looking for, it didn't really take him that long to spot the counterfeits. He set them aside, one by one, four twenties and four tens. While he was doing that, Dunleavy sank into his chair and looked sick.

"One hundred and twenty dollars," John Henry said when he was finished. "That's what you charged Hanson for the buggy, right?"

"Yes," Dunleavy croaked. "That money, it . . . it's no good, isn't it?"

"I'm afraid so."

Dunleavy clenched a fist and slammed it down on the desk.

"Cheated! By God! Cheated! If I ever get my hands on that son of a—"

"What did he look like?" John Henry broke in. "Was he a middle-aged man, heavily built, with graying red hair?"

"What?" Dunleavy frowned in confusion. He shook his head and went on, "Who's that?"

John Henry had just described Ignatius O'Reilly, but instead of explaining that to Dunleavy, he said, "That's not the man who rented the buggy?"

"Not at all. This man was fairly young, around thirty, I'd say. He had brown hair and a mustache. Quite respectable looking. He was well dressed, too. He wore a gray suit and a bowler hat."

John Henry stiffened. The description Dunleavy had just given him was vague enough to fit any number of men, but John Henry had seen someone who looked like that this very morning: Clive Denton, the stranger who had engaged him in small talk on the ferry as they were crossing the bay from San Francisco.

Denton couldn't have been on the ferry if he was the man who had picked up Penelope Smith in the buggy . . . or could he? He could have taken Penelope somewhere, dropped her off or left her with the buggy, and returned to the ferry. To keep watch for someone trailing her? Someone in particular who matched the description of a certain deputy United States marshal from Indian Territory . . . ?

It was starting to look like the gang was even larger than John Henry had suspected.

Dunleavy must have noticed John Henry's reaction to the description. He asked, "Do you know the man, Marshal?"

"I'm not sure. Maybe."

"I must say, he didn't strike me as the sort to be a prospector at all."

That statement put a puzzled frown on John Henry's face. He asked, "Why would you think Hanson is a prospector?"

"While I was drawing up the agreement for the buggy, he stepped over to the map on that wall and studied it rather closely." Dunleavy gestured toward a big map of California pinned to one wall of the office. "When I asked him if he was looking for anywhere in particular, he said he was interested in the mining towns up in the Sierra Nevada. Said he thought he might try his luck up there, that he'd heard there was quite a bit of money to be made. I told him it wasn't like back in the Gold Rush days, that a man couldn't just stumble over a fortune in a streambed anymore. I came out here back in those days myself, and that's the way it was then. No more."

"What did Hanson say to that?"

"He seemed rather amused, actually. Said a man's fortune was wherever he made it." Dunleavy shrugged. "I suppose there's some truth to that."

"You don't know for sure that's where Hanson was headed, though."

"I can't be absolutely certain, but it sounded to me like he was serious about making a trip up there."

John Henry didn't really doubt it. The gang could probably amass a considerable poke of nuggets and dust in exchange for a stack of worthless currency. That might be just what they needed to wrap up this operation.

The possibility was strong enough that he felt like he had to investigate it. He would check at the Golden State Hotel first, just to make sure that Hanson or Denton—or whatever his name really was—wasn't still in town, but if there was no sign of him or Penelope at the hotel, then John Henry would have no choice except to get his hands on a horse and head for the Sierra Nevada himself.

Maybe he could catch up to the buggy. A man on horseback could travel faster than a vehicle.

"I'm obliged to you for your help, Mr. Dunleavy," he said. He shook hands with the wagon yard owner.

"I'm glad to do whatever I can, Marshal." Dunleavy looked at the counterfeit bills that John Henry had left lying on the desk. "What do you suggest I do with that worthless money?"

"That's up to you," John Henry said, "but I wouldn't try to spend it if I was you."

Chapter Twenty-one

Just as he suspected, "Alfred Hanson" had checked out of the Golden State Hotel early that morning. A clerk was able to tell John Henry that Hanson had stayed there for several days and hadn't left a forwarding address when he checked out. The clerk didn't recall Hanson mentioning anything about where he was headed next when he checked out, either.

John Henry needed a good horse if he was going to head for the mountains. He thought he might as well go back to Dunleavy's, since the man's business included a livery stable. He could take another look at that map in Dunleavy's office, too, and see if he could figure out the route he wanted to follow.

Since the hour was approaching midday and the only breakfast John Henry had was that cup of coffee in the stationmaster's office, he stopped at a restaurant for a meal before returning to Dunleavy's. The food was good but pricey. Judge Parker would probably have a thing or two to say about that when he went over John Henry's expense account.

Dunleavy seemed a little surprised to see John Henry again, but he was happy to rent the lawman a saddle mount. Dunleavy accompanied John Henry out to the corral himself and suggested a big, strong-looking buckskin gelding.

"You want a horse with some bottom if you're traveling in the mountains," Dunleavy said. "This one will get you where you're going."

John Henry liked the horse's lines and the intelligence and alertness in the animal's eyes. He asked, "Does he have a name?"

"Not really. Some of the hostlers call him Buck, because of his color." Dunleavy shrugged. "I've never seen the point in giving an animal a name, myself."

For a man who worked with horses, Dunleavy didn't seem to have much understanding of the bond that could spring up between horse and rider. John Henry didn't bother pointing that out. He just said, "I'll need tack, too."

Twenty minutes later he was on his way. He had used part of that time to sketch a crude map based on the one that hung on Dunleavy's office wall.

Many of the mining camps and boomtowns of the Gold Rush era were gone now, having dried up and blowed away when the nuggets and dust in the nearby creeks played out, but a number of other towns in the Sierra Nevadas still existed where veins of gold-bearing quartz had proven to be long-lived. John Henry had traced out a route that would take him to half a dozen of those settlements that seemed to be likely targets for the counterfeiting gang.

But first he had to cross the broad Central Valley before he reached the mountains. Having been raised on a farm back in Indian Territory, John Henry was able to appreciate this outstanding agricultural region as he rode through it. The fertile soil produced some fine crops. He had heard that enough food came out of this valley to feed the entire western part of the United States, and he could believe that.

Although the mountains were visible in the distance, they were still at least a day's ride away when John Henry stopped for the night in the town of Stockton. It appeared to be a pleasant community surrounded by farmland.

"It's been pretty easy going so far, Buck," he told the horse as he led him into a livery stable stall. "Might get a little harder tomorrow. It'll be a longer day for you, at the very least."

Buck tossed his head as if to say that he was looking forward to it.

The liveryman recommended the San Joaquin Hotel to John Henry. He got a room and left his gear there, then walked down the street to the marshal's office.

A sign on the building's front wall identified the local lawman as Marshal Fred Gainey. John Henry went inside and introduced himself to Gainey, who turned out to be a tall, spare man with a mostly bald head and a bristly brush of a mustache.

"Federal man, eh?" Gainey said after they had

shaken hands. "What brings you to Stockton, Marshal? Chasing down a fugitive?"

"Actually I'm on the trail of some counterfeiters," John Henry explained. "I've tracked them from Los Angeles to San Francisco, and then they were headed in this direction."

That put a frown on Gainey's face. He asked, "Do you know what they look like?"

John Henry described Penelope Smith, then for good measure he threw in descriptions of Clive Denton and Nick Prentice, even though he wasn't sure if either man was part of the gang, and then concluded by telling the local lawman what Ignatius O'Reilly looked like. Gainey listened attentively but then shook his head.

"Can't say as I recall seeing anybody like that around today. You sure they can't be more than one day ahead of you?"

"That's right, at least where the blonde and the two younger men are concerned. They just reached San Francisco early this morning."

"Well, I'll have a word with the merchants around town and let them know to be on the lookout for any phony bills. And I'll pass along those descriptions to my deputies. Don't see what else I can do to help you, Marshal."

"That's plenty," John Henry assured him. "I'm obliged to you. The only other thing I'd ask is if you can point me toward a good place to have supper."

That put a smile on Gainey's face, which normally seemed to wear a more hangdog expression. He said, "The Red Top Café is your best bet. On the other side of the street in the next block."

"I'm obliged again," John Henry said. He left the lawman's office and found the café, which was a stone building with a red tile roof in the Spanish style.

After washing down a pretty good meal of steak, potatoes, and beans with several cups of coffee, John Henry went by the livery stable to check on Buck. Satisfied that the horse was being well cared for, he started for the hotel, intent on getting a good night's sleep. Some men would have sought out a saloon and had a few drinks, but John Henry intended on making an early start the next morning and didn't want anything interfering with that.

Night had fallen, and a lot of businesses were closed already. In a farming community such as this one, most folks probably got up and went to bed with the sun.

He was walking in front of one of the few lighted windows on the main street when the sharp crack of a rifle split the night air. From the corner of his eye John Henry saw a muzzle flash at an angle across the street. In the same heartbeat as the flash and the rifle's report, he felt the hot wind of a bullet passing within an inch or so of his left ear.

The window behind him shattered as the glass exploded inward.

John Henry reacted instantly, letting his instincts take over as he leaped off the boardwalk and dashed behind a parked wagon. He crouched there and drew his Colt as another shot cracked. The slug thudded against the wagon somewhere. John Henry straightened and triggered two swift shots in the direction of the muzzle flashes he had seen.

He could see now that the bushwhacker had hidden behind another wagon. John Henry couldn't tell if the rifleman was still back there or had fled into the mouth of a nearby alley. In the thick shadows it was hard to be sure of anything.

Angry shouts came from inside the building with the bullet-shattered window. From the sound of the man's voice, he was just hopping mad, not hurt. John Henry hoped that the shot hadn't wounded anybody, but right now he couldn't check. If he tried to get into the building he would be silhouetted against the light again, a perfect target.

More shouts sounded down the street. Unlike some frontier settlements, Stockton probably didn't have many gunfights breaking out in the middle of the night. People would want to know what was going on, but if they had any sense, John Henry thought, they would stay inside until things quieted down.

With all the commotion, it was a miracle that John Henry heard a plank in the boardwalk creak behind him. He twisted around and saw a figure looming ominously out of the shadows. Whoever it was might be an innocent bystander, John Henry realized, so he held off on the trigger even though his first impulse was to shoot.

Then he saw the figure thrust something long and menacing at him and he dived for the ground. A shotgun erupted with a deafening boom as a huge tongue of flame spurted from one of its barrels. Buckshot smashed into the side of the wagon and ripped through the air next to John Henry as he rolled underneath the vehicle. The only thing that saved him was that the range was close, so the charge hadn't had the chance to spread out much.

As he came to a stop on his belly, John Henry tipped the revolver up and fired from underneath the wagon. The shotgunner cried out and staggered to the side. John Henry heard the thud as the double-barreled weapon fell to the boardwalk. The man who had wielded it collapsed on top of it.

The original bushwhacker was still in the game. His rifle cracked twice more as he emerged from cover and started across the street toward John Henry, throwing lead as fast as he could work the rifle's lever.

John Henry rolled again as slugs plowed into the ground so close to his head that they kicked dust into his eyes. Half-blinded, he tried to swing the Colt around and bring it to bear on his attacker, but he had a grim hunch that he wasn't going to make it in time.

Another handgun blasted somewhere nearby. In the confusion, that was all John Henry could tell for sure. But the rifleman suddenly stumbled and dropped the repeater. John Henry snapped a shot at him but couldn't tell if he hit the man. Then his hammer fell on an empty chamber.

The bushwhacker turned and ran. He was moving fast enough that he couldn't be injured very badly. John Henry scrambled out from under the wagon, jammed the empty revolver back in its holster, and gave chase.

Shadows swallowed the bushwhacker as he ran into that alley across the street. John Henry flattened against the front wall of the building next to the alley and quickly thumbed fresh cartridges into the Colt's cylinder. Going down a dark alley with an empty gun was a recipe for disaster for a lawman.

But as he snapped the cylinder closed, he heard a swift rataplan of hoofbeats from the other end of the alley. John Henry bit back a curse. Clearly, the bushwhacker had had a horse hidden back there, and now he was galloping away as fast as the animal could carry him. John Henry knew that by the time he retrieved Buck from the stable and threw a saddle on him, the would-be killer would be long gone.

But the one with the shotgun wasn't going anywhere. John Henry could see him lying motionless on the boardwalk in the light that came through the broken window. Even though his instincts told him that the man was either dead or unconscious, he kept the Colt trained on the still form anyway as he approached.

The man was lying facedown on top of the shotgun he had dropped. John Henry hooked a boot toe under his shoulder and rolled him over onto his back. The front of the man's homespun shirt under his coat was dark with blood where John Henry had drilled him twice.

To the best of his recollection, John Henry had never seen the man before.

The sound of footsteps made him turn quickly toward them. A vaguely familiar voice called, "Hold your fire, damn it!"

"Marshal Gainey?" John Henry said.

"That's right," the local lawman answered. "Who's there?"

"It's John Henry Sixkiller."

"Marshal Sixkiller! What's going on here?"

Gainey, carrying a shotgun, came into the light. His eyes widened as he looked from the Colt in John Henry's hand to the dead man on the boardwalk.

"That's Floyd Matthews," he said. "Did you kill him?"

"Reckon I did," John Henry said, "but only after he came within a whisker of blowing my head off with that Greener."

Gainey grunted and said, "Can't say as I'm surprised. Matthews has been in trouble with the law more times than I can count."

"He's a local man?"

"Yeah. His pa and brothers have a farm north of here. Good folks, all of them. But Floyd was always off a little. Didn't want to work, so he got sent to prison twice, once for robbing a store and once for holding up a stagecoach. I figure he's committed other crimes nobody could prove on him, too. Did he try to rob you, Marshal?"

"No," John Henry said, "he was out to kill me, and so was the fella with him."

"There was another one?"

"Hombre with what sounded like a Winchester." John Henry pointed at the wagon across the street. "He was waiting for me over there and opened up on me first. When he missed and I returned his fire, Matthews moved in from behind me with the shotgun."

Gainey let out a low whistle and said, "You're lucky to be alive if they had you in a crossfire like that."

"I know," John Henry said. "I probably wouldn't be if somebody else hadn't pitched in and winged the gent with the rifle. That wasn't you, Marshal?"

Gainey shook his head and said, "I just got here. I was in my office when I heard all the shooting. Sounded like war had broken out again. You say somebody helped you? You didn't get a look at him?"

"I never saw him," John Henry said, "but there's a good chance he saved my life."

And he had no idea who could have done such a thing.

Chapter Twenty-two

They found the Winchester the bushwhacker had used lying in the street where he had dropped it, but it was just like a thousand other rifles and didn't tell John Henry anything that would help to identify its owner.

By the time he rode out of Stockton the next morning, he still didn't have any idea who had fired the shot that winged the rifleman and made him flee.

He had a hunch about the identity of the bushwhacker, though: Clive Denton. John Henry was becoming more convinced that Denton had sent Penelope Smith on into the mountains with the rest of the bogus bills while he kept an eye on her back trail. Somehow they had discovered that a federal lawman was tracking the gang and they wanted to stop him before he caught up to Penelope.

Buck kept up a ground-eating pace all day, and by evening John Henry rode into the foothills settlement of Sonora. Originally a mining camp, it had hung on after the boom days to become a reasonably prosperous town serving the needs of the mines that were still operating in the area.

The local law was a small, wiry man named Sam Meldrum, whose sweeping mustaches seemed much too big for his body. When he heard what had brought John Henry to Sonora, he suggested that they go around to the local businesses together and search for counterfeit bills. That sounded like a good idea to John Henry.

They found one of the phony ten-dollar bills at the livery stable, where the proprietor remembered the good-looking blonde in a buggy who had passed through around midday.

"She wanted to buy some grain for her horse," the man explained. "I sold her some, of course." The liveryman glanced back and forth as if to make sure no one was eavesdropping and lowered his voice as he went on, "Hell, I'd have given her the grain if I hadn't been worried that my missus would catch on. She does all the bookkeepin', and she's got an eagle eye for any unexplained losses. But I tell you, fellas, ain't many men'd ever say no to a gal as good-lookin' as that yellow-haired filly. And I reckon she knowed that, too."

"You know if she went anywhere else here in town?" Meldrum asked.

The liveryman scratched his jaw and pondered, then said, "While I was grainin' her horse, I think she went up the street to the milliner's. Can't be sure about that, though." When the lawmen started to leave the barn, he added, "That money she give me, you say it's fake?"

"That's right," John Henry said.

"Well . . . I reckon it's worth the price of the grain her horse et, just to get to talk to somebody like her for a few minutes."

As they were walking up the street, Meldrum said, "This woman must be a mighty fine looker."

"She is that," John Henry agreed. "Crooked as a dog's hind leg, though, and not to be trusted at all."

"That's a shame. I guess just 'cause a gal looks like an angel, that don't mean she's gonna act like one."

"That's about as true a thing as any man ever said," John Henry agreed.

Not surprisingly, the stout, white-haired woman who ran the millinery shop wasn't nearly as impressed with Penelope Smith as the liveryman had been. In fact, her face pinched with disapproval when John Henry described the blonde.

"Yes, she was here," the woman said. "I sold her a scarf. She said she needed something to keep the dust out of her mouth and nose while she was traveling. I can understand that. This is a dreadfully dusty country."

"But something about her rubbed you the wrong way, didn't it?" John Henry guessed.

"Well . . . young women who look like that, they have a certain arrogance about them. As if the rest of the world should kowtow to them simply because so many men fall prostrate at their feet with desire. I can only imagine."

Meldrum muttered something under his breath.

"What did you say, Sheriff Meldrum?" the woman asked with a frown.

"Oh, nothin', nothin' at all," Meldrum replied hurriedly. "So you sold her a scarf, did you?"

"That's right."

John Henry said, "And she paid you with either a ten- or a twenty-dollar bill, didn't she?"

"How in the world did you know that?"

"We'd better take a look at it," John Henry said, sighing. He was pretty sure Penelope had struck again.

By now he had seen enough of the bogus bills to recognize what he was looking for almost right away. He pointed out the slight flaws in the printing, prompting the owner of the shop to exclaim, "Good heavens! A bill like that is worthless!"

"Yes, ma'am," John Henry said. "I'm afraid so."

"I knew a woman who looked like her couldn't be trusted! I just knew it!"

"Do you know if she went anywhere else?" John Henry asked.

"I have no idea. If you catch her, Marshal Sixkiller, are you going to put her in jail?"

"That'll be up to a judge and jury, ma'am, but I expect that's what'll happen."

"Good. Her looks won't do her much good there, will they?"

John Henry couldn't answer that.

He was thinking more about the fact that Penelope was only half a day ahead of him now. He was closing in on her.

Which meant he would have to keep his eyes open even more. He couldn't shake the feeling that there might be another ambush ahead of him somewhere.

He spent the night in Sonora and rode out the next morning after saying good-bye to Sheriff Sam Meldrum. From here on the going would be considerably more rugged as the trail rose into the mountains. The good thing was that the terrain ought to slow Penelope down in the buggy even more than it did John Henry on horseback.

"It's up to you now, Buck," he said as he patted the big horse on the shoulder.

Buck responded admirably, taking the steep trails with apparent ease. He was sure-footed, too, which was a good thing because there were places where a sheer drop-off of a couple of hundred feet bordered the road. Luckily, it was wide enough so that whenever John Henry met a wagon coming down, as he did a few times, he was able to pull off to the side and let the vehicles pass.

By afternoon John Henry and Buck had climbed high into the mountains. With the drop-off to the right, a steeply sloping rock face rose to John Henry's left as the trail circled the shoulder of a snow-capped peak. The Sierra Nevadas were rugged but beautiful, he thought. Previous cases had taken him to New Mexico Territory and he had seen the mountains there. If anything, this California scenery was even more spectacular.

The trail entered a level stretch of a quarter of

a mile or so, which would allow Buck to rest a bit as John Henry reined him back to an easy walk. The dizzying drop-off still loomed to the right, the cliff topped by rugged rimrock to the left.

John Henry had reached the midpoint of that level stretch when a sudden boom made his head jerk up. That sounded like dynamite, he thought.

As he saw a cloud of dust and smoke billow up from the rimrock, he knew his hunch was right. Somebody had just set off a blast up there. And there was only one good reason for somebody to do such a thing.

Somebody was trying to drop an avalanche right on top of his head.

It looked like they had a pretty good chance of succeeding, too. The slope here wasn't sheer, but it was steep enough that once rocks started sliding and bouncing down it, nothing was going to stop them. Just such a deadly gray wave was coming toward John Henry now.

That realization of danger went through his brain in a fraction of a second. Almost as soon as the dynamite exploded, John Henry had jabbed his boot heels into Buck's flanks and sent the horse leaping ahead.

"Run for all you're worth, Buck!" John Henry shouted over the growing rumble of the rock-slide.

Whoever had set off that blast had chosen a good spot. Whether John Henry turned around and tried to retreat or charged ahead, he and Buck had about the same distance to cover to get clear of the avalanche.

Retreating hadn't even crossed his mind. Even if he survived, that would have cut him off from where he needed to go.

Besides, the Good Lord hadn't put much backup in John Henry Sixkiller's nature. His instincts always kept him moving forward.

He leaned forward in the saddle as Buck's hooves pounded the trail. John Henry watched the ground in front of them. A misstep would be fatal for both man and horse.

But from the corner of his eye he saw the rocks coming closer and closer. Already some of the smaller bits of debris that had been thrown into the air by the blast were raining down around John Henry. Running at top speed, Buck could get them clear of the avalanche's main path in a little less than a minute.

John Henry didn't think they had that much time, though. He leaned forward even more and urged Buck on, as tons of rock swept toward them with breathtaking speed.

Chapter Twenty-three

John Henry had found himself in life-or-death races before, but never one as urgent as this. Larger rocks, some as big as boulders, began to crash onto the road only a few yards behind the madly galloping buckskin. John Henry saw one looming right beside him and ducked, flattening out on Buck's neck. He felt the rock brush against the back of his coat. If he had reacted a split second slower, it would have knocked him out of the saddle and he would have fallen to his death.

A big slab of rock hit the trail about ten yards in front of them and gouged a hole out of it before continuing to plummet toward the canyon below. That left a gap some eight feet wide. A narrow ledge remained against the cliff, and if John Henry had had time to dismount, he could have led Buck along that ledge without much trouble.

But there was no time, and anyway, Buck was going too fast to stop. John Henry had no choice but to jab his heels into the horse's flanks again and lift Buck's head with the reins. Buck reached the gap and sailed into the air, soaring over the empty space in a magnificent jump. He landed on the far side with a teeth-rattling jolt and lunged ahead, never breaking stride.

Thanks to the big buckskin's strength, stamina, and speed, they were almost clear, John Henry saw. Just a few more yards, and while they wouldn't be completely out of danger the main body of the rockslide would be behind them. With John Henry urging him on, Buck seemed to reach down inside himself and find a last surge of energy. They reached the end of the level stretch. Buck lunged up the now-sloping trail as the avalanche roared on behind them, filling the air with ear-wracking noise and choking clouds of dust.

John Henry hauled back on the reins and slowed Buck to a gradual stop. The horse's sleek hide was covered with sweat, and his sides heaved. His gallant heart had to be hammering at an incredible pace, John Henry thought as he slipped from the saddle. He hoped that in saving his own life, he hadn't killed Buck in the process.

He stood there watching the devastation behind him and stroked the horse's shoulder, murmuring, "Good boy, Buck, good boy. You saved my life, big fella. Good boy."

Buck's head hung low, but he didn't seem to be breathing quite as heavily now. John Henry began to hope that with some rest, the horse would be fine. He led Buck higher up the trail so that no stray rocks tumbling down in the wake of the avalanche would endanger them.

They had climbed about fifty yards and the echoes of the rockslide were beginning to die away when John Henry heard more rocks rattling above them. This wasn't the same sort of menacing rumble as before, but it served as a warning anyway. He looked up and saw the sun glint on metal along the rimrock.

That could mean only one thing.

A second later, as John Henry lunged toward the cliff and dragged Buck with him, a rifle cracked and a bullet smacked into the trail where he had been standing.

Dynamite and several tons of rock hadn't done the job of wiping him out, so now whoever wanted him dead was making another effort with a rifle.

John Henry figured the man must have used all the dynamite he had, or else the varmint would have tried again to blow the mountain down on top of him.

"Be thankful for small favors, eh, Buck?" he said wryly to the horse.

As long as they stayed where they were, pressed against the rock face, the rifleman couldn't get a good shot at them. The angle was wrong for that.

John Henry began working his way slowly along the trail, leading Buck. About a hundred yards ahead of him, the trail took a bend to the left, around a jutting pinnacle of rock, and John Henry knew that if he could reach that bend, it would shelter him from the would-be killer hidden above him.

Unless the rifleman was able to change his position and move along the rimrock until he had a clear shot again. The gun fell silent, and John Henry had a feeling that was exactly what was going on. The man wasn't going to give up that easily.

Or woman. It was remotely possible that was Penelope Smith up there with a Winchester. He wouldn't put it past her. He thought it was more likely to be Clive Denton or Nick Prentice or even Ignatius O'Reilly himself, though.

Whoever it was, they were mighty stubborn about wanting John Henry dead.

With Buck following him, John Henry edged around the bend in the trail. The rock spire towered high above him. While he was sheltered by it, he swung into the saddle.

"I know you just made a hard run, big fella, but I've got to ask you to do it again. Let's go."

John Henry urged Buck into motion. The gelding took the slope in front of him in great, lunging strides. Horse and rider emerged from the shade of the pinnacle.

John Henry heard the crack of a rifle and knew the bushwhacker had just taken another shot at him. He didn't feel the impact of a bullet, though, and Buck didn't break stride, so he was certain the shot had missed.

Ahead and above them, the trail entered an area littered with massive boulders. John Henry knew those rocks would provide plenty of cover if he could get among them.

Something whipped past his head. Another bullet, but as long as it missed, it didn't matter how close it came.

The giant slabs of rock loomed just ahead of him. A splash of gray suddenly appeared on one of them where a slug splattered against it. A heartbeat later Buck dashed along the trail where it entered a gap between two of the giant rocks, and once again he and John Henry were protected from the varmint trying to ventilate them.

John Henry slowed Buck to a walk again. The trail led through the rocks all the way to the crest of a ridge. He figured they would be relatively safe until they got there. He didn't know what he would find on the other side of that ridge, but he would deal with that once he got there.

That avalanche was going to play hell with people wanting to travel into and out of the mountains, he thought. It would take a while to clear away all the fallen rocks and repair any damage to the road, such as that gap Buck had leaped over. There were other trails in the Sierra Nevadas, but anybody in the mining towns where he was headed would have to go a long way around if they needed to reach the Central Valley, and vice versa.

He reached inside his coat and pulled out the map he had drawn in Dunleavy's office, unfolded it, and took a look at it. The first settlement he would come to was named Copperhead.

That was an ominous-sounding name, John Henry thought, and he figured the original settlers wouldn't have named the place after a venomous snake unless there were plenty of the scaly critters around. He resolved to keep his eyes open. It wouldn't do to survive everything he had gone through already and then die from a blasted snakebite.

He kept an eye on his back trail, too, not wanting that bushwhacker to come up behind him and make another stab at killing him. The rugged landscape seemed to be peaceful again now, but John Henry knew how fast that could change with little or no warning.

He reached the top of the ridge and rode over it before stopping, so that he wouldn't be skylighted. Once he felt like it was safe, though, he reined Buck to a halt and took a minute to look out over the little valley spread before him.

The terrain wasn't as rugged on this side of the ridge, although the slopes were still fairly steep. They were covered with trees instead of giant boulders and outcroppings of rock. The clean smell of pines was strong in the air. Down below, a couple of miles ahead of him, a good-sized creek brawled its way along the valley floor. Back in the Gold Rush days, a lot of dust had probably been panned out of those cold, rushing waters.

The miners who were left had sunk shafts in the hillside. As John Henry scanned the landscape, he saw piles of tailings here and there, marking the location of the mine shafts. Chimney smoke rose into the blue sky in a few places.

Off to his right lay the town of Copperhead, built on both sides of the creek. He took his field glasses from one of his saddlebags and studied the settlement. Most of the buildings had been constructed of either logs or roughly planed boards sawed from trees felled in the area, but he saw a few more-impressive structures of stone or brick. There were still some tents pitched around the town, too, as there must have been during its days as a rough-and-ready mining camp, along with shacks made from tin, tar paper, and canvas. The layout didn't have much rhyme or reason to it, either, as a hovel might sit right next to a respectable-looking house. That was common in places that had grown quickly, fueled by some sort of boom.

A few people were moving around the streets of Copperhead, but it seemed to John Henry that there ought to be more folks visible in the middle of the afternoon like this.

Nor would he have been surprised to see a group of men from the town on their way toward him. That avalanche had been so loud the citizens must have heard it, and he would have thought that some of them would want to find out what had happened. After all, the settlement depended on the road to get goods and people in and out.

He could see the trail as it wound down into the valley, though, and no riders or wagons or buggies were moving along it.

That was puzzling, but there might be a logical explanation for it, he decided. The best way to find out would be to ride down there and see what was going on in Copperhead.

He had high hopes of catching up to Penelope

Smith here. She couldn't be that far ahead of him now, and the next settlement was a good distance farther on, too far to reach before nightfall. That meant there was an excellent chance Penelope had stopped in Copperhead to spend the night . . . and to pass more of her counterfeit money, as well.

Well aware that whoever had tried to kill him could still be on his trail, John Henry put away the field glasses and nudged Buck into motion again. As they started down the slope toward the valley and the town, John Henry told the buckskin, "Keep your eyes peeled for snakes, big fella . . . the sort that slither on the ground, and the two-legged kind, too!"

Chapter Twenty-four

The first buildings John Henry came to were a stamp mill and the offices of the Copperhead Mining Corporation. The mill wasn't working at the moment, which again came as a bit of a surprise. A CLOSED sign hung in the office window.

Maybe the vein that the Copperhead Mining Corporation had been working had played out. If the mines were failing, that might explain why the settlement wasn't very busy. Without the mines, Copperhead would have no reason for existence. If all of them closed down, more than likely the place would turn into a ghost town within a year.

He passed an assay office, also closed. Across the street was a livery stable. Its double doors were open, and a stringy man in overalls, a flannel shirt, and a battered old felt hat stood in the opening, his thumbs hooked in the front pockets of the overalls. John Henry angled Buck in that direction.

"Howdy," he said as he approached the liveryman.

The man didn't return the greeting. He just asked sharply, "You come up the trail from Sonora, mister?"

"That's right," John Henry said.

"I ain't surprised. Guess they ain't got word yet."

"Word of what?"

The liveryman didn't answer the question. Instead he asked another of his own.

"What was that big ol' racket on the other side of Cougar Ridge a while ago? Sounded like an earthquake, but I didn't feel the ground shakin' any."

"Cougar Ridge is the one the road from Sonora comes over?"

"Yup."

"I'm a stranger here," John Henry explained. "I don't know the names of all the landmarks."

"Reckon I knowed you was a stranger. What about all that noise?"

"Avalanche," John Henry said.

The liveryman's eyes narrowed in his leathery old face.

"Thought I heard somebody doin' some blastin', too," he commented.

"So did I," John Henry said. He didn't add that the explosion and the resulting rockslide had been directed at him.

Nor did he haul out his badge and identify himself. Something had started gnawing at his nerves, a vague, indefinable feeling that things weren't right here in Copperhead. He decided that it might be better to keep the fact that he was a deputy U.S. marshal under wraps for a while, until he found out more.

"You see this here avalanche for yourself?" asked the liveryman.

"I did. I was lucky not to get caught in it." John Henry patted Buck's shoulder. "This big fella got me out of the way of it."

Whatever was bothering the liveryman, he forgot about it for a moment as he studied Buck appreciatively, with the eyes of an experienced judge of horseflesh.

"That's a mighty fine-lookin' animal you got, mister. I'd plumb admire to take care of him tonight. That is, if you weren't gonna be turnin' around and lightin' a shuck outta Copperhead just as quick as you can."

"Why would I do that?" John Henry asked. "I just got here."

"You won't want to stay." The liveryman changed the subject again by asking, "What happened to the road? That rockslide wipe it out?"

"I'm afraid so. Some of the men from town need to get out there and see about clearing it off and repairing the damage. It's liable to take a few weeks."

The liveryman turned his head and spat into the dust.

"Take longer than that," he said glumly. "Nobody in these parts is gonna feel like goin' and movin' rocks."

"Why not?" It took an effort for John Henry to

keep his feelings of frustration and impatience reined in.

The liveryman shook his head.

"I've said too much already. Take my advice, mister. Turn around and ride out. You ought to be safe if you don't ride any farther into town."

"Safe from what, blast it?"

The liveryman didn't answer. He turned and walked into the barn, disappearing into its gloomy shadows.

Short of going after the man and trying to beat some information out of him—which, as a lawman, John Henry wasn't supposed to do—he didn't see any options other than trying to find somebody else in Copperhead who could give him answers that made sense.

John Henry turned Buck and rode slowly along the settlement's main street. He passed a blacksmith's shop, a gunsmith's, a lawyer's office, a couple of general stores, an apothecary, a grocer's, a butcher shop, and a newspaper office. A bank, one of the buildings in town made of brick, loomed up on his right. Across from it was a doctor's office. On the next corner was the local marshal's office and jail. Across the street on the other corner was a two-story frame hotel.

The street was empty now. A few people had been in it or moving along the boardwalks when John Henry rode into town, but they had all disappeared, almost as if they were hiding from him. One by one they had vanished into the buildings as he made his way up the street.

He felt eyes watching him as he rode past. He

even saw faces in windows here and there. The citizens of Copperhead weren't actually hiding, he realized. They didn't care if he knew they were there.

They just didn't want anything to do with him.

He couldn't figure out why they would be so hostile, but maybe the local peace officer could tell him. John Henry brought Buck to a stop at the hitch rail in front of the marshal's office and swung down from the saddle. He looped the reins around the rail and stepped up onto the boardwalk.

The door of the marshal's office creaked open before John Henry could reach it. He stopped. He didn't see anybody inside. It was almost like the door had opened by itself.

John Henry didn't spook easily. Nobody in his line of work could if they wanted to stay in the law business for very long. But something about this whole situation made a cold shiver go along his spine, like somebody with icy fingers was tickling it.

The door hadn't opened by itself. A man spoke from behind it. But what he said in a strained, hollow voice didn't make John Henry feel any better.

"Better get back on your horse and ride out, mister," the unseen man advised, "while you still can."

John Henry ignored the warning and asked, "Are you the town marshal?"

"That's right, and I'm tellin' you to git."

"No offense, but I reckon I outrank you." It looked like he was going to have to reveal his identity after all if he wanted to get any answers. "I'm a deputy United States marshal, name of John Henry Sixkiller."

For a long moment there was only silence inside the local lawman's office. Then the same strained voice said, "Trust me, Marshal, you don't want to be here." The man moved around the door so that John Henry could see him. "Turn your horse around and leave. I been watchin' you. You ain't been close enough to anybody yet to catch it."

John Henry stiffened in the saddle in response not only to the words but to the sight of the town marshal as well. The man was tall and lean, or at least he would have been under normal circumstances. Right now he was hunched over as if in pain. He had graying brown hair and a close-cropped, grizzled beard. A tin star was pinned to his vest.

His face was haggard and lined, making him look older than he probably was. His eyes seemed to have trouble focusing as he peered at John Henry. He blinked owlishly.

"Good Lord, Marshal," John Henry exclaimed. "You're sick."

"Half the town is," the man croaked. "Four people dead so far, and a heap more to come, I'm thinkin'."

"What is it? What sort of sickness?"

"Hell, do I look like a sawbones to you?"

"Don't you have a doctor here in town?"

"Two of 'em," the marshal said. "They come down with the stuff, too, almost right away. That's one reason we knew it was catchin'. Now everybody who ain't sick is stayin' as far away as they can from them that are. When one person in a family gets it, though, it spreads through the rest like wildfire."

John Henry had heard of outbreaks of sickness like that. They could devastate an entire community. Usually there wasn't much doctors could do to help, either. They just tried to halt the spread as much as possible and let the stuff run its course.

"What are the symptoms?" he asked.

"You mean what's wrong with us?" The marshal of Copperhead squinted at him. "You ain't a pill roller, neither. You said you was a star packer workin' for Uncle Sam. Why do you want to know?"

"I just thought I might be able to help."

The man shook his head and said, "Ain't nothin' nobody can do. But since you asked . . . when you come down with this stuff you get chills and fever first, and then you start to hurt all over. Most folks can't keep nothin' on their stomach. Then the fever climbs higher and higher until it bids fair to blister a man's insides and cook his brain. That's what kills folks."

Fevers were some of the deadliest ailments on the frontier, all right, John Henry thought. They had wiped out towns, decimated entire Indian tribes.

"You said both of your local doctors are sick. Is there anybody else in town with medical training?"

"A few ladies who done a spot of nursin'. They've been tryin' to help, but it's a losin' battle. You see now why I said you need to turn around and ride out, Marshal. You still got a good chance of not gettin' sick if you do."

John Henry rested both hands on the saddle horn and leaned forward to ease his muscles. He had come a long way on the trail of Penelope Smith and whoever else was part of the counterfeiting gang. He wasn't going to just turn around, ride off, and give up on this assignment.

"I followed a woman here," he said. "She's a fugitive, and I have to corral her, Marshal. Maybe you saw her. She's blond, good-looking, would have come into town earlier this afternoon in a buggy. She might have had one or two men with her."

"Ain't you heard a word that I said?" the local lawman demanded. "This town's a pesthole! It'll be the death of you if you stay."

"What about the woman?" John Henry pressed.

The town marshal shook his head and said in exasperation, "I ain't seen nobody like that today, but I'm sick myself. Been layin' down on a cot in the back room all day. I just happened to be up and see you ridin' in. So don't ask me if there are any other strangers in town, because I plumb don't know."

That was fair enough, John Henry supposed. A lawman was supposed to keep up with the comings and goings in his town, but sometimes an hombre was just too sick to do his job. He would have to take a good look around himself. If Penelope was here, her buggy would be, too, and Copperhead wasn't so big that John Henry couldn't find it.

"I'm obliged to you for your help, Marshal, and sorry that you're sick," he said. "If there's anything I can do . . ."

The man groaned and said, "Just let me go back inside, lay down, and die."

"I hope that won't happen," John Henry said sincerely. He turned his horse toward the hotel across the street.

If Penelope had reached Copperhead and didn't know that the town was in the grip of sickness, she probably would have gone to the hotel, which appeared to be the only one in town. Under the circumstances, when she found out what was going on here she might have driven on anyway, even though the next town was quite a few miles away. She might have thought that spending the night on the trail was better than staying in a place where she might contract a deadly illness.

Maybe somebody at the hotel could tell him, he mused. But before he went inside, he rode around back to check on something else.

The livery stable where he had stopped when he rode into town was the only one in Copperhead. Penelope's buggy could have been parked inside the barn, but John Henry considered that unlikely. He probably would have seen it if it had been there.

But as he suspected, there was a corral behind the hotel, where guests could leave their horses, next to a long, covered shed.

Several horses were milling around inside the corral.

And under the shed, a buggy with the team unhitched from it was parked.

He couldn't be absolutely sure just yet, but John Henry had a strong hunch that he had caught up to Penelope Smith at last.

Chapter Twenty-five

He unlatched the corral gate and rode Buck inside, reaching out to swing the gate closed behind him. He dismounted, tied the reins to a snubbing post, unsaddled, and carried the tack through another gate that led into the covered area under the shed. Several sawhorses sat there, so he put his saddle on one of them and slung the saddlebags over his shoulder.

Using a piece of blanket and a brush he found in the shed, he gave Buck a good rub-down and brushing. Buck had cooled down and seemed to be recovered from the two hard runs earlier, but John Henry knew the horse had to be worn out. He turned Buck loose to get a drink from the water trough and sample some hay from a pile in a corner of the corral.

Then he went back into the shed and paused beside the buggy he was pretty sure belonged to Penelope Smith. Well, the one she had rented from Dunleavy, anyway, John Henry amended silently. A glance in the back of it revealed that the area behind the seat was empty. Whatever Penelope had brought with her, she or somebody else had carried into the hotel.

John Henry was well aware that anybody in the rear part of the hotel, on either story, could look out the window and see him poking around out here, so he stayed alert for any movement. From the corner of his eye, he watched for somebody raising a window and sticking a rifle barrel out.

Nothing of the sort happened while he was examining the buggy. When he was satisfied that it didn't have anything to tell him, he walked toward the hotel's back door. His right hand hung near the butt of the Colt on his hip.

He knew he could be walking into another ambush, but his quarry was in there. Every lawman's instinct in his body told him that. After coming so far, he wasn't going to let anything stop him now.

The back door wasn't locked. John Henry let himself into the hotel and paused just inside the door to look and listen. A short hallway led toward the lobby. The hotel was quiet. Hushed, in fact. It almost reminded John Henry of a hospital.

Which was appropriate, he supposed, considering the wave of sickness that had washed through Copperhead. He wondered if any of the hotel's guests had come down with the fever or if they were all holed up in there trying to avoid it.

He went ahead and rested his hand on his gun as he stepped from the rear hallway into the lobby. It was dusty and deserted. Nobody sat in the overstuffed armchairs next to the potted plants. The writing desk in the corner was empty. No clerk waited on duty behind the counter with the cubbyholes for room keys on the wall behind it.

Even though John Henry now knew that the tense atmosphere hanging over Copperhead had a logical reason, there was still something eerie and almost otherworldly about the place. His nerves were stretched taut just from being here.

He walked over to the counter where the registration book lay open. If he had expected to find Penelope's name in it, he would have been disappointed. The last person to check in had signed himself "Edward Munroe." The name meant nothing to John Henry. The date Munroe had checked in was a week earlier.

According to the register, he hadn't checked out.

That was interesting, John Henry thought, but it didn't have to mean anything. Maybe Munroe had left town and the clerk had simply failed to make a note of it. Maybe he was lying upstairs in one of the rooms, too sick to move. It was even possible that Munroe was one of the four people who had died from the fever.

Or maybe Munroe was the man who, a couple of days earlier, had introduced himself to John Henry on the ferry as Clive Denton. John Henry let the theory spin out in his mind. Denton could be the gang's advance man, traveling ahead of Penelope to the places where she planned to distribute the counterfeit bills. After scouting out each location, Denton doubled back to meet Penelope, send her on ahead, and then watch to make sure no one was following her. If there was any pursuit, it would be Denton's job to get rid of it . . . obviously by any means necessary.

As far as John Henry could see, that idea hung together. He had no proof, but it was certainly possible.

Any connection between "Denton" and "Munroe" was sheer speculation, however. But there was one way to check it out, he thought as he leaned over the book and studied it closer. Someone with different handwriting had put the number "14" in tiny print next to Munroe's name. The clerk must have done that, John Henry thought, and fourteen was the number of Munroe's room.

John Henry glanced up at the pegboard where room keys hung. The peg in the space marked "14" was empty.

Somebody was up there in that room.

John Henry's gut told him he needed to find out who.

The sudden creak of hinges made his head jerk up and his hand move quickly to the Colt on his hip. A door behind the counter had opened, and a man peered out at him in surprise.

The man's face was narrow and pasty. It looked even more pale because of the contrast with his unruly jet-black hair. His eyes were huge behind a pair of thick spectacles that perched on his nose. His ears stuck out from the sides of his head. He wore a string tie, and his shirt collar was buttoned up but still loose around his scrawny neck. His black suit and white shirt continued the striking contrast.

"Didn't know anybody was out here," the man said in a high-pitched voice. His head swayed forward on his skinny neck and then pulled back. "You shouldn't be here, mister. The hotel's closed. Not taking any new guests. The town's got sickness in it."

"So I've heard," John Henry said. "But I've got important business here, so I'll have to risk it."

"No business is worth your life."

"You're still here," John Henry pointed out. "But I guess you've already got the fever, don't you?"

"Me?" The man sounded surprised by that. He shook his head and went on, "I'm as healthy as a horse. Nobody here is sick yet, and I plan to keep it that way. So you need to get out, in case you're carrying the contagion with you."

"I'm not," John Henry said. "You're only the third person I've talked to in this town."

"Who were the others?"

"The liveryman—"

"Jacob Gaston. Last I heard he wasn't sick."

"And your town marshal."

The man's face took on a pinched look. "Marshal Ledbetter's got the sickness. I know that for a fact."

"He does," John Henry agreed, "but I stayed well away from him. I never got close enough to catch it. So you can see, it ought to be safe enough for me to stay here."

He had a hunch that money would sway the man's opinion, so he slipped a hand in his pocket and went on, "I need a room, and I can pay."

"Well . . ." The man came all the way out of the little room. "Reckon it might not hurt anything, if you're telling the truth."

"I give you my word," John Henry said.

The man nodded toward the registration book and said in a surly voice, "Sign in. Rooms are a dollar and a half a night without meals, two dollars with."

"You've got your own dining room, then?"

"Yeah. And a good supply of food in the kitchen. Good thing, too, because nobody wants to venture out to find any grub."

"Reckon I can understand that."

John Henry took the pen from the inkwell next to the registration book and signed "Henry Johnson" on the line under Edward Munroe's name. In the space for where he was from, he wrote "Fort Smith, Arkansas," which wasn't exactly true but close enough for government work, which was what had brought him here.

The sallow-faced man evidently had mastered the skill of reading upside down. He said, "You're a long way from home, Mr. Johnson."

"Like I said, I'm on business, Mr. . . . ?"

"Weaver," the man said. "I own this place."

"Pleased to meet you, Mr. Weaver," John Henry said, even though he really wasn't. "If I can get the key to my room . . ."

"Room Eight," Weaver said as he reached for one of the keys hanging on the pegboard.

John Henry didn't argue. He just took the key and nodded.

"Any bags?" Weaver asked.

"Just these," John Henry replied as he tapped a fingertip against the saddlebags slung over his left shoulder. Keeping his voice casual, he asked, "Anybody else checked in today, or am I the first one?"

"You're the first one," Weaver said.

John Henry tried not to frown. That didn't really make sense. He was convinced that was Penelope's buggy out in the shed. She couldn't have arrived that far ahead of him.

"You want anything else?" Weaver asked.

John Henry shook his head and said, "No, I reckon not." Then a thought occurred to him and he asked, "What time is supper?"

"There's a pot of beans on the stove in the kitchen. Go in there and help yourself whenever you're ready. Wash up after yourself, too."

And yet the man had the gall to charge an extra fifty cents a night for meals, John Henry thought wryly. He turned and walked to the stairs. As he started up them, he saw Weaver watching him. The man's head darted forward a little on his scrawny neck and then pulled back several times, as it had been doing sporadically throughout the conversation. It must have been a nervous habit. For some reason it reminded John Henry of a lizard, and that made him dislike the pasty-faced hotel keeper that much more.

He put all that out of his mind as he reached the second floor landing. Right now he wanted to find out who was in Room 14: Edward Munroe . . . or Penelope Smith. He walked quietly along the rather threadbare carpet runner in the corridor, being careful and testing each board before he put his weight on it. Whoever was in there, he wanted to take them by surprise.

If Edward Munroe turned out to be who he claimed to be and was completely innocent, it was going to be a mite embarrassing to bust in on him, John Henry told himself. He was willing to risk some embarrassment not to take any chances, though.

The key to Room 8 was in his pocket, but he went right on past it and came to a stop in front of a door with a pair of flat brass numbers—"1" and "4"—nailed to it. He leaned closer to the door and listened intently.

Faint sounds told him that someone was in there and moving around. He heard what was probably a wardrobe door open and close. Still moving slowly and carefully, he wrapped the fingers of his left hand around the shiny brass doorknob and tested it.

Locked.

John Henry didn't think that would be too much of a problem. The jamb was warped a little and flimsily built to start with, so he figured he could pop the door open, locked or not.

He tightened his grip on the knob and placed his left shoulder against the door. With his right hand he slid his revolver from its holster with just the faintest whisper of steel against leather.

Then he drew in a deep breath and abruptly

rammed his weight against the panel while pulling up on the doorknob. Just as he expected, the door flew open and he moved rapidly into the hotel room, sweeping the gun from side to side.

He wasn't expecting the sight that met his eyes, though. With a startled gasp, Penelope Smith whirled away from the wardrobe on the left side of the room to face him and then stood there staring at him in shock.

She wasn't any more shocked than John Henry was.

Penelope didn't have a stitch of clothing on.

Chapter Twenty-six

John Henry had been raised to be a gentleman, and that upbringing betrayed him now. He jerked his head to the side to avert his eyes from that display of creamy female flesh, totally forgetting for an instant that the naked female in the room was also a wanted fugitive.

Penelope hadn't forgotten it, though. She recovered from her surprise and lunged toward the dressing table. John Henry saw a little pistol lying there and knew he didn't have the luxury of worrying about being chivalrous anymore.

He flung himself across the room, moving even faster than she was. His left arm hooked around her waist. He twisted, pulling her away from the dressing table when her fingers were mere inches away from the gun. A heave sent her flying through the air to land with a bounce on the bed. As she rolled over, John Henry leveled the Colt at her and said, "Don't move, Miss Smith. It'd be a mighty big shame to shoot you, but I'll do it if I have to."

She stopped moving. She was in an extremely indelicate position, but that didn't stop her from pushing herself up on her elbows and glaring at him. He saw plenty of anger on her face, but not an ounce of shame.

"Are you going to just stand there and stare at me?" she demanded.

"I'm not staring," John Henry said. "I'm keeping you covered."

"*Covered* is a pretty far cry from what I am right now!"

She was correct about that. John Henry said, "You can sit up and wrap the bedspread around you." He paused. "You don't have a knife hidden under the pillows, do you? Or a Henry rifle? Maybe a stick or two of dynamite?"

"What the hell are you talking about?" Still looking outraged, she sat up and tugged the quilted spread loose from the foot of the bed so she could wrap it around her nudity. "Men get lynched for breaking into a woman's room like this, you know. Especially Indians!"

"So you know who I am."

Penelope glared some more as she said, "I knew something was wrong about you as soon as you came into Campos's place with that Chinese whore."

"She's not . . . Never mind." There were more important things to consider right now than defending Wing Sun's honor. He gestured with the Colt and went on, "Stand up and move over there into that corner."

With a surly pout on her face, Penelope

followed his orders, keeping the bedspread wrapped around her as she did so.

"If you were a gentleman, you'd at least let me get dressed before you arrested me."

"And if I was a fool, I'd give you a chance to get your hands on a weapon. I like you better the way you are right now, defenseless."

Her chin jutted defiantly as she said, "You really think I'm defenseless?" She started to lower the bedspread.

"Let's not have any of that," John Henry said sharply. "Despite what you think, I was raised to be polite to ladies. And even to females who *aren't* ladies."

"You think you know so damned much," she said.

"I know you've been passing bogus bills from here to Wichita," John Henry said. "I know you're working for Ignatius O'Reilly and that Clive Denton and Nick Prentice, if those are their real names, are part of the gang, too."

A small frown that appeared genuinely puzzled appeared on her face as he spoke, but when he finished she burst out with a laugh.

"You're even more ignorant about what's going on here than I thought you were," she said.

"Enlighten me, then," John Henry told her. "Explain the whole thing to me."

She shook her head.

"I don't think so. I'm just going to let you make a fool of yourself, Marshal Sixkiller!"

He wondered for a split second why her voice suddenly went up like that at the end, but then the answer burst on his brain and he twisted toward the door, which he had pushed on with his heel but it hadn't closed all the way because he had sprung it getting into the room.

Too late. It exploded open, and the edge of it cracked against the wrist of his gun hand, knocking the Colt to the side. He was able to hang on to the gun, but he couldn't bring it to bear before Clive Denton barreled into him. The collision's impact propelled John Henry backward onto the bed.

Denton landed on top of him. The man's left hand gripped John Henry's wrist and kept him from bringing the gun around, while his right fist hammered into the lawman's face. Denton wasn't exceptionally big, but he had a lot of wiry strength and the sheer ferocity of his attack had taken John Henry by surprise.

John Henry jerked his head to the side to avoid another blow and threw a punch of his own. His fist caught Denton on the jaw and drove his head to the side. Denton hung on stubbornly, though, and tried to ram his knee into John Henry's groin. John Henry twisted away from it.

"Get out of the way!" Penelope yelled. "Get out of the way and I'll shoot him!"

She had dropped the bedspread, darted over to the dressing table, and snatched up the little pistol. She couldn't get a shot at John Henry, though, while Denton was so close to him. John Henry grappled with his opponent, trying to keep Denton between him and the muzzle of Penelope's gun.

As the two men lunged back and forth, straining

against each other, they slid off the edge of the bed and crashed to the floor. That was enough to break them apart. Denton rolled and lashed out with a foot. The heel of his boot connected with John Henry's wrist, and this time he couldn't hold on to the Colt. It flew from his fingers and went spinning and sliding under the bed. Penelope dived after it, maybe thinking that she wanted a bigger-caliber weapon.

Denton leaped on John Henry and wrapped both hands around the lawman's throat. His fingers clamped down cruelly and his thumbs dug in as he tried to crush John Henry's windpipe. John Henry hooked a couple of punches into Denton's ribs, but they failed to loosen the man's grip. Denton was fighting with the strength of insane desperation.

"I've got his gun!" Penelope cried exultantly. "Clive, I've got his gun!"

John Henry clawed at Denton's fingers around his throat. The room was starting to spin crazily now. He knew he was on the verge of passing out. He tried cupping his hands and slapping them against Denton's ears, but the man hunched his shoulders and pulled his head down, and John Henry's hands skidded off the sides of his head. Despite his rather mild appearance, Denton obviously had plenty of experience at this sort of bare-knuckles brawl.

He lifted John Henry's head from the floor and then slammed it down against the boards. John Henry was barely hanging on to consciousness now.

He might have blacked out if Denton hadn't

let go of him. Denton reared back and staggered to his feet. He reached over, said, "Give me that!" and jerked John Henry's Colt out of Penelope's hands. He stood over John Henry and pointed the revolver at him.

"What are you going to do?" Penelope asked.

"I'm going to shoot him, of course!" Denton said. "Finish off the troublesome bastard with his own gun!"

"Wait!"

Denton glanced over at her in surprise. His brown hair was askew from the battle, with strands of it hanging over his eyes. He raked it back with his free hand and said, "Wait? Why would I do that?"

"I . . . I wasn't really thinking when I said that before about shooting him. Surely we don't have to kill him."

"Of course we have to kill him," Denton snapped. "He's been dogging your trail for days. If he wasn't the luckiest son of a bitch I've ever seen, he'd already be dead!"

He pulled back the Colt's hammer.

"But . . . but if you shoot him, it'll make a lot of noise," Penelope objected. "People will come to see what happened."

"Nobody in this cursed town will care about a gunshot. The poor devils are all too worried about surviving that fever." Denton sneered. "But I suppose if you'll hand me one of those pillows, I'll use it to muffle the shot. We might as well be discreet . . ."

John Henry was thinking clearly enough again to consider making a desperate roll to the side. Maybe while he was doing that, he could sweep Denton's feet out from under him and turn the tables yet again.

Suddenly Penelope exclaimed in surprise, a sound followed immediately by a dull thud. Denton's eyes rolled up in their sockets as he sagged forward. A man's hand reached around him and plucked the Colt from Denton's fingers. Denton pitched to the floor and landed facedown next to John Henry, out cold.

Nick Prentice pointed the gun he had just used to knock out Denton at Penelope, who was naked again, having dropped the bedspread when she scrambled to retrieve John Henry's gun. A grin spread across the big man's face as he looked from Penelope to John Henry and said, "Well . . . this is a mighty interesting situation, Marshal."

Chapter Twenty-seven

John Henry pushed himself up on an elbow and groggily shook his head. He wasn't sure he was any better off than he had been a moment earlier, since he suspected that Prentice was part of the gang, too.

But then his thoughts began to clear and he realized that couldn't be right. If Prentice was one of the counterfeiters, he wouldn't have stopped Denton from shooting John Henry. Not only that, but Prentice currently held two guns, and he wasn't pointing either of them at John Henry. He covered the unconscious Clive Denton with the weapon in his left hand while the gun in his right was pointed toward Penelope.

John Henry reached up, caught hold of the sheets, and used them to brace himself as he pulled himself to his feet. He gave a little shake of his head and asked, "What's going on here?"

Before Prentice could reply, Penelope said coldly, "I'm naked, you know."

"So I noticed," Prentice said, still grinning. "I sort of like you that way, Miss Smith. Not only for the obvious reasons, mind you, but because I can tell at a glance that you're unarmed."

"Don't tell her that," John Henry said. "She doesn't like it."

"Why don't the two of you trade places?" Prentice suggested. "Marshal, you step over Denton and move around me."

John Henry did so, and when he had, Prentice moved back a little and motioned with the Colt for Penelope to slide past him and stand next to the unconscious man.

"That's better," Prentice said. "Now I've got you where I can keep an eye on both of you at the same time. Marshal, I suppose you can hand the bedspread back to the lady. Wouldn't want her to catch a chill."

John Henry's eyes narrowed. He didn't much care for the way Prentice was giving orders, and the man's last comment made John Henry think that maybe Prentice didn't know about the outbreak of sickness in Copperhead. That would indicate that the man had just gotten to town.

John Henry picked up the bedspread and tossed it to Penelope. As she wrapped herself in it again, he told Prentice in a flat voice, "I'll take my gun back now."

Prentice hesitated for a second, but then he shrugged, reversed the Colt, and held it out butt-first to John Henry. John Henry felt a little better about things once he had wrapped his fingers around the revolver's walnut grips.

Prentice wore a brown tweed suit and had a dark brown bowler hat set at a jaunty angle on his head. A gold watch chain was looped across his vest. The gun he had used to knock out Denton was a short-barreled Smith & Wesson .38 that he carried in the shoulder rig visible under his open coat.

"I appreciate the helping hand," John Henry went on.

"I'd say it was more than a helping hand. I saved your life, Marshal, just like I did when Denton ambushed you in Stockton and hired a local badman to help him try to kill you."

"That was you?"

"I wouldn't know about it if I hadn't been there, would I? I'll bet if we took off Denton's coat and shirt, we'd find the wound where I grazed him and made him drop his rifle when he was about to ventilate you."

Prentice had a point about that. John Henry said, "So you've been following me."

"Not really. I've been following *her.*" Prentice nodded toward Penelope. "You were just between us part of the time."

"You were on her trail in Los Angeles," John Henry said as the picture began to clear in his mind. "That's why you were at Campos's place, pretending to be a gambler. You barely caught the same train for San Francisco that she did."

"That's right. I would have closed in on her eventually, but then you showed up in Frisco, too, and I figured why not let you be the stalking horse. I knew she had to be working with somebody, and sure enough, you drew Denton out of the woodwork."

"How do you know his name?" John Henry asked. "Or did he introduce himself to you on the ferry, too? I'm assuming you *were* on the same ferry."

"Sure," Prentice said easily. "I'm good at blending in with crowds. That's not easy for a big fella like me to do, but I've learned how to manage. And no, I didn't talk to Denton on the ferry, but I saw him talking to you and when we got to Oakland I wired his description to my boss. Before I left town to follow you and Miss Smith, I got a wire back tentatively identifying him as Clive Denton. Born in London, but he's been over here in the States most of his life, making a name for himself as a crook. Mostly as a confidence man, but he's dabbled in embezzlement, extortion, and blackmail, too. And now counterfeiting."

"Who are you?" John Henry asked. "Who do you work for?"

"Nick Prentice happens to be my real name. I work for the Secret Service."

John Henry had heard of the Secret Service. He said, "Pinkerton's bunch."

"Well, not exactly. Allan Pinkerton formed what was called the Secret Service during the war, but it was more of an espionage and intelligence outfit. The agency I work for is part of the Treasury Department, and it's our job to track down counterfeiters . . . like Miss Smith here."

"I'm in no mood for a history lesson," Penelope snapped. "I'd like to get dressed."

"Not just yet," Prentice said. "And don't try telling us that you're embarrassed, my dear. After some of the entanglements you've been in, I know better."

She just said, "Hmmph," and glared at him.

"So once I'd drawn Denton into the open, what was your plan then?" John Henry asked Prentice.

"Keep an eye on him and follow all of you, of course, until the trail led to the ringleader."

"Ignatius O'Reilly."

John Henry saw something flicker across Penelope's face when he said the name. He couldn't tell for sure what the response meant, but he thought she didn't like hearing O'Reilly's name.

"Yep," Prentice said. "They have to be planning on rendezvousing with him sometime. I would have preferred to hang back and wait for that, but then when I took a peek through that door and saw Denton about to shoot you, I knew I had to step in."

"Thanks," John Henry said dryly. "Sorry I ruined your plans."

Prentice's broad shoulders rose and fell in a shrug.

"It's all right," he said. "We'll just have to make the girl tell us where to find O'Reilly."

"You're not going to make me do anything," Penelope snapped. "Anyway, I don't know where this man O'Reilly is, because I don't know him. I never even heard of him."

Prentice shook his head and said, "It's not going to do you any good to lie, darling. Those fake bills you've been passing for the past six weeks are O'Reilly's work. Not his best work, mind you, but we're convinced that he printed them."

"I'm not saying anything else," Penelope insisted.

"There are still a couple of things I'm not clear on," John Henry said. "How did a Secret Service agent and a deputy U.S. marshal wind up on the trail of the same bunch of counterfeiters?"

"You don't know much about Washington, do you, Marshal? Those bureaucrats back there are always falling all over themselves trying to get a jump on some other agency or department. Then there's the matter of one hand seldom knowing what the other is doing. If everybody in Washington would just cooperate, they could get things done a lot easier. But then there wouldn't be a need for so many people to work in the government, would there?"

"Sounds to me like a loco way to do things," John Henry muttered.

"Ah, now you're beginning to understand! What was the other thing you wanted to ask me about?"

"Denton used dynamite to cause an avalanche that nearly buried me under tons of rock. Where were you when that happened?"

"Following you, of course. I was about half a mile behind you. There was nothing I could do to help you. And then it took me a good while to get here because I had to find another trail and take the long way around. To tell you the truth,

I was a little surprised to see you, Marshal. I thought there was a good chance Denton had gotten you that time."

"He came closer than I like to think about," John Henry admitted.

Penelope frowned. She said, "There wasn't supposed to be any killing. That was the plan all along. Nobody was supposed to die."

"Obviously you didn't know all the plan," Prentice said, "because Denton tried three times to kill Marshal Sixkiller. Who knows what else he did since the two of you started this whole thing in Wichita?"

"I didn't want anybody to die," Penelope insisted.

"So that's why you caused that duel between me and Quentin Ross?" John Henry said. "Ross wound up dead, too."

"I know." Penelope looked down at the floor. "I just wanted to stage some sort of distraction so I could get out of there. It was time for me to leave Los Angeles. I guess I just didn't think about what might happen. It wasn't my intention for him or anybody else to be killed, though."

"You know what they say about the road to hell," Prentice told her. "Now, where do we find Ignatius O'Reilly?"

Chapter Twenty-eight

Penelope remained stubborn, continuing to insist that she had never heard of O'Reilly. She sat on the edge of the bed with the spread wrapped around her and shook her head to every question Prentice asked her.

While that was going on, John Henry tied Clive Denton's hands behind his back and propped the man in a corner. Denton was starting to come around. He shook his head slowly from side to side and moaned softly.

With a sigh, Prentice finally gave up and told Penelope, "You might as well get dressed. I don't suppose we can take you over to the local jail and lock you up like that."

"We can't lock her up in the jail at all," John Henry said.

Prentice frowned and asked, "Why not?"

John Henry felt a little satisfaction because there was something he knew and the big, self-assured Secret Service agent didn't. That was probably petty of him, he thought, but he enjoyed it anyway.

"You don't know what's going on here in Copperhead, do you, Prentice? Half the town is sick. There's some sort of fever on the loose, and the town marshal has it. None of us are setting foot in that jail."

A worried frown creased Prentice's forehead. "So there's a little fever—" he began.

"That's killed four people so far. No telling how many more it'll kill before it runs its course."

Prentice looked even more worried.

"What are we going to do with these two?" he asked.

"The hotel is safe, as far as I know. We'll have to keep them here until morning. Then I suppose we can take them on to the next town, since we can't go back to Sonora because of that avalanche."

"What about O'Reilly?"

John Henry went over to a small table with a carpetbag sitting on it. He unfastened the catches and opened the bag. Inside were several tied-together bundles of bills. He picked up one of the bundles, riffled through the ends of the bills, and studied the printing on the currency.

"These are the fakes, all right," he said as he tossed the bundle back into the carpetbag. "If nothing else, we've stopped these two from distributing the rest of the counterfeit money."

"That doesn't get us O'Reilly."

"Maybe when Miss Smith realizes that she's going to spend a number of years in federal prison, she'll be more inclined to talk," John Henry suggested.

Penelope's voice held a slight note of panic as she said, "I'm telling you, I don't know where he is."

"I notice you're not denying anymore that you know who O'Reilly is," Prentice said.

"All right!" Penelope burst out. "My God, you're a persistent bastard. Of course I've heard of Ignatius O'Reilly. Everybody who's involved in our line of work has heard of him. But that doesn't mean I have any connection to him or know where to find him."

Prentice shook his head and said, "I don't believe you, sweetheart."

"Don't call me sweetheart! Or darling or dear or anything else like that." Penelope's lips twisted in a snarl. "I hate you. I hate both of you!"

"Might as well get over that. We'll be spending a lot of time together for a while, starting with tonight."

"You can't mean to stay in this room," Penelope said.

"If you think I'm letting you out of my sight, you're crazy. Don't get shy on us now. You can't be too worried about propriety when you've been working with this English crook, and probably doing a lot more than that."

John Henry said, "There's no need to be rude."

"All you cowboys are always gallant with the ladies, aren't you?" Prentice said scornfully. He turned back to Penelope and went on, "Get your clothes on, or I'll just tie you up the way you are now."

Through gritted teeth, she said, "You'd probably enjoy that, but I wouldn't give you the satisfaction."

Defiantly, she dropped the bedspread and reached into the open wardrobe for some of her clothes.

John Henry was just as glad Prentice was there. If he hadn't been, John Henry would have felt duty bound to keep an eye on Penelope, even while she was getting dressed. This way, he could let Prentice do that while he hunkered on his heels in front of Clive Denton and took hold of the man's chin. He lifted Denton's head.

"I know you came to a little while ago and heard what we were talking about," John Henry said. "Maybe you'd like to tell us where we can find Ignatius O'Reilly, Denton. Cooperating could help you in the long run."

Denton opened his mouth and spewed out a string of profanity. He concluded by saying, "I should have pulled the trigger right away when I had the chance and splattered your brains all over the floor, Sixkiller."

"Well, you missed your chance, and I don't intend to give you another one. In fact, you're not going to have any sort of chance for anything except a lot of years of iron bars and gray walls."

"So there's no point in me helping you, is there?" Denton asked with a sneer.

John Henry glanced toward the other side of the room and saw that Penelope was dressed now, in a simple traveling gown. She sat on the foot of the bed and took turns glaring at her two captors.

John Henry looked out the window, past the gauzy curtains that hung over the glass, and saw that night had fallen. Prentice must have been thinking the same thing that he was, because the Secret Service man said, "I could do with something to eat."

"The man who runs the hotel told me there's a pot of beans on the stove in the kitchen," John Henry said. "One of us could go down and bring some back up here."

Prentice cocked an eyebrow and said, "That would require both of us trusting the other one."

"Yeah, I thought of that," John Henry said. "You don't trust a deputy United States marshal?"

"You don't trust an agent of the United States Secret Service?"

"I haven't seen a bit of identification," John Henry pointed out. "All I've got is your word that you work for the Secret Service."

Prentice looked like he was going to argue, but then he shrugged again and said, "I suppose you've got a point. I have identification papers."

He moved the gun from his right hand to his left and used the right to reach inside his coat. He brought out a thin wallet and handed it to John Henry, who opened it and removed a folded document. It looked official and identified the bearer as Nicholas Prentice, an agent of the United States Secret Service.

"Anybody could carry this around," John Henry said.

"Anybody can carry a marshal's badge, too," Prentice said. "Look, if we weren't on the same side, why the hell did I stop Denton from killing you?"

John Henry didn't have an answer for that, other than the thought that Prentice might be carrying out some sort of particularly deep deception.

He didn't actually believe that was the case, though. Prentice's words earlier had carried the ring of truth. There came a time when you had to trust *somebody*, and right now the odds were a lot more in Prentice's favor.

John Henry handed the wallet back and said, "All right. I'll fetch some bowls of beans."

"You might look around and see if they've got any bottles of beer down there, too," Prentice suggested.

John Henry grunted, but he didn't argue. He supposed it made sense that they would need something to wash down the beans. He preferred coffee, though, and hoped that there would be a pot of it simmering on the stove, too.

He went downstairs, not seeing anyone along the way. He supposed all the other guests in the hotel were staying in their rooms, hoping to avoid as much contact with other people as possible in order to increase their chances of not getting sick. He looked around and found the kitchen. It was empty, too.

The cast-iron pot of beans was half-full. John Henry rummaged in the cabinets, found bowls and utensils and a tray on which to carry them. He filled four bowls and put spoons on the tray with them. He took cups from a shelf and filled them with coffee from the pot sitting next to the pot of beans.

A faint smile touched his mouth as he thought about the night ahead. He and Prentice would have to take turns standing guard, so he hoped the coffee would fortify them and help them stay alert when the time came. The fact that all four of them were going to eat beans for supper and then spend the night together in a relatively small room was a little daunting, but nothing could be done about that.

When he had the tray ready, he carried it out of the kitchen and up the stairs. As he approached Room 14, he saw that the door was pushed up but not caught, just the way he had left it. He used his shoulder to push it open, since he had his hands full with the tray.

He had just stepped inside when he spotted Nick Prentice lying motionless on the floor. There was blood on his head.

Chapter Twenty-nine

The split second that it took for John Henry to realize what he was looking at was almost his undoing. In that fraction of a heartbeat, he heard a slight noise to his left and twisted in that direction, ducking his head and thrusting the tray hard in front of him.

The gun that Clive Denton tried to use to bash his brains out struck John Henry on the shoulder instead. The blow was painful, but it didn't slow him down. He crashed the tray into Denton's face. Denton cried out, not only from being hit but from having hot coffee and beans splattered all over his head as well.

John Henry bulled into Denton and drove him backward, ramming him against the wall. He still had hold of the tray, so he swung it like a club and smashed Denton across the face with it again. Then he dropped the tray and grabbed the wrist of Denton's gun hand. John Henry lifted his knee and brought Denton's wrist down on it. The gun flew from Denton's fingers.

While Denton was still half-stunned, John Henry lifted his right elbow. It caught Denton under the chin and drove his head hard against the wall. Denton went limp. His feet slid out from under him. John Henry stepped back and let the man crumple to the floor.

He hadn't seen Penelope Smith since he came into the room, but he hadn't really had time to look for her, either. He'd been busy fighting for his life against Denton.

Now John Henry swung around, palming out his Colt in case he faced a new threat.

Right away, though, he spotted Penelope lying on the rug next to the bed, at right angles to where Nick Prentice was sprawled on the floor. She was moving around a little, so John Henry knew she was alive. The side of her face was red where evidently something had struck her.

John Henry picked up the gun Denton had dropped. It was Prentice's .38, he saw. He stepped over to Prentice and knelt next to him.

The Secret Service agent lay on his side. John Henry rolled him onto his back and was glad to see that Prentice's chest was rising and falling. Prentice was alive. From the looks of the wound on his head, he had been walloped with something, probably the same pistol that Denton had tried to use on John Henry.

John Henry checked quickly and found that Prentice wasn't wounded anywhere else. He had been knocked out cold, but that was all.

That probably wouldn't have been the end of it, though, if John Henry hadn't come back in when he did. He had seen how vicious Clive

Denton was and had no doubt that Denton would have murdered Prentice if he'd had the chance.

That didn't explain how Penelope had gotten knocked out, though, unless it had happened while she and Denton were struggling with Prentice.

There was also the question of how Denton had gotten free, but when John Henry looked around some more, he found what he thought was the answer to that. A small knife lay on the floor, its blade shining in the light from the lamp. He found the cord he had used to tie Denton, too, and the loose ends of it definitely had been cut.

He used the pieces to bind Denton's wrists again and pulled the knots even tighter this time, not worrying about how uncomfortable it was going to be for the prisoner. As many times as Denton had tried to kill him, John Henry wasn't inclined to be lenient.

While he was doing that, Penelope moaned a couple of times. As John Henry finished with Denton, she got her hands under her and pushed herself up to lean against the bed as she sat on the floor. She blinked and shook her head as if trying to clear out the cobwebs, and a moment later as her vision cleared she looked up at John Henry in surprise.

"You're alive," she said. Her breath caught in her throat and her eyes widened as she started to look around. "Prentice . . . !"

"He's alive, too, no thanks to you," John Henry said harshly.

A humorless laugh escaped from her lips. She said, "That's where you're wrong, Marshal. I think he's alive, thanks to me. If I hadn't tried to stop Clive from cutting his throat, he'd be dead now. And what did it get me? A clout across the face that knocked me silly."

"And how did Denton get his hands on a knife in the first place?" John Henry shot back at her. "I'm guessing that you slipped it to him somehow. You either cut him loose, or you gave him the knife and let him do it himself."

"Prentice doesn't know how many hiding places there are in a woman's dress. He watched me like a hawk and still didn't see the knife until it was too late. I dropped it next to Clive while I was giving him a drink of water." She nodded toward the pitcher of water and the glass that now sat on the night table. John Henry supposed they had been there all along; he had been too busy to notice. "Then I kept Prentice's attention on me by talking while Clive cut himself loose. And you know what? You would have done the same thing if you'd been faced with going to prison for something that's not really your fault."

"How do you figure it's not your fault?" John Henry asked. "You're the one who passed out all that counterfeit money."

"Yes, but it was all Clive's idea! He's the one who got his hands on it, I don't know where. He planned the whole operation. That's why I kept telling you blasted lawmen that I don't know anything about that damned Ichabod O'Reilly!"

"Ignatius," John Henry corrected her.

"Ignatius, Ichabod, what the hell does it matter?" Penelope's lip curled in disdain, but it seemed to be directed at herself as she went on, "I'm just another foolish woman who convinced herself she was in love with a man and let him talk her into doing something stupid. That's no crime, Marshal. Just a damned shame, that's all it is."

"I reckon a judge and jury will have to sort that out," John Henry said. "What happened after Denton got loose?"

"What do you think? He jumped Prentice and they fought over the gun. Everybody underestimates Clive. He was a boxing champion, and you wouldn't think it to look at him but he's strong as an ox."

John Henry nodded. He had seen evidence of those things and bore the bruises to prove it.

"Clive managed to wrestle the gun away from Prentice and knocked him out with it," Penelope went on. "Then he was going to cut Prentice's throat to dispose of him quietly. I argued with him. I told him it wasn't necessary to kill anybody. I said we should wait for you, knock you out when you came in, tie you both up, and then take the buggy and get out of here tonight." A note of bitterness came into her voice as she continued, "He called me a stupid bitch and was going to kill Prentice anyway. I grabbed his arm and he backhanded me and . . . and that's really all I know until I woke up a few minutes ago and you were here. You must have come in right after Clive knocked me out."

John Henry had listened to her story all the

way through. Everything she said was reasonable enough. It might even be true, he thought.

But it might be a pack of lies, too. He didn't know that it really mattered, one way or the other. Penelope was still guilty of distributing all that counterfeit money, and she would have to answer for it in a court of law.

He had to admit, though, that she had sounded sincere as she explained her version of what had happened while he had gone down to the kitchen. And he could believe that Denton was handsome and charming enough to have talked her into becoming his accomplice.

That didn't explain the connection between Denton and Ignatius O'Reilly, if there was one. Denton had to get those bogus tens and twenties from somewhere, John Henry mused. It was still possible that Denton could lead the law to O'Reilly.

But all that could be hashed out later. Right now, Nick Prentice was coming around. The Secret Service agent grimaced and moved his head from side to side. That made him wince. He lifted a hand to the bloody lump on his head as his eyes tried to flutter open.

"Take it easy," John Henry told him. "You're all right, but you're going to have a headache, I imagine."

"Sixkiller?" With an effort, Prentice lifted himself onto an elbow. He looked back and forth between John Henry and Penelope Smith. "What the hell happened here?"

"I reckon the score is a little closer to even

between us now," John Henry said. "Denton was going to carve you a new grin."

"I'm the one who stopped him, not you," Penelope said sullenly. "You can at least give me a little credit for that."

"The worst of it is that we lost our supper," John Henry said as he nodded toward the mess that had been made when he walloped Denton with the tray. Coffee stains were on the wall, and there were puddles of coffee and bean juice on the floor. A lot of the spilled beans had been tromped into paste while John Henry and Denton were fighting.

Prentice closed his eyes and let his head rest on the floor again.

"I don't think I could eat now anyway," he said. "I feel a little sick."

John Henry tensed. With things the way they were in Copperhead right now, feeling a little under the weather might just be a death sentence.

Chapter Thirty

Prentice drank some of the water from the pitcher, then poured a little in his hand and splashed it in his face, rubbing it in. That perked him up, or at least so he claimed. John Henry figured it would be a good idea to keep an eye on the big Secret Service agent anyway.

He helped Prentice into the room's lone chair. Penelope sat down on the bed, crossed her arms over her bosom, and continued glaring at them.

"If you're going to keep on being so hostile, it'll make for a long night," John Henry told her.

"I don't care," she said. "If you think I'm going to go out of my way to help you put me in jail, you're crazy." She paused, then went on, "Making counterfeit money doesn't really hurt anybody, you know."

"It's the same thing as stealing from the government."

"Ha! How does that hurt anybody?"

"Well, then, it's the same thing as stealing from the people you give those phony bills to,"

John Henry said. "Like that woman in Sonora you bought the scarf from. It didn't cost as much as what you paid her, so she owed you some change. You got the scarf, and you got a handful of real money in return, to boot. That's robbery as far as I'm concerned."

"Nobody loses enough that way for it to really matter," Penelope insisted.

"It all adds up."

She fell into a sullen, pouting silence and didn't look at him anymore.

The bad part about it was that she had a point, John Henry thought. Not about counterfeiting being harmless, of course. It did hurt people, as he had just pointed out to her. It was a crime, too, and John Henry was sworn to uphold the law.

But in the past he had gone after murderers and outlaws who robbed on a much grander scale. Counterfeiting was a petty crime, and John Henry felt a little resentment toward Judge Parker for saddling him with this chore.

On the other hand, Clive Denton had tried to kill both a deputy United States marshal and a Secret Service agent, so John Henry supposed that elevated the case to a more serious level. Denton had demonstrated that he was vicious enough and ruthless enough to be a danger to folks, so getting him behind bars was a worthwhile objective. The same held true for Ignatius O'Reilly, who had a history of bloody violence behind him.

Prentice spoke up, saying, "I'm feeling better now. I think I could use some coffee. Was there any left in the pot when you got some, Sixkiller?"

"Yeah," John Henry said. "I could use a cup, too, if you feel up to fetching it. *And* if you're sure you're not coming down with whatever it is that ails these folks around here."

"I just felt a little sick at my stomach from getting hit in the head. I'm fine now." Prentice stood up. "But I think it would be better if you stayed here and kept an eye on these two. I can find the kitchen all right."

John Henry took Prentice's place in the chair. He propped his right ankle on his left knee, then drew his Colt, draped his thumb over the hammer, and rested the gun on his crossed leg. The barrel pointed about halfway between Penelope and Denton.

"Go ahead," John Henry told Prentice. "I think things are under control here."

Prentice grunted and said, "That's what I thought, until that she-devil pulled her tricks."

"It's not my fault you're dumb as a rock," Penelope said without looking at the Secret Service man.

"You're the one who's going to prison. I'm still free as a bird. Who does that make dumb?"

With a haughty sniff, Penelope ignored the question and still didn't look at him.

"Go ahead," John Henry said again. "We'll be fine."

"If either of them try anything . . . shoot 'em. Shoot 'em both, for all I care."

Prentice jerked the door open and stalked out of the room.

John Henry saw a trace of a smile hovering around Penelope's lips. She knew she had gotten under Prentice's skin, and that pleased her.

That cup of coffee was going to please John Henry, if he ever got around to drinking it.

The night was a long one, just as John Henry expected. He was able to doze a little while Prentice stood guard, but by morning he was pretty tired. Both of them were.

Penelope, on the other hand, had curled up on the bed and apparently slept soundly.

Obviously that didn't require a clear conscience where she was concerned.

When the sky began to lighten outside with the approach of dawn, John Henry left Prentice guarding the prisoners and went downstairs to the kitchen. He found Weaver there, removing a pan of biscuits from the oven.

"My regular cook is sick," the hotel keeper said. "I don't know if these biscuits I made will be fit to eat or not, but maybe they're better than nothing. There's a fresh pot of coffee on, too. Will you be leaving Copperhead today, Marshal?"

"I'll be riding out, all right," John Henry said.

"Still looking for that woman you asked me about yesterday?"

"No. I found her."

That made Weaver turn toward him and frown in surprise.

"Where was she?"

"Right here in the hotel. You just didn't know

it. The fella who called himself Edward Munroe gave her the key to his room, and she slipped in without you seeing her."

Weaver's head did its little darting-forward-and-back motion. He pushed the thick spectacles up on his nose.

"This is my hotel," he muttered. "People shouldn't sneak around."

"There's some damage up in Room Fourteen, too," John Henry went on. He took a double eagle from his pocket, one of several coins he had found in Denton's pockets when he searched the man. As far as he could tell, it was genuine, although he supposed that with Denton, you never could be sure.

He laid the double eagle on the table and said, "That ought to be enough to cover it, along with breakfast this morning and some of those biscuits to take along for the trail. You got a canvas bag I can put them in?"

When he went back upstairs, he was carrying the bag of biscuits and three cups of coffee. Denton could do without, or Penelope could share hers with him if she wanted to. John Henry didn't care one way or the other.

Before going into the room, he called out, "Prentice!" He didn't think there was any way Denton could have gotten loose again, but he wasn't going to take any unnecessary chances.

The door swung back and Prentice appeared in the doorway, holding his .38 Smith & Wesson.

"Everything all right this time?" John Henry asked.

Prentice scowled and said, "I didn't let this

blond hellcat trick me again, if that's what you mean."

"Just checking," John Henry said dryly. Prentice had made enough snide comments that John Henry didn't mind returning the favor a little.

Prentice jerked his head and said, "Come on in. I need that coffee."

Half an hour later, they had all eaten a couple of biscuits and drunk some coffee, with Penelope sharing her breakfast with Denton. The biscuits Weaver had cooked were edible but not particularly good. As he had said, though, they were better than nothing. With breakfast finished, it was time to start thinking about the next move.

"I'll go down, saddle our horses, and hitch the team to the buggy," John Henry said. "I suppose one of us will have to drive the buggy."

"I'll do that," Prentice volunteered. "Just throw my saddle in the back of the buggy. I'm not that fond of riding."

"Not sure there's room," John Henry said. "I figured on stashing Denton behind the seat."

"Fine, put the saddle on my horse. It doesn't really matter."

Penelope asked, "Where are you taking us?"

"Oroville," John Henry said. "It's the next town. I'm hoping they have a jail and a telegraph office there."

"Orville? What sort of name for a town is Orville?"

"Oro . . . ville," John Henry said. "Probably because somebody found gold ore near there."

"Oh. Well, I guess that makes sense."

"Stop stalling," Prentice said. "Go ahead and get everything ready, Sixkiller. I'll watch these two."

"Keep your eyes open."

"Just get it done," Prentice said. He hefted the .38. "They're not going to try anything."

John Henry wasn't so sure of that. He didn't see how Penelope and Denton could get away, but he had learned not to underestimate that shady pair. He would be glad when cell doors clanged shut behind them.

The sun was up by the time they were ready to leave. John Henry saw a few people moving around or looking through doors and windows, but for the most part Copperhead still looked like a ghost town. He would be glad to put this place behind him. It gave him the fantods.

He had tied Prentice's horse to the back of the buggy. Denton—his wrists tied behind his back and his ankles lashed together—sat on the floor behind the seat. It had taken both John Henry and Prentice to put him in there, and he had cursed them the whole time. If he kept that up, they would stop and gag him, John Henry decided.

Penelope had put on a straw hat with a flat brim and crown. It was tied in place with a couple of ribbons under her chin. She had a shawl draped around her shoulders, too, because early mornings were cool up there in the mountains, no matter what time of year it was. She sat stiffly in the front seat as Prentice climbed into the buggy and settled down beside her.

"What's the matter?" he asked her. "Don't like the company?"

"I wouldn't even if you weren't taking me to jail," she said without looking at him.

Prentice chuckled and slapped the reins against the backs of the two horses hitched to the vehicle.

John Henry had already swung up into the saddle on Buck's back. He said, "Let's go," and fell in alongside the buggy as Prentice sent it rolling along the street toward the edge of the settlement.

Good riddance, John Henry thought as they rode out of Copperhead.

About a quarter of a mile out of town, the road began to rise again. It went through a gap in a ridge with steep cutbanks on both sides, a sign that the route was man-made and not natural. The road was about forty feet wide.

The little group had just started through the gap when more than a dozen riders appeared at the far end, blocking the road. Men who had been hidden on top of the cutbanks leaped to their feet and pointed rifles at John Henry and the buggy.

One of the horsebackers spurred his horse ahead of the others, raised an arm in a signal to stop, and shouted, "Hold it right there or we'll open fire and blow you all to hell!"

Chapter Thirty-one

John Henry hauled back on Buck's reins. Beside him, Prentice brought the buggy to an abrupt halt as well. John Henry's first impulse at being confronted like this was to reach for the gun on his hip, but they were too outnumbered to fight their way through the blockade.

Besides, he regarded the prisoners as his responsibility, too. If lead started to fly here in the gap, there was a good chance some of it would find Penelope and Denton.

"What the hell?" Prentice muttered. "Road agents?"

"They don't look like it," John Henry said.

The leader of the group blocking the road, the man who had called out to them, wore an expensive, western-cut black suit and a black Stetson with silver conchos studding its band. He had a bright blue bandanna tied loosely around his neck. He moved his horse a few feet closer and shouted, "Get on back to Copperhead, now! Don't make us kill you!"

"Stay here," John Henry told Prentice.

"What do you think you're—" the Secret Service agent began.

John Henry didn't wait for him to finish the question. He started Buck forward at a slow walk. The men on horseback raised their rifles, and so did the ones on the cutbanks. John Henry felt the tension in the air. One little bit of pressure on a trigger, and all hell would break loose.

"Mister, I think there's been some sort of mistake," he called to the black-suited leader.

"You made it," the man said flatly. John Henry was close enough now to see that he had a weathered, deeply tanned face and white hair under the brim of that black Stetson. "We're not allowing anybody out of that pesthole to spread your filthy contagion. You reckon we haven't heard over in Oroville that the whole town's sick?"

So that explained it. This wasn't the holdup it had appeared to be at first.

It was a quarantine.

A quarantine enforced at gunpoint.

John Henry had brought Buck to a halt. Fifty or sixty feet still separated him from the man in black. He had a hunch that if he came any closer, the other men would start shooting.

"None of us are sick," John Henry said. "We're not carrying the disease."

"How do you know that? You came through Copperhead, didn't you? You've been exposed to it, and you don't know how long it takes after that before you actually get sick. We don't aim to take a chance on you spreading the damned fever!"

The only person John Henry had seen in Copperhead who was actually sick was the town marshal, but from the looks of him, the fever was indeed pretty bad. He couldn't really blame outsiders for wanting to keep it contained to the settlement. But at the same time, he and Prentice needed to get through with their prisoners.

"Listen, I'm a deputy United States marshal," he said. He edged Buck forward as he reached inside his coat. "I can show you my badge—"

"Hold it!" the man in black yelled. "One more foot and we'll shoot!"

He pulled the bandanna up over his mouth and nose as his horse moved around skittishly. The animal must have sensed the bloody violence hanging in the air.

John Henry brought Buck to a stop again. Since he already had hold of the leather wallet containing his badge, he brought it out and opened it, holding it up so that the badge was visible, shining in the morning sun.

"You see? I'm a lawman, just like I said. Now let us pass, and that's an order!"

One of the men on the left cutbank shouted, "You can take your orders and go to hell! I'd rather risk jail than let my family get sick and die!"

Mutters of agreement came from the other men.

John Henry glanced back over his shoulder at Prentice, who was watching the exchange tensely. If his deputy marshal's badge didn't sway the blockaders, he doubted if Prentice's Secret

Service credentials would make any difference, either.

What made it worse was that he understood how these men felt. Disease was one of the biggest fears on the frontier, along with other natural disasters like fire, flood, and cyclones . . . all the things that human beings had little or no control over. Probably most of these men had wives and children, and all they wanted to do was protect those loved ones. He didn't want to try to shoot his way through them, even if he had stood any chance of doing so.

"Mister, what's your name?" John Henry asked the man in black.

"What does that matter to you?"

"I like to know who I'm talking to, that's all."

The man hesitated for a moment, then answered in a voice slightly muffled by the bandanna over his face, "I'm Baird Stanton. I own the Sunburst Mine, over by Oroville."

"I'm Deputy Marshal John Henry Sixkiller. The man in the buggy back there is Nick Prentice, an agent of the Secret Service from Washington, D.C. We have a couple of federal prisoners, and we need to get them to the nearest jail so we can lock them up. We need to find a telegraph office, too, so we can send wires to our bosses."

"Let's say I believe you," Stanton said. "I'd like to help you, Marshal, I really would, but you're coming from Copperhead and we can't let you through. You know good and well why we can't."

"How come you don't have the road blocked on the other side of the settlement?"

"We were going to do that today, but some fellas we sent around there yesterday to check it out came back and said the road's already blocked. There's been an avalanche."

John Henry looked down, smiled wryly, and shook his head slightly. Quarantine by rifle on one side of Copperhead, quarantine by avalanche on the other. The settlement was cut off, all right. Of course, people could probably still get in or out through the rugged mountains surrounding the town, but it wouldn't be easy.

He lifted his head and said to the mine owner, "I give you my word none of us are sick, Mr. Stanton. We were in the hotel the whole time, and no one there is sick."

"You can't guarantee that," Stanton insisted. "You can't know where everybody's been or who they've been around." The man shook his head. "No, sir, it's just too risky."

John Henry had been trying to keep his temper reined in, but angry words welled up in his throat at last. He said, "So you'd commit murder? You think that's what your wives and children would want you to do? You think they want you to become killers?"

"It wouldn't be murder," Stanton snapped. "No more so than shooting down a rabid dog. What we're talking about here is self-defense, nothing more, nothing less."

"The law won't see it that way." John Henry raised his voice a little so that all the men from Oroville could hear. "You kill us and you'll hang for it. I can promise you that."

"Nobody will ever know," Stanton said, his

voice as hard as flint. "If we have to shoot you, we'll leave you where you fall for a few days, then burn the bodies just to make sure there's no danger." A shudder went through Stanton as powerful emotions gripped him. "By God, I'd burn the whole town to the ground if I didn't have to go into that den of contagion to do it!"

John Henry stared at him, struggling to believe what he'd just heard.

"You'd wipe out a whole town full of innocent people? They didn't do anything to cause themselves to get sick!"

"Doesn't matter. That fever's got to be stopped." Stanton dragged in a deep breath. "But nobody's going to bother the folks in Copperhead as long as they stay there. And when the sickness finally goes away, then things can get back to normal. You can avoid any trouble, Marshal, by just turning around and riding back to town." He squared his shoulders. "I'm done talking now. Make your choice."

In a low voice that only the mine owner could hear, John Henry said, "Your men can't kill me quick enough to stop me from getting a bullet in you, Stanton. You'll die, but it won't be from a fever."

"I'll die to protect my town, and don't you doubt it for a second, Sixkiller."

John Henry didn't doubt it. He saw the fires of fanaticism burning in Stanton's eyes. The man had gotten himself so worked up that he really wasn't afraid of death, his own or anybody else's.

There was only one thing John Henry could do.

He lifted Buck's reins and turned the horse back toward the buggy.

"What are you doing?" Prentice demanded. "They have to let us through!"

"They're not going to," John Henry said. "We'll have to turn back. We can hole up in Copperhead until the fever burns itself out. It might take a week or two, but there's no reason we can't figure out a way to lock up these two until it's safe to leave."

Prentice looked angry and exasperated, but he must have realized that they couldn't shoot their way through twenty or thirty determined and well-armed men. Muttering curses under his breath, he started turning the buggy around. He had to maneuver it back and forth a couple of times to get the vehicle pointed back toward Copperhead.

John Henry cast one more look over his shoulder at Baird Stanton. The mine owner still sat there on his horse, a sentinel determined to keep anyone from passing.

"I suppose we head back to the hotel now," Prentice said. "Maybe there's a storeroom or something like that where we can lock up these two."

Penelope said, "You're going to stick me in a stuffy storeroom with a cot or just a blanket on the floor to sleep on? For a week or more?"

"You should have figured that things might not work out too well before you decided to break the law," Prentice told her.

She stared at him with narrowed eyes and

said, "I'm going to make your life a living hell, lawman."

Prentice laughed.

"Better than you have tried, sweetheart."

"There you go with that sweetheart business again. I wouldn't be your sweetheart if you were the last man on earth, Prentice."

"If I was the last man on earth, you'd be out of luck, Miss Smith, because I'd rather cuddle up to a diamondback rattler than you."

As he rode beside the buggy, John Henry fervently hoped that the two of them weren't going to keep up this squabbling the whole time they were all stuck in Copperhead.

If they did, he might be ready to shoot them himself by the time they got out of town.

Chapter Thirty-two

The settlement hadn't changed in the short time they'd been gone, not that John Henry expected that it would have. He saw a lot of curious faces peering at them through windows in the buildings they passed. He suspected that he and his companions were the first ones to discover the town was quarantined.

Prentice brought the buggy to a stop in front of the hotel. He told Penelope, "You sit right there and don't make a move while we're getting Denton out of the back. Try anything funny and I'll knock you out, I swear it."

"I'm not surprised that you'd threaten to beat a woman," she said.

"You're not a woman. You're a counterfeiter."

Penelope sniffed and looked away.

John Henry dismounted while Prentice looped the reins around the buggy's brake lever. The Secret Service man put a hand on the brass trim and vaulted to the ground. A step brought him to the back of the vehicle. He reached behind the seat to grab hold of Clive Denton while John Henry stood by waiting to help.

Suddenly, Prentice recoiled as if he had reached into the back and closed his hands around one of those diamondback rattlers he'd mentioned earlier. He took a step away, and his head snapped around so that he could look over at John Henry. Surprise and something else—horror?—were etched on his face.

"Denton," he said. "I touched his jaw when I went to take hold of his coat." Prentice swallowed. "He's burning up. He's got the fever."

John Henry stiffened. He knew that Denton hadn't said much since cursing him and Prentice as they put him in the buggy. John Henry hadn't noticed anything unusual about the man then, nor had he given any thought to the fact that Denton had gotten quiet.

Now he stepped closer to the buggy and peered into the back. Denton was conscious, but his eyes had a glassy look to them, as if he wasn't really seeing what he was looking at. His face was flushed, too.

"Good Lord!" Penelope exclaimed. "Let me out of here."

She started to scramble down from the buggy in an obvious attempt to get away from Denton. Prentice caught hold of her arm. She let out a little scream.

"Let go of me!" she cried. "You touched him! You've probably got the stuff!"

Prentice had gone pale under his tan. John Henry felt a little washed out himself. He remembered how his face had been only inches away from Denton's when they were fighting in the hotel room. Denton's breath had blown in his face again and again.

The contagion might already be in his body, John Henry realized, growing and spreading, even though he felt fine at the moment.

Maybe Baird Stanton had been right to turn them back after all, he thought.

"All right, let's all settle down," he said, trying to inject some reason back into the conversation. "Prentice, how do you feel?"

"Fine right now," the Secret Service man answered. "I still have a little headache, but that's just from being pistol-whipped. It's bound to be."

John Henry thought that was likely, too. He turned to Penelope and asked, "What about you?"

"I'm not sick, if that's what you mean," she said. "But I don't want to be. I'm scared."

"There's no point in being scared," John Henry said. "You're either infected or you're not. That's true for all of us. There's not much we can do about it. We're stuck here anyway, so we'll just take care of Denton the best we can and wait it out."

"He was here several days ago," Penelope said. "That must be when he caught it. He scouted the place, then came back down to Oakland to meet me . . ." A shudder ran through her. "My God. He kissed me . . ."

"All we can do is wait," John Henry said again, keeping his voice level and calm. "People can be exposed to an illness without catching it."

"One like this, that spreads so fast and is so

dangerous?" Penelope sounded skeptical. "What are the chances of that?"

"I reckon we'll find out," John Henry said. "Come on, let's get Denton back inside the hotel."

Prentice let go of Penelope's arm, but he pointed a finger at her and warned, "Don't run off. The mood I'm in right now, if you try to I'm liable to just shoot you."

"You wouldn't dare," she told him with a toss of her head. "That would be murder, and you're supposed to enforce the law, not break it."

John Henry stepped over to the buggy. He was loath to reach in and take hold of Denton, but somebody had to. He told himself that it wasn't any riskier than fighting with the man had been. Probably less so.

The front door of the hotel opened, and Weaver stepped out onto the boardwalk with a shotgun in his hands. He pointed the twin barrels toward the buggy and said in a quavery but loud voice, "You folks aren't coming back in here. I was in the lobby and I heard what you were saying about that fella being sick. Not one of you is setting foot in this hotel!"

John Henry reined in the angry, frustrated response he wanted to make. Instead he said, "Be reasonable, Mr. Weaver. We've all been in there already. We spent the night there. Keeping us out now won't make you or your other guests any safer."

"You don't know that," Weaver snapped. "You're a lawman, not a doctor. So the way I see it, the best thing I can do is keep you out. I don't want to shoot anybody, but I will if I have to."

John Henry realized that the sickness gripping Copperhead had one bad side effect nobody had mentioned so far: it made folks loco. Actually, it made apparently healthy people so scared of getting sick that they grabbed guns and tried to keep the sickness at bay with threats.

Vowing not to succumb to those feelings himself, John Henry said, "We need someplace to stay. Some men from Oroville have closed off the road east of here. They're not going to let anybody in or out of Copperhead until the sickness has had time to run its course."

"That sounds like something those no-good skunks from Oroville would do," Weaver said, demonstrating that even under these dire circumstances he still had some civic pride. "But I can't help you anyway, Marshal. I don't care where you go, you just can't stay here."

"What about the jail?" Prentice suggested. "I know you said the town marshal is sick, but if we've already been exposed, what does it matter?"

"I suppose we can give it a try," John Henry said.

He pointed out the lawman's office, which was close by. Prentice got back into the buggy, casting leery glances toward Denton as he did so, and swung the vehicle around so that it was in front of the marshal's office and jail. John Henry walked over to the building, leading

Buck and herding Penelope along with a hand on her arm.

"We're all going to die, aren't we?" she muttered.

"Not if I have anything to say about it."

"That's just it. You don't. None of us do."

John Henry hoped the situation wasn't quite that bleak, but for all he knew, Penelope was right. Their fate was probably in other hands now.

Prentice had gotten out of the buggy by the time John Henry and Penelope stepped up onto the boardwalk in front of the marshal's office. He banged a fist on the door and called, "Marshal! Marshal, are you in there?" He turned his head to look at John Henry. "Do you know his name?"

"Ledbetter, I think," John Henry said.

Prentice tried again, calling, "Marshal Ledbetter! Hey!"

There was still no response. John Henry said, "Keep an eye on Penelope," and stepped past Prentice. He tried the knob.

The door wasn't locked.

John Henry's instinct was to put his hand on his gun as he opened the door with his other hand, but he reminded himself that the only threat inside the office wasn't the kind you could deal with by using a bullet. He pushed the door back and said, "Marshal Ledbetter?"

When there was no answer, he stepped inside. The office was cloaked in gloom because the shutters were closed over the windows. A rectangle of light slanted in through the open door, though, and it revealed the denim-clad legs of a man sticking out from behind an old, paper-littered desk with a scarred top.

"Marshal Ledbetter?" John Henry said again, but the sight of those motionless legs told him he wasn't likely to get a reply. He moved deeper into the office, circling so that he could see behind the desk.

Ledbetter lay on his belly with his head turned to the side so that his face was visible. He looked a little like he was asleep. John Henry couldn't tell if the local lawman had collapsed like that, or if the last of his strength had deserted him and he'd stretched out on the floor to rest.

Either way, he wouldn't ever be getting up again under his own power. His eyes were open wide and staring, but he couldn't see anything. They were as glassy as marbles. John Henry approached the marshal warily and reached down to rest the back of his hand against Ledbetter's cheek.

He wasn't burning up with fever anymore. He was cold.

Cold and dead.

Chapter Thirty-three

The day before, when John Henry had talked to Marshal Ledbetter, he'd been able to tell that the man was very ill. Obviously Ledbetter had been in the final stages of the fever, and it had claimed his life either later that day or during the night.

He stepped back outside and told Prentice, "The marshal's dead."

Penelope said, "Does that mean it's safe to go in there now? We can't catch the fever from him?"

"I'm no doctor, but that seems reasonable to me. We've still got Denton to deal with."

"Are the cells empty?" Prentice asked.

"Yeah. The place is empty except for Ledbetter's body."

"We can lock Denton in one of them, then, and his lady friend here can take care of him."

"Clive and I were business partners, nothing more," Penelope snapped. "Well . . . maybe a little more. But I never signed on to play nursemaid to him while he's dying of some pestilence."

"You're really warmhearted, aren't you?" Prentice said.

"I don't see you volunteering to wipe his forehead with a wet cloth."

Wearily, John Henry said, "Let's just get him inside. You want the shoulders or the feet, Prentice?"

"I'll take the feet," the Secret Service man said. He nodded to Penelope and went on, "Hadn't we better put this one in a cell first? Otherwise she's liable to make a break for it while we're occupied with Denton."

"Really?" Penelope said. "Where the hell would I go? The road's blocked in both directions, and I'm not exactly the sort to go traipsing off over the mountains."

"She's got a point there," John Henry said with a faint smile.

"All right. But don't you try to run off," Prentice said to Penelope. "If you do, I'll paddle your butt until you're too sore to walk, let alone run."

"Try it," she snarled at him, "and I'll carve your heart out with my fingernails if I have to."

While Penelope stood by watching, John Henry and Prentice lifted Denton out of the buggy. The man was muttering incoherently, but he wasn't actually conscious. As John Henry gripped Denton under the arms, he could tell even through the clothing how hot the man was. Denton's brain had to be baking inside his skull.

After making Penelope go in first so they could keep an eye on her, they carried Denton through the marshal's office into the cell block and placed him on the bunk in the first cell on the right. As they went back into the office, John Henry said, "Actually, wiping his face with a wet cloth is a good idea. That might cool him off a little. I'd like to keep him alive if we can."

"So would I," Prentice said. "He's our only real lead to O'Reilly . . . assuming Miss Smith is telling the truth."

She sneered at him.

"You're going to be Denton's nurse, whether you like it or not," Prentice went on.

"You can't make me do that."

"Damn right I can. You're our prisoner."

"You can't force me to associate with somebody who's deathly ill. It . . . it wouldn't be humane!"

"He's your partner, remember." Prentice nodded toward the marshal's body. "Or maybe you'd rather drag that corpse down to the undertaker's."

Penelope glared, as usual, but after a moment she said, "All right. Find me a basin or a bucket and some water and rags, and I'll see what I can do."

While Prentice was doing that, John Henry walked back over to the hotel, stood in front of the two-story building, and called, "Mr. Weaver!"

The nervous-looking proprietor opened the door and stuck his head out.

"What do you want now?"

"You've got an undertaker in this town, don't you?"

"Of course we do. Claude Richardson. Two blocks down and around the corner. Is that fella Munroe dead already?"

"His name's really Denton," John Henry said, although once he thought about it he realized he didn't know if Clive Denton was any more the man's real name than Edward Munroe was. "And no, he's not dead, but your marshal is."

"Marshal Ledbetter? Damn it! Where's this filthy stuff going to end?"

"I don't know, sir," John Henry said. "I wish I did."

He found the undertaking parlor and called Claude Richardson's name. A mild-looking, mostly bald man came to the door. He looked to be healthy enough at the moment.

"What can I do for you, son?" he asked.

"I'm Deputy U.S. Marshal Sixkiller," John Henry introduced himself. "I came to tell you that Marshal Ledbetter has passed away and needs your attention."

Richardson grimaced. He sighed and said, "Can't really say that I'm surprised. Put him out front of the jail. I'll bring my wagon and come get him."

"You're not afraid to handle him?"

"Pestilence rarely survives the death of its host, Marshal. It should be safe enough to lay him to rest properly." The undertaker sighed again. "Lord knows I've had to do it often enough the past few days, and I'm still all right as far as I can tell. I sent all my helpers home to their families. I won't put them at risk."

"You're digging the graves by yourself?"

"That's right."

"I'll give you a hand. Got to warn you, though,

I've been exposed to the sickness myself. Feel fine so far, but you never know."

"It's possible the whole town has been exposed," Richardson said. "We don't know how long it takes before symptoms start to appear."

"That's what I figured, too. It doesn't hurt anything to be careful, though."

"No, it doesn't. Although man's caution doesn't really amount to much in the face of destiny, does it?"

"Not a whole lot," John Henry agreed.

When he got back to the jail, he looked in the cell block and saw that Penelope was sitting on a three-legged stool next to the bunk where Denton lay. A bucket was on the floor beside her. She dipped a rag into the bucket, soaked it with water, wrung it out until it wasn't dripping, and swabbed it over the unconscious man's face.

Prentice stood across the aisle with a shoulder propped against the iron bars of another cell. With a note of reluctant admiration in his voice, he said, "She's doing a good job. It may be my imagination, but I don't think Denton looks quite as flushed now."

"He's still really hot," Penelope said without looking up from her task. "So hot his skin dries the rag out almost as quick as I can get it wet."

"Keep it up," John Henry told her. "That's all anybody can do for him right now. If we were back in Indian Territory, I could probably find some old Cherokee woman who could make a tea from some roots and herbs that would help him, but I don't know anything about the plants around here."

"And if we were someplace civilized," Prentice said, "there would be more doctors, and they would know what they were doing. No wonder people out here are so afraid of fevers. They make you feel helpless."

"We'll do what we can," Penelope murmured.

Prentice grunted and asked, "Since when did you become so compassionate? I thought you didn't care what happened to Denton."

"I'd hate to see even an animal that was this sick."

"I'd probably feel more sympathetic if it was an animal."

"That's because you don't have any human feelings."

John Henry said, "You know, the two of you really ought to try to get along better. We're liable to be stuck here in each other's company for a while, and squabbling won't make the time pass any quicker or more pleasantly."

"Tell *him* that," Penelope said. "I'm at least trying to help."

"At least until you try to kill us and escape again," Prentice said.

John Henry sighed, shook his head, and said, "I'm gonna go tend to the horses."

Chapter Thirty-four

John Henry was right about the ordeal facing them. Denton continued to rave and burn up with fever the rest of that day and on into the night. Sometime after midnight he began yelling incoherently and thrashing around. Penelope couldn't calm him down. John Henry went into the cell and used Denton's own belt to lash him to the bunk.

None of them got much sleep that night.

Marshal Ledbetter had coffee on hand and there was a pump out back, behind the jail, so John Henry was able to get a pot of coffee boiling the next morning. There was no food in the office, though.

He had spotted a café in the next block, so he walked down there and found that the place had a CLOSED sign in the window. Taking a chance that someone might be there, he knocked on the door anyway.

A woman answered from inside, "Go away! We've got the sickness here!"

"You've got food, don't you?" John Henry asked. "My friends and I need something to eat, and we've been taking care of a sick man, so we've already been exposed to the fever. I can pay you . . ."

He heard a key turn in the lock, and the door opened a crack. He could see a narrow slice of a middle-aged woman's haggard face. She asked, "You say you're taking care of someone who's got the fever?"

"That's right."

"I can't turn you away, then, and you don't have to pay, either. I've got biscuits and bacon, and I was getting some ready to send to the houses where there's illness. Those of us who are fightin' it have to stick together, I think. I'd be glad to share with you and your friends, especially if you'll deliver some of those meals for me."

John Henry summoned up a tired smile and touched a finger to the brim of his hat.

"I'd be glad to do that, ma'am. You're right, we've all got to help each other as much as we can."

The woman got a stern look on her face as she said, "Mind you, I think folks ought to stand on their own two feet most of the time. This is an emergency, though. People got to pull together to get through it."

"Yes, ma'am."

"What's your name, young man? You're not from around here, are you?"

"John Henry Sixkiller." He left off the part about being a deputy U.S. marshal. That didn't amount to a hill of beans under these circumstances. "I'm from Indian Territory."

"Well, Mr. Sixkiller, wait right here, and I'll bring you some food. You can come back and make those deliveries after you and your friends have eaten."

"If it's all right with you, ma'am, I'd just as soon go ahead and take care of those chores for you. Our breakfast can wait. Folks here in Copperhead have had it bad for longer than we have."

The woman's weathered face creased in a smile.

"You're a good man, Mr. Sixkiller."

"Make it John Henry," he said, returning the smile.

The woman who owned the café was Mrs. Smalley. Over the next three days, John Henry got to know her, her married daughter Edith Parton, who worked in the café with her, Edith's husband, Calvin, and their children. It was Calvin who had the fever, but he was a big, strapping man who worked as the blacksmith's assistant, and he seemed to be fighting off the sickness.

John Henry became acquainted with the blacksmith, Lon Williams, too, and several dozen other people in town as he delivered meals, milked cows, fed horses and pigs, and did anything else he could to help people get on with their lives while they fought the sickness that threatened to destroy Copperhead. He dug graves, as three more people passed away after Marshal Ledbetter. He pumped water.

Meanwhile, in the jail, Penelope sat up nearly around the clock for several days, bathing Clive Denton's face and spooning broth from Mrs. Smalley's kitchen into his mouth. Slowly, Denton's condition improved, until finally one morning he was drenched in sweat, so much sweat that it soaked the bunk. John Henry and Prentice had to move him to another cell.

His fever had broken. He was still very weak and not lucid yet, but it was starting to look like he might live.

Surprisingly, as Denton began to grow stronger, Penelope offered to go with John Henry when he made his rounds of the town looking for ways to help.

"What happened to you?" Prentice asked her. "You get religion during these past few days or something?"

"None of your damned business," she snapped. "Is it a crime to want to help people?"

"No, but it's a crime to distribute fake money, and I'm sure you've crossed plenty of other lines, too. If you're just trying to make yourself look good so you'll get a lighter sentence once you're convicted, I don't think it'll work."

"Go to hell," Penelope muttered. She looked at John Henry and jerked her head toward the door. "Let's go. I've been shut up in here for days. I need some fresh air."

Whatever her reason for doing it, John Henry

had to admit that Penelope threw herself into the work of caring for the people of Copperhead. She had a smile for everybody, and folks seemed to perk up when she was around. She had to be exhausted. She had gotten even less sleep than John Henry and Prentice while she was taking care of Denton. Yet she kept going, as long as there was anything she could do to help someone.

As dusk settled down one evening, the two of them paused on the boardwalk. Penelope rested her hands on the railing and leaned forward as a cool breeze, laden with the scent of pines from the surrounding mountains, swept along the street. She closed her eyes and said, "Mmmm."

John Henry leaned a shoulder on one of the posts holding up the awning over the boardwalk and asked her, "How are you feeling?"

She opened her eyes and looked over at him. "No fever yet," she said. "How about you?"

"Tired." He rasped his fingers over the beard stubble on his jaw. "I could use a bath and a shave. But no fever. I reckon I'm fine."

"How did we both manage to keep from catching it? Or did we? Has it just not shown up yet?"

John Henry shook his head and said, "I don't know. Sickness is a funny thing. Some people just don't catch much. I've barely been sick a day in my life, that I remember." He smiled. "I guess what it comes down to is luck. Or the Good Lord taking a liking to you, if you want to think about it that way."

She laughed and said, "It's sure not because the innocent are being spared, or I'd have been a goner a long time ago."

"Maybe you're not as wicked as you seem to think you are. The past few days I've seen a different Penelope Smith."

"Yeah, well, what about Prentice? He's not sick, either. Which means that jackasses can't catch this stuff, I guess."

"Prentice is all right. A little full of himself, maybe."

"You're being too kind to him. He hates me." She shrugged. "Maybe according to his standards, he's got good reason to."

Actually, over the past few days John Henry had seen Prentice looking at Penelope with a puzzled frown on his face, as if he were feeling something that he couldn't quite figure out. He still gibed at her from time to time, but not as much as he had been doing at first. Now it was almost like a habit, rather than any real hostility directed toward the blonde.

"I'm not sure you're right about that, either," John Henry said.

Penelope might have argued with him some more, but at that moment something happened that neither of them expected.

In the hills to the east of town, gunfire erupted. John Henry stiffened as he heard the flat boom of pistol shots mixed with the sharper cracks of rifles.

Penelope heard the sounds, too. She straightened and stared into the gathering shadows.

"What in the world?" she muttered as the shooting continued.

"I don't know," John Henry said, "but if I didn't know better I'd say that a small-scale war just broke out up there."

Chapter Thirty-five

The two of them hurried back to the jail, which was about a block away. Nick Prentice was sitting at the desk, playing solitaire with a grubby deck of cards he'd found in one of the drawers, when John Henry and Penelope burst in. His head jerked up, and he exclaimed, "What the hell?"

"Listen," John Henry said.

Prentice dropped the cards and came to his feet. With the door closed, he must not have been able to hear the shots, John Henry thought, but they were clearly audible now.

"Good Lord!" Prentice exclaimed. "What's all that shooting about?"

From the cell block, Clive Denton called, "What's all the commotion out there? Is that gunfire I hear?"

"Sounds to me like it's coming from that gap Stanton and the other men from Oroville blockaded," John Henry said. "Somebody must be trying to shoot their way out."

Prentice let out a scornful grunt.

"Have you seen anybody in this town who'd try something like that, Sixkiller? These people are sheep. Sick sheep."

Penelope suggested, "Maybe somebody's trying to shoot their way *in.*"

"Who'd do a thing like that?" Prentice asked her.

She shrugged.

"I don't have any idea. But it makes as much sense as somebody shooting their way out, doesn't it?"

John Henry listened again and said, "I don't hear the guns anymore. Whether they were trying to get in or out, either way it sounds like the fight is over."

"So what happens now?" Prentice asked in the thick silence.

"Your guess is as good as mine," John Henry said. "It might be a good idea to get ready for trouble, though."

The marshal's office had a gun rack on one wall, with two Winchesters, three shotguns, and an old Henry repeater in it. John Henry got all the weapons down and laid them on the desk, then opened the drawers in search of ammunition.

He found a couple of boxes of .44-40 cartridges for the rifles and a box of shotgun shells. He started loading them.

"Do you really think there's going to be a fight?" Penelope asked worriedly.

"I don't know, but whatever just happened up there in the hills, somebody was willing to start shooting, that's for sure. I want to be prepared if they ride in here still in the same mood."

When he had finished loading the long guns, he took a cartridge from one of the loops on his shell belt and slipped it into the empty chamber in the Colt's cylinder where he usually carried the hammer. Prentice did the same with his .38.

Denton must have heard enough to figure out what they were doing, because he called from the cell block, "Hey, how about giving me a gun?"

"Have you lost your mind?" Prentice said. "Why would we do that, after all the times you've tried to kill us?"

"If there's a gunfight, I might need to defend myself," Denton insisted.

"If any bullets start flying around, you'd better just duck your head and pray, because you're not getting a gun and that's for damned sure."

Denton continued grousing, but John Henry ignored him. He told Penelope, "The walls of this building are nice and thick. They'll stop a slug. So if there's trouble, you stay in here and keep your head down, too."

"I can handle a gun, you know," she said. "After the last few days, don't you think I'm trustworthy?"

"You pitched in to help and did a lot of good," John Henry admitted. "I admire you for it, too. But that doesn't mean I'd be inclined to trust you with a gun."

"You'd trust that Chinese girl, and her father's one of the biggest crooks in Los Angeles! You know he's grooming her to take over, don't you?"

"More than likely." John Henry smiled faintly. "But she's a hell of a shot, too."

"So am I," Penelope insisted.

"You're not getting a gun," Prentice said. "That's final."

"Fine," she snapped. "You'd better hope you don't need me to save your lives, the both of you."

Night was falling rapidly now. John Henry said, "I'm going to go scout around town a little. You might want to lock the door after me."

"Be careful," Prentice said. "You don't know what's out there."

"Maybe I can find out."

Taking one of the Winchesters, John Henry slipped out of the marshal's office. He heard Prentice turn the key in the lock behind him. There was also a bar that could be lowered into a pair of brackets on either side of the door to make it even more secure if necessary.

Although Copperhead was still far from back to normal, more lights burned in the buildings now than had been common for the past couple of weeks. A lot of people who had been sick were recovering at last, thanks in small part to the efforts of John Henry, Penelope, and others who had pitched in to help, but mostly thanks to their own sturdy constitutions. As widespread and potent as the sickness had been, the casualties could have been a lot worse, John Henry thought as he made his way quietly along the boardwalk.

"Hsst! Mr. Sixkiller!"

John Henry recognized the voice. He looked

toward the café across the street and saw Mrs. Smalley standing in the doorway. She beckoned for him to come over.

He did so, looking both directions along the street before he stepped out. He didn't see anyone moving around.

"What is it, Mrs. Smalley?" he asked as he stepped up onto the boardwalk in front of the café.

"We heard a lot of shooting a little while ago," the woman said. "Is there going to be trouble?"

"I don't know," John Henry replied honestly. "That's why I'm out taking a look around. What you should do is stay inside, and keep your family inside, too, just in case."

"Calvin's gettin' a mite restless," she said, referring to her burly son-in-law, who was recuperating from the fever. "Now that he feels better, he wants to be out and about again. He said to tell you that if you need any help, you can count on him. He's got an old cap-and-ball pistol that belonged to his pa."

"I appreciate that, ma'am. I'm hoping it won't come to that."

Mrs. Smalley regarded him shrewdly and said, "You're some sort of lawman, aren't you, Mr. Sixkiller? Or a military officer? I can tell."

He smiled and told her, "I'm a deputy U.S. marshal. Would've told you before now, but with so many people sick and all, it didn't really seem to matter what any of us do for a living."

"That's the truth," she agreed. "Just remember, Marshal, if you need help, there's plenty of good folks in Copperhead who'll give you a hand if they can."

John Henry nodded and said, "Yes, ma'am, I'll remember. For now, just go on back inside, lock your door, and lay low."

"You be careful," she told him as she eased the door closed.

John Henry moved along the street, thinking that it would be a good idea to warn as many of the other citizens as he could to keep their heads down for a while. There hadn't been any more shooting. If trouble was on its way to Copperhead, it ought to be here soon, he told himself.

Several minutes went by while he stopped at a few more places along the street and told the people whose acquaintance he had made to stay inside and keep their heads down in case of trouble. He was about to turn around and head back to the marshal's office when he heard a familiar sound drifting through the evening air.

Hoofbeats—a lot of them—approaching the settlement from the east.

John Henry stiffened as he remembered what Baird Stanton had said about wishing he could burn Copperhead to the ground. Had the mine owner decided to risk that drastic move anyway? Maybe some of his men had had second thoughts and tried to stop Stanton from carrying out that wanton destruction. That would explain the gunfire, John Henry thought.

Although to be honest, the shooting had sounded like more than a skirmish among the members of the group that had blocked the road. John Henry wouldn't have thought there would be that many guns up there.

He had a hunch he was about to find out the reason for the violence, because a big bunch of riders was closing in on Copperhead. John Henry turned and trotted into an alley, drawing back as far as he could into the shadows. He wanted to find out what was going on here before revealing his presence.

He didn't have long to wait. The riders swept into town, close to forty strong, John Henry estimated. He couldn't see them very well. Even though lights were burning in some of the windows, the glow didn't really reach that far into the street. All he could make out was a dark mass of mounted men.

The one who was in the lead held up a hand to signal a halt. He wore a flat-crowned, narrow-brimmed beaver hat of the sort that had been stylish several decades earlier. John Henry couldn't see the man's face.

The leader turned his horse toward the others and called in a voice that was obviously used to giving orders, "Spread out! Search the whole town if you have to, but find my daughter and bring her to me!"

Daughter? John Henry thought. *Whose daughter?* The leader of this bunch wasn't Baird Stanton; John Henry was certain of that. Stanton sounded like a westerner. This man had an eastern accent of some sort.

Baffled, John Henry remained in the shadows and watched as the men began to dismount and fan out. As they walked through patches of light, he got a better look at some of them, and he didn't like what he saw. They were heavily armed, hard-faced men of a sort he had encountered before. He knew hired killers when he saw them.

This bunch must have approached Copperhead along the road from the east, and when Stanton and his men tried to stop them, gunplay had broken out. The fact that these strangers were here now told John Henry that they had won the fight.

He wondered if Stanton and the other men from Oroville had been wiped out.

Then he put that question out of his mind, because the leader had swung down from his saddle and stepped up onto the boardwalk across the street to light a cigar. A match rasped into life, and as the stranger held the flame to the end of his cheroot, the harsh light washed over his face.

John Henry had never seen the man before, but he recognized the description. The man was stockily built, of average height, and probably in his late forties. Curly red hair with a considerable amount of gray in it was visible under that old-fashioned beaver hat. His nose was crooked, probably from having been broken sometime in the past. His beefy face had two scars on it, one over his left eye and a longer, thinner scar on the right side of his jaw.

John Henry saw all that in the brief moment that the match illuminated the man's face, and he knew without any doubt that he was looking at Ignatius O'Reilly.

Chapter Thirty-six

As soon as John Henry realized who the leader of the gunmen was, his mind made the next logical leap. O'Reilly was here looking for his daughter, and who else could that be except the blonde who called herself Penelope Smith?

But how could O'Reilly have known that the law had her in custody here in Copperhead and that he needed to rescue her? John Henry couldn't answer that unless O'Reilly had a spy here in town. He supposed that was possible, but the likelihood of such a thing struck him as far-fetched.

The answers to those questions could wait. Right now John Henry had to figure out a way to keep O'Reilly from freeing Penelope and Clive Denton. He also needed to take the master counterfeiter himself into custody.

And he was only outnumbered forty to one, he told himself with a bleak smile.

His business was to take care of the impossible jobs for Judge Parker, though, so he had to figure out a way. The key, he realized, was to get his hands on O'Reilly. Once he had the mastermind in custody, he could use O'Reilly as a hostage while he and Prentice got out of here along with their other two prisoners.

In order to do that, John Henry had to avoid being discovered by the hired killers who were searching the settlement, and he had to maneuver into a position where he could jump O'Reilly and overpower him.

He retreated farther along the alley until he reached the rear of the building. O'Reilly was on the other side of the street, so John Henry had to get over there somehow. He would go all the way down to the livery stable on the edge of town, he decided, and try to cross there without being seen.

Using all the shadows and other cover that he could in order to avoid being spotted, he hurried along behind the buildings. He heard O'Reilly's men calling to one another as they searched. He hoped the townsfolk they encountered would have enough sense to cooperate. Men like those tended to shoot first any time they were challenged and sort things out later.

Even though John Henry was still puzzled about several things, the last few minutes had cleared up some of his confusion. Baird Stanton and his men must have tried to stop O'Reilly's bunch from getting through. John Henry wondered if Stanton or one of his group had had a chance to explain why Copperhead was quarantined, or if O'Reilly's gunmen had started shooting before that came about. If the latter was true, the hired killers wouldn't know they were exposing themselves to a potentially deadly fever.

John Henry wasn't going to waste any sympathy on them if they got sick.

He was almost to the livery stable when two figures suddenly loomed up in front of him. The searchers hadn't been talking or making any other noise, so he hadn't known they were there until they rounded the rear corner of a building and he nearly ran into them.

"Hey!" one of them exclaimed. "Hold it right—"

John Henry reacted instantly, leaping forward and lashing out with a fist. He didn't want any shots, because that would just draw the attention of the other gunmen. He aimed at the sound of the man's voice and smashed a terrific blow to his jaw.

Luck played a big part in the punch landing so perfectly, but there were two men, not just one. John Henry wheeled and saw movement and knew the second man was clawing at the gun on his hip. John Henry left his feet in a diving tackle and caught the man around the waist. The man went over backward and hit the ground so hard it knocked the breath out of him. That was another lucky break, because he couldn't yell without any air in his lungs.

John Henry hammered a punch at the man's head. He felt teeth gash his knuckles and knew he had hit the man in the mouth. John Henry hit him again, and this time the teeth gave under the impact. The man gurgled and went still as he lost consciousness.

John Henry hit a third time, just for good measure.

He scrambled to his feet and left the two unconscious gunmen where they had fallen. They would be out for a few minutes, and that would be long enough to give him a chance. He checked to make sure his Colt hadn't fallen out of its holster, picked up the Winchester he had dropped when he tackled the second man, and ran toward the livery stable.

He had just reached the big barn and circled around it when he heard a spattering of gunfire somewhere up the street. The shots sounded like they might be coming from the marshal's office, and John Henry hoped that Prentice hadn't decided to shoot it out with O'Reilly's men.

At the same time, the gunfire provided a distraction, and John Henry took advantage of it. He saw several of O'Reilly's men running in the street, but they were all looking toward the shots. John Henry ran across the street, too. None of the gunmen paid any attention to him.

He ducked into the shadows and headed for the last place he had seen O'Reilly, the boardwalk in front of the hotel.

The counterfeiter was still there, John Henry saw as he approached cautiously. O'Reilly stalked back and forth, visibly impatient. John Henry paused at the corner of the building, pressing his back against the side wall for a moment as he waited for any indication that he had been spotted. When none came, he risked a better look.

From where he was, he could have easily dropped O'Reilly with a rifle shot. But that would be cold-blooded murder, and even though O'Reilly was a killer himself, John Henry wasn't prepared to execute the man.

John Henry also knew that shooting down O'Reilly wouldn't save him and Prentice. With their boss dead, there was no telling what sort of bloody rampage the hired guns might go on. Everyone in Copperhead could be in danger.

No, their chances would be better if O'Reilly was alive and a prisoner. Then they could use him as a bargaining chip.

John Henry hadn't heard any more shots. He looked across the street at the marshal's office and felt his heart sink a little when he saw that the door was open. Prentice should have kept it locked, even barred. If he had blown out the lamp and barred the door in time, O'Reilly's men might not have known that anyone was in there.

On the other hand, someone in town, fearing for their life, could have told the searchers about the beautiful blonde who could be found in the jail. John Henry was still convinced that Penelope was O'Reilly's daughter. Prentice would have put up a fight when the gunmen tried to take her . . .

John Henry hoped the big Secret Service man was still alive.

O'Reilly stopped pacing as figures appeared

in the doorway of the marshal's office. A group of men emerged, prodding several people in front of them.

John Henry spotted Nick Prentice. The government man crossed the street reluctantly, a rifle muzzle jabbing him in the back.

Clive Denton was next to Prentice. From the looks of how he was being treated, he hadn't exactly been "rescued." He was being shoved along at gunpoint, too.

That left Penelope. Instead of her stalking across the street in triumph, one of the gunmen had hold of her arm and forced her toward the hotel. She struggled, and John Henry could hear her spitting curses at her captor.

He frowned. Maybe he'd been wrong about Penelope's relationship to Ignatius O'Reilly.

O'Reilly clasped his hands behind his back, rocked forward on his toes and then back on his heels in obvious satisfaction. Even from the side, John Henry could tell that the master counterfeiter was smirking.

"It's about time," O'Reilly's voice rang out as the three prisoners were brought in front of him. "I've gone to a great deal of trouble to track you down. But a reunion long delayed is that much sweeter, wouldn't you say, my dear?"

"I'm not your dear," Penelope snarled at him. "I'm not anything to you."

"On the contrary," O'Reilly insisted. "You're my darling daughter."

"Just because you married my mother doesn't

make me your daughter. You never gave a damn about her or me!"

"I'm sorry you feel that way. Just like I'm sorry that you decided to run away after your mother passed on, rest her poor soul."

"She didn't *pass on,*" Penelope said. "She killed herself because she couldn't stand being married to a monster like you anymore. You think I'll ever forget finding her hanging from that beam with a rope around her neck?"

O'Reilly stiffened.

"We'll speak no more about that," he snapped. "You're coming home with me now, Penelope. I forgive you for what you've done." O'Reilly turned his gaze on Denton. "You, on the other hand, Clive . . . you're a bitter disappointment. You were almost like a son to me, and what do you do? You steal from me."

"It . . . it was all her idea, Mr. O'Reilly," Denton stammered. "I knew you weren't satisfied with that batch of currency and were going to destroy it. Penelope said that it would still fool most people and that it . . . it would be a shame to just waste it—"

"That's not true," Penelope said. "That's what he told me. He said we'd take a trip across the Southwest and make enough money to set up our own operation." She laughed humorlessly. "And I was a big enough fool to believe you, Clive! You're no better than *he* is. You just wanted to use me."

"That's enough," O'Reilly said. "We're wasting

time here." He nodded toward Prentice. "Who's this?"

"He . . . he's a Secret Service man," Denton babbled, clearly trying to get back in O'Reilly's good graces. "He's been after us for weeks, but he thought he was chasing you, Mr. O'Reilly. Him and that U.S. marshal."

"What U.S. marshal?"

"His name's Sixkiller," Denton said. "He's around here somewhere."

O'Reilly's head jerked to the side as he glared at his men.

"You didn't find this lawman?" he demanded.

One of the gunmen answered, "We didn't even know he existed until now, boss."

"Find him. I don't want any loose ends."

Some of the gunmen who had congregated in front of the hotel began to spread out again.

O'Reilly turned back to the prisoners and said, "Thank you for that bit of information, Clive."

A grin spread across Denton's face. He said, "I helped you out, didn't I, Mr. O'Reilly?"

"Indeed you did, and because of that I'm going to do a favor for you in return. I'm going to make sure you die quickly."

O'Reilly extended his right arm as one of the men gave Denton a hard shove in the back that sent him stumbling forward. John Henry saw the derringer appear in O'Reilly's hand as if by magic and knew it came from a spring-loaded sleeve holster. The little gun cracked wickedly, flame leaping from its muzzle. Denton was only a couple of feet away, and his head rocked back as a small but lethal bullet hole appeared in his forehead. He fell to his knees and then pitched over onto his side, dead.

O'Reilly lowered his arm and said, "Kill the Secret Service man. My daughter and I are leaving. And what I said about loose ends still goes. Once you've found that marshal and made sure he's dead . . . burn the whole town."

Chapter Thirty-seven

John Henry could hardly believe his ears. O'Reilly had just cold-bloodedly pronounced a death sentence on the whole settlement. He knew he had to make his move now before the hired killers began to carry out that destruction.

Something else happened first, though. A tall, powerfully built young man John Henry recognized as Calvin Parton stepped out of the café and shouted, "Let Miss Penelope go!"

The old cap-and-ball pistol in his hand boomed as he fired at the knot of gunmen in the street. One of them fell as the heavy lead ball smashed into him.

Calvin dived for cover as the other gunmen reacted instinctively and returned fire. They were so surprised that they had hesitated for a split second, though, and that gave Calvin time to throw himself back through the café door. The barrage of lead smashed into the front wall of the building.

At the same time the owner of the hotel,

Weaver, who appeared as jittery as ever, lunged out onto the boardwalk with his shotgun in his hands.

"You won't burn down our town!" he shouted as he triggered the double-barreled weapon. The charges of buckshot ripped through several of the hired gunmen and blasted them off their feet.

John Henry stepped into the open and started cranking off rounds from the Winchester as fast as he could work the rifle's lever. His shots were deadly accurate. One of the killers fell with each crack of the Winchester.

Meanwhile Prentice had turned on the man guarding him and grabbed the man's rifle. They swayed back and forth as they struggled over the weapon. Prentice was bigger and stronger, though, and he ripped the rifle out of the man's hand and brought it up sharply, slamming the stock against the gunman's jaw. Prentice hit him so hard and shattered the jaw so thoroughly that the man's chin wound up practically under his ear as he collapsed.

O'Reilly's derringer had another barrel in it. He whirled and fired at Weaver, who was trying to reload the shotgun. Weaver cried out, dropped the shotgun, and slumped to the boardwalk. O'Reilly leaped down to the street, grabbed Penelope's arm, and dragged her with him as he retreated into the hotel. She screamed and fought but couldn't tear loose from his brutal grip.

John Henry heard the scream and from the corner of his eye saw O'Reilly forcing Penelope into the hotel. He didn't have time to help her just then, however, because he was crouched beside a hitch rack returning the fire from several gunmen who were charging him. He blew one of them off his feet with the final shot in the Winchester, then flung the empty rifle aside and threw himself forward on his belly as he palmed out the Colt.

The revolver blasted three times and spilled the other attackers, even as their slugs kicked up dirt around John Henry. He surged to his feet and turned toward the hotel entrance. He saw that Prentice had armed himself with a couple of pistols from fallen gunmen and had the same idea. The two of them converged on the door.

All along the street, shots roared as the citizens of Copperhead mounted a stiff resistance against the invaders. They had been through so much already, surviving the outbreak of fever that had threatened to wipe out the town, and they weren't about to just surrender now to a bunch of no-account killers from outside.

John Henry hoped they would be all right, but he had done all he could to help them.

Now he was going after Ignatius O'Reilly.

The larger Nick Prentice bulled him aside, though, and charged through the door into the hotel lobby first. A shot roared. Prentice grunted in pain and staggered. He dropped one of the guns he had picked up as his left arm hung useless, drilled by a bullet. As John Henry darted past Prentice, he saw O'Reilly backing up the stairs, holding Penelope in front of him as a shield.

His left hand was around the blonde's waist, dragging her up the stairs as she continued to struggle. O'Reilly's right hand held a six-gun he had picked up somewhere. Flame spurted from the muzzle as he fired at John Henry.

The lawman felt the hot wind-rip of the slug as it sizzled through the air next to his ear. He couldn't shoot back because the chances were too great that he would hit Penelope. John Henry was an excellent shot, but the risk was too great even for him.

They were almost at the top of the stairs when Penelope thrust a foot between O'Reilly's calves and heaved as hard as she could. O'Reilly's left leg went out from under him. Both he and Penelope fell hard against the banister, which bowed out under their weight and then gave with a sharp cracking of wood. Penelope fell, screaming, but O'Reilly caught himself.

He might have been just as well off if he hadn't, because without Penelope to shield him, John Henry and Prentice both fired at him, triggering several shots each. The bullets pounded into O'Reilly's chest, making him dance a grotesque little jig at the top of the stairs. With blood welling from half a dozen wounds, he dropped the gun, groaned, and pitched forward to tumble wildly down the stairs, leaving crimson smears on the steps behind him.

Prentice dropped his gun and lunged forward. Penelope hung from the broken banister, having made a desperate grab for it as she fell. Prentice called to her, "Go ahead and drop! I'll catch you!"

The distance wasn't that far. The fall wouldn't have killed her, probably wouldn't even have hurt her very badly, but even with one arm wounded, Prentice was there to wrap the other arm around her and cushion her with his broad chest as she dropped. He staggered a little but caught himself, then stood there with his arm around her, holding her tightly against him as she looked up into his face.

Then his mouth came down on hers and she didn't pull away.

John Henry kept his gun leveled as he approached the crumpled body at the foot of the stairs. He was pretty sure that Ignatius O'Reilly was dead. Anybody with that many bullets in him ought to be.

Then John Henry saw the unnatural way O'Reilly's neck was twisted and the grotesque angle at which the counterfeiter's head was turned. If by some miracle the gunshots hadn't killed O'Reilly, the broken neck from the tumble down the stairs had.

Either way, he was dead as could be.

Footsteps from the entrance made John Henry swing around. Baird Stanton was coming into the hotel with his arm around Weaver's waist, holding up the proprietor. Stanton was hatless and had a bloody bandage wrapped around his head. Weaver's shirt was stained with blood, but he was walking mostly under his own power and didn't seem to be wounded too badly. The bullet from O'Reilly's derringer must have just creased him, John Henry thought.

"You're not here to make more trouble, are you?" he asked the mine owner from Oroville.

"Hell, no!" Stanton exclaimed. "As soon as we patched up our wounds, my friends and I came after that loco bunch that blasted their way through us a while ago. Killed half a dozen good men, they did, and I was damned if I was gonna let them get away with that, even if it meant riding into this pesthole of a town!"

"Even with half the people sick, Copperhead is a better town than Oroville," Weaver insisted. "But I have to say, you fellas were a mighty welcome sight, riding in that way and finishing off those gunmen. They planned to burn down the town!"

"Yeah, that's, uh, terrible," Stanton said. He glared at John Henry, who let out a grim chuckle and decided it wouldn't do any good to point out that a few days earlier, Stanton had threatened to do the very same thing. Stanton hadn't really meant it, though; John Henry saw that now. The man was just so afraid of the fever that he hadn't been thinking straight.

John Henry started thumbing fresh cartridges into his Colt as he asked, "So everything's mopped up outside?"

"Yeah," Stanton said. He helped Weaver sit down in one of the armchairs. "What in blazes was all this about, anyway? Who were those lunatics?"

"It's a long story," John Henry said. He glanced at Prentice and Penelope, who were still embracing, and added, "But it looks like we've got time."

* * *

"So everybody in this town"—Judge Parker glanced at the report in his hand—"Copperhead. They all recovered from the fever?"

"Yes, sir," John Henry said. "Less than a dozen people died. From the fever, anyway." His face took on a regretful cast as he remembered the aftermath of the battle along Copperhead's main street. "Another four men were killed in the fighting with O'Reilly's men."

Parker tossed the document onto his desk. His bushy eyebrows lowered slightly as he looked at John Henry and said, "I believe I asked you to apprehend O'Reilly alive if possible."

"Couldn't be done," John Henry said blandly. "Mr. Prentice and I fired in self-defense, and in defense of Miss Smith's life as well."

"The slippery Miss Smith," Parker said. "The one who . . . got away."

"There was a lot of confusion that night. Lots and lots of shooting, Judge, and wounded folks everywhere. But Miss Smith pitched in to help, just like she did when so many people were sick with the fever, and to tell you the truth, I just lost track of her."

"As did Mr. Prentice, a trained agent of the Secret Service."

"Well, in all fairness, Judge, he'd lost quite a bit of blood from that arm of his O'Reilly ventilated. I'm not surprised he was a mite addled."

Parker sat forward, glared, and said, "If you think for one moment—"

He stopped short, blew out an exasperated breath, and shook his head.

"Never mind," the judge went on. "So what it amounts to is that you went to California, befriended a Chinese criminal overlord and his daughter, got in a fight at a notorious gambling den, killed a master counterfeiter that various people in Washington very much wanted to interrogate and send to prison, and then lost a prisoner who happened to be that master counterfeiter's daughter."

"Stepdaughter," John Henry corrected. "And I think it's safe to say they weren't close."

"Still, that's a fair summing up?"

"Well, I put a stop to them passing the rest of that counterfeit money. They would have kept it up for a while longer, probably in half a dozen more towns there in the Sierra Nevadas."

"There's that to be thankful for, I suppose." Judge Parker leaned back in his chair. "I could assign you to track down Miss Smith, you know."

"I reckon you could, Judge, but I'd bet that it'd be a waste of time. She's a mighty smart young woman. I think she'll lie low for a long time, long enough that we'll never see her again."

"Mm-hmm. Mr. Prentice is retiring from the Secret Service, you know. The doctors believe that he'll get most of the use back in his left arm, but it'll never be like it was. I'm told that he thought it best that he move on to something else."

"Yes, sir, he told me he might see about going to work for Allan Pinkerton," John Henry said.

"Since he's got some experience in that line of work, so to speak."

"Yes." Parker's voice took on a brisk tone as he continued, "I believe we're done here, Marshal Sixkiller. Thank you for your good work."

"Just did the best I could at the time, Judge," John Henry drawled. He stood up, put on his hat, and turned to leave the office.

Parker stopped him by saying, "One more thing."

John Henry looked back at the judge.

"I realize you just got back from a long, hazardous assignment," Parker said, "but a band of outlaws is raising hell over in the Nations right now and somebody needs to put a stop to it. You've heard of Clyde Wolverton?"

John Henry's eyes narrowed.

"Fella who claims to wear a necklace made out of teeth he pulled from the mouths of deputy marshals he killed?"

"That's the one," Parker said. "Judging by the reports I've received, he's assembled a group of desperadoes, all of them almost as evil as he is. How would you feel about rounding them up, Marshal Sixkiller?"

Before leaving California, John Henry had bought Buck from Dunleavy, using his own money, and brought the gelding back here with him on the train. So now he had two good horses, Iron Heart and the big buckskin. He might need them both on a job like this.

"I think I can run Wolverton and his bunch to ground, Judge."

"I'm glad to hear it. Good luck, Marshal."

Billy Rainbow had called him a dead man walking, John Henry recalled as he left the red-brick courthouse, because of all the badmen who wanted to kill him. That number was about to go up again.

But he wasn't dead yet. He still had plenty of fight in him. Clyde Wolverton and the other varmints in his gang would find that out soon enough.

And as John Henry Sixkiller rode out of Fort Smith later that day, there was a smile of anticipation on his face. He could practically smell the gunsmoke already.

He wouldn't have it any other way.

Keep reading for a special excerpt of the next explosive book in the Luke Jensen, Bounty Hunter series.

BURNING DAYLIGHT
by WILLIAM W. JOHNSTONE *and* J. A. JOHNSTONE

Bounty hunter Luke Jensen has always relied on his guns, his brains, and his guts to bring in the deadliest outlaws in the West. But when a family needs his help, he'll have to use something else: his heart . . .

BLOOD IS THICKER THAN SLAUGHTER
Luke Jensen has seen some sorry-looking bounties in his time, but this one takes the cake. A wanted poster is offering a reward of one dollar and forty-two cents—plus one busted harmonica—to capture Three-Fingered Jack McKinney. Turns out, McKinney's twelve-year-old son Aaron wants revenge on his daddy for abandoning him and his mom. The reward is all the money Aaron can scrape together. Luke can't say no to the poor boy—or his beautiful mother—so he agrees to go after McKinney and his bank-robbing gang.

Good deeds, however, are like good intentions—the road to hell is paved with them. And when Aaron McKinney decides to tag along, it puts Luke in the middle of a father-and-son reunion that's life-or-death, blood-for-blood, and kill-or-be-killed . . .

The Jensen Family
First Family of the American Frontier

Smoke Jensen—*The Mountain Man*
The youngest of three children and orphaned as a young boy, Smoke Jensen is considered one of the fastest draws in the West. His quest to tame the lawless West has become the stuff of legend. Smoke owns the Sugarloaf Ranch in Colorado. Married to Sally Jensen, father to Denise ("Denny") and Louis.

Preacher—*The First Mountain Man*
Though not a blood relative, grizzled frontiersman Preacher became a father figure to the young Smoke Jensen, teaching him how to survive in the brutal, often deadly Rocky Mountains. Fought the battles that forged his destiny. Armed with a long gun, Preacher is as fierce as the land itself.

Matt Jensen—*The Last Mountain Man*
Orphaned but taken in by Smoke Jensen, Matt Jensen has become like a younger brother to Smoke and even took the Jensen name. And like

Smoke, Matt has carved out his destiny on the American frontier. He lives by the gun and surrenders to no man.

Luke Jensen—*Bounty Hunter*
Mountain Man Smoke Jensen's long-lost brother Luke Jensen is scarred by war and a dead shot—the right qualities to be a bounty hunter. And he's cunning, and fierce enough, to bring down the deadliest outlaws of his day.

Ace Jensen and Chance Jensen—*Those Jensen Boys!*
Smoke Jensen's long-lost nephews, Ace and Chance, are a pair of young-gun twins as reckless and wild as the frontier itself . . . Their father is Luke Jensen, thought killed in the Civil War. Their uncle Smoke Jensen is one of the fiercest gunfighters the West has ever known. It's no surprise that the inseparable Ace and Chance Jensen have a knack for taking risks—even if they have to blast their way out of them.

Chapter One

Luke Jensen froze with the glass of whiskey halfway to his lips as he heard the metallic ratcheting of a gun being cocked above and behind him. He glanced at the nervous-looking bartender and asked quietly, "He's on the balcony, isn't he?"

The man's lips were tight. His double chin bounced a little as he gave a short nod.

"I'd get down, if I were you," Luke advised, then he dropped the whiskey and threw himself to the side as a gun roared.

The deafening blast filled the saloon. From the corner of his eye Luke saw a bullet gouge out a piece of the hardwood bar and send splinters flying.

By the time he hit the sawdust-littered floor a split second later, his long-barreled Remingtons filled both hands. The guns roared and bucked as he triggered them. The .44 slugs smashed into the chest of the man standing on the balcony and rocked him back a step before he stumbled forward against the railing.

Luke recognized the man who had just tried to kill him. His name was Son Barton, a West Virginia mountaineer who had fled his home state because he had a habit of shooting people who annoyed him. He had headed west, fallen in with several other killers and outlaws, and ridden the dark trails for the past few years. Luke had tracked the gang to this Arizona Territory settlement and intended to collect the rewards on them.

The wanted posters said DEAD OR ALIVE, but it looked like Son Barton was going to be dead because life was fading fast in his eyes. The gun he had fired at Luke slipped from nerveless fingers and fell to the saloon floor. As Barton tipped forward over the railing and followed, he turned over once in the air and landed on his back with a resounding thud. He gurgled once but didn't move and didn't make any more sounds after that, either.

Still holding the Remingtons, Luke put a hand on the floor, pushed himself to one knee, and tried not to groan from the effort. These days, he felt every one of his years. He stood the rest of the way up and glanced out the window.

The four horses he'd been looking for were tied up at the hitch rail outside. Barton's three friends were still unaccounted for.

The bartender poked his bald head up enough to gaze wide-eyed over the hardwood.

The few men who had been drinking in the saloon had stampeded out as soon as the shooting started.

Luke said, "The other three upstairs, too?"

The bartender shook his head. "Just two of 'em. Only got three girls workin' for me. The fourth man said he was goin' over to the store to pick up some supplies."

Since the settlement was small that man was bound to have heard the shots. He'd be heading to the saloon to see what had happened, but it would take him a while get there, so Luke didn't worry about him for the time being. The other two upstairs concerned him more. And with good reason.

A man burst through the door of the room where he'd been frolicking with one of the soiled doves and began spraying lead from a Winchester as fast as he could swing the barrel back and forth and work the rifle's lever.

The bartender ducked again.

Luke dived forward and slid through beery sawdust underneath a table. Bullets whapped against the wood above him. His head and shoulders emerged from the other side. He tipped the Remingtons up and fired two more shots. One missed, but the other caught the rifleman in the throat and jerked his head back as it bored on up into his brain. Blood shot out a good three feet from the wound as he went over backward.

The rifleman's frenzied firing had served as a

distraction, Luke realized. The third member of the gang had made it almost all the way down the stairs while Luke had been dealing with the rifleman. And this hombre held a shotgun. He leveled it and squeezed off one barrel as Luke desperately tried to roll aside.

The buckshot hit the floor, except for one piece that plucked at Luke's shirtsleeve. He wasn't hurt, though, and as he came up on a knee again, he thrust the Remingtons out in front of him and triggered them.

The shotgunner jerked. Luke bit back a curse as he saw that his aim had been a little off. He'd hit the varmint in the left arm and left shoulder. He might bleed to death eventually, but he was still on his feet and still had hold of that scattergun.

Luke jammed the revolvers back into their holsters and grabbed hold of another table. As he swung it up, the wounded outlaw fired the shotgun's second barrel. Luke felt the table shiver as the charge struck it. Then he lunged forward and shoved the table out in front of him. It hit the shotgunner and knocked him back against the wall behind him.

Luke rammed the table into the man twice more, then, panting from the effort, shoved it aside and drew one of the Remingtons, even though the outlaw wasn't a threat any longer. He had dropped the shotgun, which was empty, and slumped to the bottom of the stairs, stunned. Luke twirled the Remington around and rapped the butt against the outlaw's head, knocking him out cold. No point in taking any chances.

Outside, a swift rataplan of hoofbeats sounded in the street. Luke hurried to the entrance and shoved the batwings aside. Only three horses stood at the hitch rail. The fourth one was making tracks out of town with a cloud of dust curling up from its hooves. The rider leaned forward over the animal's neck and frantically swatted his hat against its rump to urge it on to greater speed.

"Well, hell," Luke said.

The bartender stuck his head up again. "Is . . . is it over?"

"Yeah. The fourth one lit a shuck, and I don't feel like chasing after him. Reckon I'll have to be satisfied with the three I got . . . for now." Luke started reloading the Remingtons, keeping an eye on the man he had knocked out. "You have any law in this town?"

The bartender stood up. "Got a marshal. A deputy sheriff from Singletary, the county seat, swings by now and then, but you can't ever tell when he's gonna come through."

"A jail?"

"Well . . . a smokehouse where Marshal Hennessy locks up fellas when he has to."

Luke pouched the iron he'd been reloading and took out the other revolver. "I suppose a telegraph office would be too much to hope for."

"I'm afraid so. The railroad didn't come

through here, so we never got a telegraph line. Summerville is just a sleepy little place, mister."

"That's the name of this town?"

"Yes, sir. Summerville, Arizona Territory."

Footsteps sounded on the boardwalk. A middle-aged, leathery-faced gent peered over the batwings and asked, "What in blazes is goin' on in there, Doolittle? Sounded like a damn war broke out."

The bartender waved a pudgy hand at Luke. "This fella came in and was about to have a drink when some of my other customers started shootin' at him."

The newcomer pushed the batwings aside and took a step into the room, revealing the lawman's star pinned to his vest.

Luke holstered the second Remington. "You'll take note of how this gentleman phrased that comment, Marshal. All three of those men shot at me first. That makes this a clear-cut case of self-defense."

The bartender, Doolittle, nodded, making his double chin wobble again.

"I take it they had a good reason for trying to ventilate you?" the marshal asked.

"They considered it a good reason. They knew I've been tracking them and planned to collect the rewards that have been posted for them."

Marshal Hennessy's lips tightened. "Bounty hunter, eh?"

"That's right." Luke gestured toward the body lying on its back. "That's Son Barton. The one over there at the bottom of the stairs is Jimmy

McCaskill. He's just knocked out. You'll find another dead one up on the balcony, but I don't know which one he is. Didn't get a good enough look at him, and I didn't see the fourth man, the one who got away, at all. But Barton and McCaskill ran with Ed Logan and Deuce Roebuck, so I'm sure the dead man will turn out to be one of them."

As if he hadn't heard what Luke was saying, Marshal Hennessy said, "I don't like bounty hunters."

Luke sighed. "Most lawmen don't. I understand that, Marshal. But we do serve a useful function, you know."

"Yeah, so do buzzards, but that don't mean I got to cozy up to 'em."

"I'll be satisfied if you'll just agree to lock my prisoner up for the night. I'll have him out of your hair tomorrow morning. We'll ride up to the county seat where I can turn him over to the sheriff there."

Hennessy rasped his fingers over his beard-stubbled chin, then nodded. "All right, I suppose I can do that. You're responsible for feedin' the varmint, though. I'm not gonna ask the town to stand the cost of that."

"Fair enough." Luke went over to McCaskill, bent and took hold of his collar, and started dragging his senseless form toward the door. "Lead the way, Marshal."

Hennessy did, trudging along Summerville's only street until he came to a small but sturdy-looking smokehouse. Brackets had been attached on either side of the door, and a thick beam rested in them. He struggled to lift it, saying, "I keep telling the town council . . . uh . . . they oughta build me a real jail . . . but they say the town can't afford it."

Luke let go of McCaskill's collar and reached to help the marshal. "I don't imagine you have much call for one."

"Nope. I have to throw a liquored-up cowpoke in here every once in a while, but that's about it."

Luke motioned for Hennessy to step aside. He took hold of the beam and lifted it out of the brackets. When he started to lean it against the smokehouse wall, he spotted McCaskill trying to crawl away. The outlaw had regained consciousness. Luke wondered how long he'd been shamming.

McCaskill must have thought he could crawl off for a few yards, then leap to his feet and make a dash for his horse. He tried to jump up, but Luke tossed the beam and it caught the outlaw across the back. The weight was enough to knock McCaskill facedown on the street and brought a groan from him.

Luke planted a booted foot on McCaskill's head and said, "You're a determined one, aren't you? I suppose I can see why, since you're bound to hang. But you're starting to annoy me, Jimmy." He drew one of his Remingtons. "It would be a lot easier just to haul your carcass to the county seat."

"Here now," Marshal Hennessy blustered. "Gunning a man when he's trying to shoot you is one thing, but that'd be pure murder, mister."

"Don't worry. I'm a patient man . . . within reason." Luke stepped back and kept McCaskill covered while the outlaw climbed to his feet and stumbled into the smokehouse. Luke replaced the beam, effectively locking him in.

Now that he had a thick door between him and Luke's guns, McCaskill regained some of his bravado. "You're gonna be sorry, you damn bounty hunter. Deuce is gonna get me outta here, and we'll see to it that you die slow and painful."

"Deuce Roebuck, you mean?" Luke said. "I hate to break it to you, Jimmy, but the last I saw of Deuce, he was fogging it out of here and never looked back. I expect he's at least five miles away by now. By nightfall, he'll have gone twenty miles and completely forgotten about you."

"You just wait and see," McCaskill said, but his voice had a quaver in it that revealed his confidence was slipping.

Luke turned back to the marshal. "Do you have an undertaker here in town?"

"Yeah, but I didn't figure you wanted to have those other two buried. Don't you have to take them to the county seat, too, to collect the bounties on them?"

"Yes, but I thought maybe he could clean them up a little. Blood attracts flies, you know."

Hennessy pursed his lips. "He'll do it . . . but he'll charge you for it."

"If it makes the ride a little more pleasant, it'll probably be worth it." Luke paused. "Of course, I suppose I could just cut their heads off and throw them in a gunnysack . . ."

Chapter Two

Summerville's undertaker was a tall, cadaverous man who introduced himself to Luke as Clifford Ferguson. Luke had wondered sometimes why undertakers all seemed to be either thin to the point of gauntness and dour or fat and jolly. He hardly ever ran into one of normal size, with a normal demeanor. He supposed the most likely explanation was that some men who dealt with death all the time lost their appetite, while others coped with the strains of their grim profession by embracing the pleasures of life, including plenty of good food.

Ferguson agreed to clean up the bodies of Son Barton and Ed Logan. A search of their saddlebags turned up a spare shirt and trousers for each man, so Ferguson would dress them in those duds and burn the blood-soaked clothes. He named a price of two dollars per corpse for the service.

Luke handed over a five-dollar gold piece he

had also found in one of the saddlebags and got a silver dollar in change.

"I ain't sure I ever saw a bounty hunter quite so picky about the carcasses he hauled in to collect the blood money on 'em," Marshal Hennessy commented as he and Luke stood on the boardwalk in front of the saloon watching Ferguson and his stocky Mexican assistant load the bodies onto a wagon.

"It's summer, and Singletary is half a day's ride away," Luke said. "I actually considered asking Mr. Ferguson to go ahead and embalm them, just to cut down on the stink, but I decided that would be too much of an expense. The bounty on the three I'm taking in only adds up to eighteen hundred dollars, eight hundred for Barton and five hundred apiece on the other two, and they had less than twenty dollars between them in their saddlebags. They went through the loot from their recent jobs quickly."

"Eighteen hunnerd bucks is a damn fine chunk of money." Hennessy added sourly, "The town only pays me sixty dollars a month, plus half the fines I collect. That's better than cowboying, but not by much."

"In that case, Marshal, let me buy you a drink," Luke suggested.

Hennessy shook his head. "My stomach won't take whiskey no more. They call it rotgut, and it surely lived up to its name." He inclined his head toward a small frame building diagonally across the street and went on. "I've got a pot of coffee on the stove in the office, though, if you're of a mind."

"Thank you, Marshal. That sounds good."

The coffee probably *wasn't* good—Luke had come across very few local lawmen who could brew a decent cup—but he didn't figure it would hurt anything to accept Hennessy's invitation. The likelihood that he would ever pass through Summerville again was small. He couldn't rule it out, though, and being on good terms with the local star packer sometimes came in handy.

They walked across to the marshal's office. The coffee actually wasn't as bad as Luke expected, although it would be a stretch to call it good. He thumbed back the black hat on his head and perched a hip on the corner of Hennessy's paper-littered desk while the marshal sagged into an old swivel chair behind it.

"Jensen," Hennessy said musingly. "I reckon you get asked all the time if you're related to Smoke Jensen, the famous gunfighter they write all those dime novels about."

"From time to time," Luke admitted.

"Well . . . are you?"

"As a matter of fact," Luke said, "Smoke is my brother."

It was true. For many years, his younger brother Kirby—known far and wide as Smoke—had believed that Luke was dead, killed in the Civil War. In reality, violent and tragic circumstances had led to Luke carving out a new life for himself after the war, with a new name as well. Only in recent years had he gone back to using the name Jensen, but he kept the profession he had chosen—bounty hunting.

Hennessy stared at him for a couple of seconds, then said, "You're joshin' me."

Luke shrugged. "It's the truth, Marshal. I haven't seen Smoke for a while. Mostly he goes his way and I go mine. He has a successful ranch over in Colorado to look after, you know."

"And you're just a driftin' bounty killer."

"We each have our own destiny. Some philosophers believe that our fates are locked into place before we're even born."

"Well, I don't know about that. Seems to me that a fella's always got the choice of takin' a different trail if he wants to."

"It's certainly nice to think so." Luke took another sip of coffee and looked idly at the papers scattered across Hennessy's desk. Most of them were reward posters. "You get these dodgers when the stagecoach brings the mail?"

"Yep. Sheriff Collins sends 'em to me."

Luke moved some of the papers around and then tapped a finger against one of them. "There's the reward poster for Son Barton. It's possible the posters for the other three are somewhere in here, too."

Hennessy frowned. "What are you gettin' at, Jensen? You think I should've known those boys were in town and tried to arrest 'em myself? I know Summerville ain't a very big place, but I can't keep track of every long rider who drifts in and then back out again."

Luke had a feeling the marshal didn't want to know when outlaws were in his town. That would mean going out of his way to risk his life for a salary that certainly wasn't exorbitant. As long as visitors to Summerville didn't cause any trouble, Hennessy was perfectly content to let them go on their way.

Luke couldn't blame him for that. "That's perfectly understandable, Marshal."

Something else among the papers caught Luke's eye. He pushed some of the reward dodgers aside and picked up what appeared to be a piece of butcher paper. The writing on it hadn't been done with a printing press, like the other wanted posters. Someone had used a piece of coal to scrawl in big letters at the top *WANTED*, and below that in slightly smaller letters *Three-fingered Jack McKinney*.

"What's this?" Luke asked.

Hennessy leaned back in his chair and grinned. "Reckon the sheriff thought I'd get a laugh out of it. He sent a note sayin' that they been poppin' up around the county. Homemade wanted posters ain't exactly legal."

"'Wanted for being a thief and a killer and a no-account scoundrel'," Luke read from the poster. "'Reward'"—he looked up at Hennessy—"'Reward $1.42 and a harmonica. The harmonica is only six months old.'"

The marshal chuckled. "It's a joke. Some kid wrote it. You can tell by the writing. He's probably got a friend named Jack McKinney and figured it'd be funny to fix up a wanted poster with his name on it."

"Maybe. But you just said Sheriff Collins told you they'd been posted in other parts of the county. Seems like an awful lot of trouble to go to for a joke."

"You can't never tell what a kid will do. It can't be real. Who'd ever go after an outlaw for a measly $1.42 bounty?"

"And a harmonica," Luke reminded him. "Don't forget the harmonica."

"Well, if you want to go after this Three-fingered Jack, whoever he is, you just feel free to take that dodger with you. You might need it to collect the ree-ward." Hennessy slapped his thigh and laughed some more about it.

As Luke finished his coffee, he folded the handmade wanted poster and slipped it into his shirt pocket.

The marshal didn't even seem to notice.

After leaving the marshal's office, Luke went by the undertaking parlor to see how Ferguson was coming along with the job on Son Barton and Ed Logan. Ferguson promised they would be done by evening, but since Luke wasn't planning to leave until the next morning, the undertaker suggested, "I can put them down in the root cellar if you'd like. Keep them cooler overnight. That might help with the smell to-morrow."

"I'd be obliged to you for that."

"Only cost you another dollar."

Luke smiled as he handed back the silver

dollar Ferguson had given him in change earlier. He suspected the undertaker had had that in mind all along.

That left Luke at loose ends. Summerville didn't have a hotel, so when he gathered up his own horse and the mounts belonging to the three outlaws and led them to the town's only livery stable, he asked the hostler, "What are the chances that I can sleep in the hayloft tonight?"

"If you've got four bits to spare, mister, I'd say the chances are real good," the man replied. "And four bits for each of the horses, so that adds up to, uh . . ."

Luke dropped three silver dollars in the callused, outstretched palm. "Give them a little extra grain and we'll call it square."

This stop in Summerville was getting expensive, but for now he was using the money he had found in the outlaws' saddlebags. If the total wound up going over that amount, he would recoup the funds when he collected the rewards in the county seat.

With that taken care of, he drifted back to the saloon. Doolittle was still behind the bar. Somebody had mopped up the blood that had been spilled earlier, and the customers who had been chased out of the place by gunplay had returned.

In addition, three soiled doves in shabby dresses sat together at a table, their services not in demand at the moment. All of them showed the wear and tear of the hard life they led. No amount of paint could cover that up.

Doolittle cast a nervous glance across the bar at Luke. "You're not plannin' on shooting up the place again, are you?"

"I wasn't planning on it the first time." Luke's voice hardened as he added, "And I'd sort of like to know how Son Barton even knew I was here."

One of the doves spoke up. "I can tell you that, mister. He had just finished with me—and mighty damn quick, I might add—and got up to look out the window. He said, 'It's that damn bounty hunter' and some other things that I'm not even comfortable repeatin'. Then he yanked on his clothes, grabbed his pistol, and ran out of the room. Nobody who works here tipped him off, if that's what you're thinkin'."

Luke nodded slowly. He hadn't been aware that the outlaws knew he was on their trail, but he supposed someone he had questioned regarding their whereabouts could have gotten word to them to be on the lookout for him and described him.

"Felicia's right, Mr. Jensen," Doolittle said. "We don't mix in our customers' affairs. Anybody's got a problem with anybody else, we try to stay out of it."

"A wise way to be," Luke said.

Doolittle reached for a bottle and a glass. "Since you didn't get to finish that drink earlier, how about you have another one now, on the house?"

"Thank you, Mr. Doolittle. You're a gentleman and a scholar."

Doolittle filled the glass and pushed it across the bar. "Not hardly, but I can pour a drink."

That was the only thing anybody in Summerville had offered to do for Luke without charging him for it.

A little later, the soiled dove called Felicia went over to the bar and made it pretty clear she wouldn't mind if Luke took her upstairs, but he wasn't sure if she intended for it to be a business transaction or not.

He had always had pretty good luck with women. They seemed to find him attractive despite his craggy features and the gray that was starting to appear in his dark hair. But unlike some men, being involved in a shooting scrape didn't leave him puffing and pawing at the ground like a bull, so he diverted Felicia's veiled suggestion as politely as possible.

The only eating place in town was a hash house owned by a pigtailed Chinaman. Luke had supper there, then went back to the stable, climbed into the loft, and settled down to sleep.

He wasn't sure how long it was after he'd dozed off that an explosion woke him.